SOLOMON VS. LORD

THE DEEP BLUE ALIBI

KILL ALL THE LAWYERS

HABEAS PORPOISE

IMPACT
(Originally published in hardcover as *9 Scorpions*)

"A breakout book, highly readable and fun with an irresistible momentum, helped along by Levine's knowledge of the Supreme Court and how it works." —*USA Today*

BALLISTIC

"*Ballistic* is *Die Hard* in a missile silo. Terrific!"
—*Stephen J. Cannell*

ILLEGAL

"Levine is one of the few thriller authors who can craft a plot filled with suspense while still making the readers smile at the characters' antics." —*Chicago Sun-Times*

PRAISE FOR PAUL LEVINE

TO SPEAK FOR THE DEAD

"Move over Scott Turow. *To Speak for the Dead* is courtroom drama at its very best." —*Larry King*

NIGHT VISION

"Levine's fiendish ability to create twenty patterns from the same set of clues will have you waiting impatiently for his next novel."
—*Kirkus Reviews*

FALSE DAWN

"Realistic, gritty, fun." —*New York Times Book Review*

MORTAL SIN

"Take one part John Grisham, two parts Carl Hiaasen, throw in a dash of John D. MacDonald, and voila! You've got *Mortal Sin*."
—*Tulsa World*

RIPTIDE (originally published in hardcover as *Slashback)*

"A thriller as fast as the wind. A bracing rush, as breathtaking as hitting the Gulf waters on a chill December morning."
—*Tampa Tribune*

FOOL ME TWICE

"You'll like listening to Jake's beguiling first-person tale-telling so much that you won't mind being fooled thrice."
—*Philadelphia Inquirer*

FLESH & BONES

"Lassiter is smart, tough, funny, and very human . . . one of the most entertaining series characters in contemporary crime fiction."
—Booklist

LASSITER

"Since Robert Parker is no longer with us, I'm nominating Levine for an award as best writer of dialogue in the grit-lit genre."
—*San Jose Mercury News*

LAST CHANCE LASSITER

"Cleverly plotted and well written. The dialogue and characterizations are first-rate." —Bookreporter.com

STATE vs. LASSITER

"The best of the best. Just when I thought 'Lassiter' couldn't get any better." —Goodreads 5-star review

BUM RAP

ALSO BY PAUL LEVINE

THE JAKE LASSITER SERIES

To Speak for the Dead

Night Vision

False Dawn

Mortal Sin

Riptide

Fool Me Twice

Flesh & Bones

Lassiter

Last Chance Lassiter

State vs. Lassiter

THE SOLOMON & LORD SERIES

Solomon vs. Lord

The Deep Blue Alibi

Kill All the Lawyers

Habeas Porpoise

THE LASSITER, SOLOMON & LORD SERIES

Bum Rap

STAND-ALONE THRILLERS

Impact

Ballistic

Illegal

Paydirt

PAUL LEVINE

BUM RAP

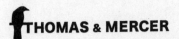
THOMAS & MERCER

Text copyright © 2015 Paul J. Levine

Published by Thomas & Mercer, Seattle

www.apub.com

Amazon, the Amazon logo, and Thomas & Mercer are trademarks of Amazon.com, Inc., or its affiliates.

ISBN-13: 9781477829868
ISBN-10: 1477829865

Cover design by Brian Zimmerman

Printed in the United States of America

For my grandchildren . . .
Jonah, Lexi, Ruby, and Violet

"*Jake Lassiter. The Jakester! The mouthpiece who took the* shy *out of* shyster *and put the* fog *into* pettifogger."

—State Attorney Ray Pincher

- 1 -

Nicolai Gorev

The gunshot hit Nicolai Gorev squarely between the eyes. His head snapped back, then whipped forward, and he toppled face-first onto his desk.

There were two other people in the office of Club Anastasia.

Nadia Delova, the best Bar girl between Moscow and Miami, stared silently at Gorev as blood oozed from his ears. She had seen worse.

Steve Solomon, a South Beach lawyer with a shaky reputation, spoke over the echo still ringing off the walls. "I am in deep shit," he said.

Nadia and the Feds

One week earlier. . .

Office of the United States Attorney for the Southern District of Florida

In Re: Investigation of South Beach Champagne Clubs and one "John Doe"

File No. 2014-73-B

Statement of Nadia Delova

July 7, 2014

(CONFIDENTIAL)

Q: My name is Deborah Scolino, assistant United States attorney. Please state your name.

A: Nadia Delova.

Q: How old are you?

A: Twenty-eight.

Q: Where were you born?

A: Saint Petersburg. Russia. Not Florida.

Q: What is your occupation?

A: What do I look like? Nuclear physicist?

Q: Ms. Delova, please . . .

A: Bar girl. I am Bar girl.

Q: What does that entail?

A: Entails my tail. [Witness laughs] Is simple job. I get men to buy cheap champagne for expensive price.

Q: How do you do that?

A: We go to nice hotel. Fontainebleau or Delano. Me and Elena on hunting parties.

Q: Do you dress as you have today? For the record, a tight-banded mini in hot pink. I'm guessing Herve Leger.

A: Is knockoff. But shoes are real. Valentino slingbacks with four-inch heels. I dress good on hunting parties.

Q: And just what are you hunting for?

A: Tourists. Men with money. We look for expensive watches. Patek Philippe. Audemars Piguet. Rolex Submariner.

Q: So you approach the men?

A: At the hotel bar. We make small talk. "Oh, you are so handsome. Tell us about Nebraska." We say we know a private club with good music.

Q: What club is that?

A: Anastasia. On South Beach.

Q: What happens when you get there?

A: Bartender serves free vodka shots, except ours—mine and Elena's—are water. When the man is drunk, we order champagne. Nicolai buys it for twenty-five dollars at Walmart. Charges a couple thousand a bottle, but the man is so drunk, he signs credit card because Elena has her tongue in his ear, or my hand is in his crotch. Or both.

Q: Just who is Nicolai?

A: Nicolai Gorev. Owner of Club Anastasia.

Q: Ms. Delova, we need you to help the government's investigation of Nicolai Gorev.

A: *Nyet.*

Q: Ms. Delova . . .

A: I am not as stupid as you might think.

-3-

Your Lawyer or Your Lover

I didn't shoot the bastard," Steve Solomon said.

"Tell me the truth, Steve."

"Jeez, Vic, I am." Sounding frustrated. Telling the story over and over. He spread his arms and held his palms upward, the gesture intended to show he wasn't hiding anything.

Victoria studied him. She'd been studying Solomon for several years now. He was her law partner and lover. Solomon & Lord.

Victoria Lord. Princeton undergrad, Yale Law.

Steve Solomon. University of Miami undergrad. Key West School of Law.

Victoria graduated summa cum laude. Steve graduated summa cum luck.

She practiced law by the book. He burned the book. But in court . . . well in court, they were a powerful team.

Solomon & Lord.

Steve had street smarts and was a master of persuasion. Victoria knew the law, which helped with judges. Plus, she was likable, a necessity with juries. Steve also had one talent Victoria lacked: he could lie with a calm certainty no polygraph could ever discover.

She loved Steve. And hated him. Sometimes they argued over "good morning." But life sizzled when they were together and fizzled when they were apart. Right now, one wrong move, and they could be apart forever.

"Tell me again," she said. "Everything."

"Why?"

"I want to see if you tell the same story two times in a row."

"Aw, c'mon, Vic."

They were sitting in a lawyers' visitation room at the Miami-Dade County jail. The metal desk and two chairs were bolted to the concrete floor. Victoria hated the place. It smelled of sweat and disinfectant and something vaguely like cat piss. Her ankle-strap Gucci pumps had slipped on something wet—and yellow—when she had walked down the corridor. She always felt nauseous visiting a client here. Now that the accused was Steve, she also felt a throat-constricting fear.

To get into the jail, she had shown her Florida Bar card. To get out, Steve would need a very good lawyer. She had tried—and won—several murder trials. But with all the emotional baggage, she felt incapable of representing Steve. A surgeon didn't operate on a loved one.

"If you didn't kill Gorev, who did?" she asked.

"Like I said, Nadia Delova, our client."

"*Our* client?"

"Okay, you were at a hearing in Broward. Nadia was a walk-in. She had five thousand in cash and said she just needed me for a one-hour meeting."

"Where's the money?"

"In an envelope in my desk drawer."

"When were you going to tell me about it?"

"That reminds me of a lawyer joke."

"Not now, Steve."

"A lawyer sends out a bill for five thousand dollars, and the client mistakenly sends him ten thousand dollars. What's the ethical question?"

"Obviously, should he return the money?"

"No! Should he tell his partner?"

Steve laughed at his own joke. He had a habit of doing that. A lot of his old habits were starting to irritate her. Accepting new clients without her approval was one. Straddling the border between ethical and sleazy conduct was another. Getting charged with murder was a new one.

"Where's Nadia now?"

"That's what I need to find out. Or you do."

"You understand your predicament?"

"The cops found me in a locked room with a dead man and a smoking gun. Yeah, I have a pretty good idea."

"Tell me everything from the top."

"Nadia was waiting when I unlocked the door to our office at about eight fifteen a.m. She said she was a Bar girl. Very up front about it."

"How admirable."

Steve ignored her sarcasm and plowed ahead. "She must have come straight from work, because she was all dolled up. Minidress. Heels. Jewelry. Gloves."

"Gloves in Miami. In July."

"Dressy black gloves. Up to the elbows. Like Holly Golightly in *Breakfast at Tiffany's*."

"Wasn't Holly a prostitute?"

"Only in the book. In the movie, she was more like a fun date."

Just outside the door, a baby wailed. It was a weirdly discordant sound in this dreadful place. The common visitation area, a dismal space with rows of benches for families, was adjacent to the lawyers' room. The baby's keening reached an impossibly high pitch, and Victoria felt a headache coming on.

"Physical description of this Nadia?" she asked.

"About your height. Nearly six feet. Without her heels."

"She took off her shoes?"

"In the office. For a minute. She rubbed her feet. Is that important?"

"I don't know. Had you ever met this Bar girl before?"

"Of course not."

"But she felt comfortable enough to take off her shoes and rub her feet in your presence?"

"Is that a lawyer's question or a girlfriend's question?"

"Just keep going. What else besides her height and her tired feet?"

"Dark hair. Nearly jet-black. Pale skin and blue eyes. Unusual combination. Very . . ."

"Striking?"

"Well . . ." He swallowed, and his Adam's apple bobbed. Victoria made a mental note that Steve—for all his bluster—might not hold up well under cross-examination.

"If you like that sort of thing," he said finally. "I always preferred blondes. Like you."

"Of course. What else about Nadia can you remember?"

"Her lips were very . . . What's the word?"

"I don't know, Steve. What is the word?"

"Big?"

"Pouty," Victoria said. "Bee-stung?"

"Yeah. Exactly."

"Unlike my very average, very Waspy lips?"

"C'mon, you have great lips. Anyway, she had a nice . . ." He made a flowing motion with both hands, the male pantomime for a curvaceous woman. Victoria figured that men had been communicating this way since they first emerged from caves. Not that today's men were that much different from those of the Paleolithic Era.

"Body?" she helped him out. "Curvy body?"

"Yeah, great body. I mean, no greater than yours, but . . ."

"Bigger boobs?"

He nodded, as if saying it aloud might shatter her fragile ego.

"Okay, so at eight fifteen a.m., this striking, long-legged, cantaloupe-breasted woman wearing gloves up to her elbows gives you five thousand in cash, and, like a puppy wagging its tail, you follow her to this South Beach club."

"Actually, I drove us both."

"And just why did she need a lawyer?"

"Her boss, Nicolai Gorev, was holding her passport. She wanted it back plus some money he owed her."

"And how exactly were you going to help her do this?"

Steve let out a long, slow breath. "Well, that's where it gets a little sticky."

"Doesn't it always?"

"I think it was maybe a language thing, her being Russian and all."

"Damn it, Steve. What aren't you telling me?"

He was quiet a moment, then gave her that twinkling smile. It was intended to distract her from whatever he needed to say but didn't want to. He was a handsome man with black hair and deep-brown eyes. *Mischievous eyes*, Victoria thought. Devilish eyes, her mother always said. She did not mean it as a compliment. He had an aquiline nose that reminded Victoria of George Washington, except that if Steve had chopped down a cherry tree, he would have lied about it.

At last, Steve said, "Well, you know how you always hated that TV commercial I did for the firm?"

"The blasphemous one? 'If you want the best lawyers in Miami, hire the wisdom of Solomon, the strength of the Lord.'"

"Nope. The one where I was a cowboy with the pearl-handled pistols?"

"How could I forget?" Victoria said. "The cease-and-desist letter from the Florida Bar is on my desk."

"Well, if you want to know exactly what happened . . ."

"I do! Word for word."

So before Victoria could begin pulling out his fingernails with pliers, Steve told her.

* * *

"Do you have one gun or two?" Nadia asks.

"What?" Steve answers. They are inside Club Anastasia, headed toward an office at the end of a corridor behind the bar. A heavyset woman in an apron is mopping the floor. Two thick-necked men in black suits are riffling through a stack of credit card receipts and using an old-fashioned, noisy adding machine with a paper scroll. The men glance at Nadia and return to their work.

"On the TV, you have two guns," Nadia says.

"You talking about my commercial?"

"I told you. I got your name from the television."

In the commercial, Steve was dressed in cowboy garb. Right down to the chaps, Stetson, and pair of six-shooters. He fired at a blowup doll—a man in a suit intended to resemble, well, The Man. The doll exploded, and Steve blew smoke from the gun barrel.

An actor's baritone voice intoned: "If you need a lawyer, why not hire a gunslinger? Steve Solomon. Have briefcase. Will travel."

On the screen, the logo of Solomon & Lord. And the phone number: 555-UBE-FREE.

"No guns," he tells Nadia as they approach Gorev's office. "I hate guns."

"Then what can you do to frighten Nicolai?"

"What I always do. Threaten to sue."

She exhales a little puff of displeasure, opens her purse, and shows Solomon what is inside. "Well, at least I have a gun," she says.

* * *

"Don't say it, Vic. I know I screwed up. That's why I need you so much now. Have you filed your notice of appearance?"

She shook her head, felt her gold hoop earrings swinging. They had been a present from Steve after they'd won their first murder trial. "I can be your lawyer or your lover, Steve, but not both."

"Jeez, Vic." His eyes went wide with surprise. "We're partners in everything."

Victoria could feel his disappointment. Didn't he realize you don't put this sort of burden on the person you love?

"You won't listen to me," she said. "As soon as you're indicted, you'll try to take over."

"No way. You'll be the boss."

"You'll push me to go over the line. Like that stupid saying of yours."

"'When the law doesn't work, you gotta work the law.' It's the truth, hon."

"Not the way I practice."

They were both quiet a moment. Somewhere inside this hellish place, a steel door clanged shut. Shouts of men could be heard on upper floors. The cat piss smell seemed to grow stronger.

"I need you, Vic."

"I already retained Jake Lassiter."

"Lassiter! I want a lawyer, not a linebacker."

"He's won some tough cases."

"He's a slab of meat. If you won't represent me, I want Roy Black."

"We can't afford Roy."

"Tell him it's me."

"Already did."

"And he didn't offer a courtesy discount?"

"He doubled his fee."

"What about Marcia Silvers? She's won some big cases."

"Marcia's in Washington, prepping for a Supreme Court argument."

"Damn! But why Lassiter?"

"Because he won't put up with your bullshit. And if you're innocent, he'll tear apart the courthouse to prove it."

"Says who?"

"He promised me. He'll be like Samson ripping down the pillars of the Temple of Dagon."

"If I recall my Old Testament," Steve said, with an air of resignation, "that's what killed old Samson."

-4-

Last Chance Lassiter

I want an innocent client.

I *need* an innocent client.

I don't mean *not guilty* because the state can't meet its burden of proof. But *innocent*. "Factually innocent," as we mouthpieces call it.

I've been trying cases for twenty years after a short, unspectacular career as a second-string linebacker with the Miami Dolphins. I made a few memorable hits on the suicide squads—the kickoff and punt teams—but mostly I sat so far down Shula's bench, my ass was in Ocala. I went to night law school in the off-season, graduated in the top half of the bottom third of my class, and passed the bar exam on my fourth try. I've been bouncing from courtroom to courtroom in the so-called justice system ever since.

My name is Jake Lassiter, and I'm a grinder. I am not called to speak at fancy conventions in five-star hotels. The governor has not offered me black robes and elevated me to the bench. I am not interviewed by CNN to comment on the latest trial of the century. And I am not rich.

Here's what I do. Burglary. Robbery. Assault and battery. Con games. Stolen cars. Embezzlement. Drug possession. And, of course, murder. For whatever reason, I'm particularly good at murder. Maybe because the stakes are so high, my engine revs to the red line. Not that a murder trial is a sprint. It's a marathon where everyone along the road throws rocks at you as you chug along. You have to be able to take a hit.

It's a lot like the kickoff team in football. The fastest man is not necessarily the one who makes the tackle. More likely, the flier will be picked off by one of the blockers. The player who's not particularly fast but senses the blocker's angle can knock the bastard aside, keep rumbling along, and make the hit. That's what kept me on the Dolphins for three years, and it's my theory of trying a murder case. Play within yourself. Predict your opponent's move before it happens, and beat him to the punch. If you're not particularly swift or shifty—meaning if you're me—a forearm blast to the throat will do.

On the field or in the courtroom, try not to get knocked on your ass, but if you do, never let them see your pain. Bounce to your feet and head for the ball.

Here's what I won't do as a lawyer. I won't represent a man accused of violence against women or children because my granny taught me that such scum do not deserve my time or effort. Otherwise, it's pretty much anything goes.

I take a lot of cases other lawyers turn down. Either the money is short or the odds of winning are long. That's earned me the name "Last Chance Lassiter."

I pick up cases here and there. Sometimes I just stand by the elevator on the fourth floor of the Richard E. Gerstein Justice Building. Someone who's headed for an arraignment naked—without a lawyer—will spot me. I'm a big guy in a suit with a briefcase, and I don't look lost. Maybe they like my broken nose or my decent haircut, or maybe they're just scared.

"You a lawyer, dude?"

"Best one you can afford . . . dude."

Money is always a problem. My first question to a potential customer—yeah, I sometimes call them that—is not "Did you do it?" It's "How much money do you have?" And, yes, I take credit cards. But not a mortgage on a customer's house. Not because I'd feel lousy about foreclosing. Because I once got burned when the IRS leapfrogged the mortgage I was holding with a lien for unpaid taxes, leaving my client without a house and me without a fee.

Sometimes former customers refer their pals. This puzzles me, because those ex-customers are nearly always in prison. I guess they don't blame me for losing. After all, they were guilty, and they watched me work my ass off on their behalf.

That's a fact of the business. Most of my customers are guilty as hell. I only win when the state can't prove its case or otherwise screws the pooch. I'm a damn good cross-examiner, and I've won cases by catching cops in lies. That doesn't mean my customer wasn't technically guilty. But if I can eviscerate the state's witnesses and then work my magic in closing argument, I can get my customer off.

How else can I win? Sometimes the cops will conduct an unconstitutional search, or the prosecutors will fail to turn over exculpatory evidence, or the trial judge will err. On the occasions I win, I receive little gratitude. No Christmas cards or baskets of fruit. Maybe a grumbling complaint about the size of my fee.

The customer sees the stage play, not the work behind it. Writing the script, building the sets, painting the props, and learning the lines. The ingrate couldn't care less. I'll never hear from the victorious client again . . . until he's arrested for something else.

Mostly I lose. Or plead my guy guilty. It's a dirty little secret, but that's the deal with most criminal defense lawyers, even the big names who pontificate on the tube. If anyone knew our real winning percentage, they'd cop a quick plea or flee the jurisdiction.

We all want to be heroes to our paying customers. John D. MacDonald, my favorite Florida writer—yeah, I read a bit—once began a book: "There are no hundred percent heroes." If you ask my customers, they'd probably give me 51 percent. MacDonald also wrote, "If the cards are stacked against you, reshuffle the deck." Well, I'm tired of holding a pair of deuces or a busted flush. Tired of the grind. Tired of losing. Which is why on this sweaty July day with a sky as gray as an angry ocean, I needed an innocent client.

I was juggling these thoughts while driving north on Dixie Highway toward I-95 on my way to the jail. Victoria Lord had called this morning while I was slicing mangoes for my nephew Kip's smoothie. Victoria's law partner and live-in lover, Steve Solomon, had managed to get himself arrested in the shooting death of some Russian club owner on South Beach.

"I don't like Solomon," I told her on the phone.

I know. I know. My marketing skills could use work.

"Do you like most of your clients?" she asked.

"Practically none."

"But you bust your hump and break down doors to win."

"I hate losing more than I hate the clients."

"That's why I'm hiring you. Plus you have street smarts and won't fall for any of Steve's bullshit."

"Has he agreed to this?"

"Not yet."

"Tell him I've punched out clients who lied to me."

"You have no idea how many times I've wanted to smack him."

In front of me, a landscaper's overloaded Ford pickup was dropping palm fronds and dead ferns all over the highway. I goosed the gas pedal and pulled my ancient Eldorado convertible into the passing lane. "Victoria, do you ever get tired of representing guilty people?"

"Steve swears he's innocent."

"And the law presumes he is. But I'm not talking about him. Does it ever get you down? That nearly everyone is guilty."

She was silent on the phone a moment. Maybe wondering if she'd called the wrong guy. Then she said, "It comes with the territory, Jake. We force the state to meet its burden of proof. If they do it, we haven't really lost. The system has won."

"So you really believe the stuff they teach in law school?"

"If I didn't, how could I go on?"

Exactly, I thought. She hadn't practiced long enough to lose her religion, the belief in the holiness of the justice system. I didn't want to be a prick, so I didn't say, "Give it ten more years, Victoria; then get back to me."

Instead, I said, "See you and your presumably innocent partner in an hour."

I knew them both a bit. They lived together on Kumquat, and I'm on Poinciana in Coconut Grove, so we're practically neighbors. I'd recently seen Solomon tooling around the neighborhood in a jazzy new Corvette with a paint job they call "torch red." Not my style. I'm also too big to fit comfortably in the driver's seat. His personalized license plate was "I-OBJECT," a pretty good summation of his temperament.

Solomon was a herky-jerky guy, always in motion, always gabbing. About six feet tall with dark hair that usually needed trimming. He weighed about as much as one of my buttocks, but he had that wiry strength. I'd seen him jogging down Old Cutler Road, and he kept up an impressive pace. In court, he badgered witnesses, pestered lawyers, and interrupted judges. His files were always a mess, and, basically, he was a pain in the ass. Showy and over the top by my standards, and I'm not exactly the shy and retiring type.

One day, in the Justice Building cafeteria, I joined Solomon at a luncheon table with several other lawyers. He was spouting off about "Solomon's Laws," rules he makes up that flout the system.

"If the facts don't fit the law, bend the facts," Solomon said, stuffing his face with eggplant Parmesan.

Everybody laughed. Except me. When I was a young lawyer, I represented an old musician named Cadillac Johnson whose song had been stolen by a hot young hip-hop artist. The copyright claim was murky and documents had been destroyed, but I knew in my gut that my guy had written the song several decades earlier.

"It's a tough case, maybe impossible," Cadillac told me.

"If your cause is just, no case is impossible," I said.

Ever since, I've tried to live by those words. Problem is, just causes are hard to come by. And, oh yeah, I won a pile of cash for Cadillac's retirement without bending the facts, though I did punch a guy out.

The first time I saw Victoria Lord, she was in court, and what I noticed was her posture. A tall, slender blonde who stood very straight and spoke with quiet confidence and authority. Tailored business suits and patrician good looks. Her table was neatly arranged with color-coded files that I'm sure were alphabetized and cross-indexed. Highly organized. A real pro at a young age. Maybe overly earnest for my taste. I could be wrong, but she seemed to be one of those anti-gluten, pro-yoga, organic wine bar, Generation-Y echo boomers. A Gwyneth Paltrow type who would name her first daughter Persimmon or whatever.

They're really different, Solomon and Lord, but as people say, opposites attract. For whatever reason—maybe because they each bring different strengths to the courtroom—they've become a damn good trial team.

Traffic slowed to a halt between Seventeenth Avenue and the entrance to I-95. A mattress lay in the middle lane. Typical. At least it wasn't on fire. I was stuck behind a muddy old Chevy that belched oily smoke. The tag was expired, and I'd bet a hundred bucks the driver had neither a license nor insurance. I squeezed my oversize Eldo into the left lane, cutting off a young guy in a white Porsche. He banged his horn, and through the rearview, I saw him shoot me the bird.

Aw, screw you, Porsche Boy. And your designer sunglasses, too.

I'm tired of Miami. For a long time, I've felt out of place, a brew-and-burger guy in a pâté-and-chardonnay world.

I got a call a few weeks ago from Clarence Washington, an old Dolphins teammate. After retirement, he picked up a master's degree and then a doctorate in education. And this from a kid who grew up in the projects. I have a lot of respect for Clarence. Now, he's headmaster at a boy's prep school in the green hills of Vermont. And to think I knew him when he tossed a beer keg off a seventh-story balcony into a hotel swimming pool. With a Dolphins cheerleader riding that keg all the way down.

Anyway, Clarence said he needed a new football coach. The guy who had the job had retired after like a hundred years. Apparently, there's very little pressure coaching a bunch of pampered skinny white boys who play against others of their ilk. It doesn't really matter if you win, as long as the uniforms don't get too dirty and the parents' cocktails are chilled. And you get to wear a sweat suit to work with the crest of the school on the chest.

So Vermont was on my mind as I drove to the stinkhole county jail, stuck in traffic, horns blaring, and the thermometer closing in on ninety-six degrees.

Steve Solomon, you may not know it, but you're the tipping point. If you're a lying scumbag murderer, I'm hanging up my shingle and heading north.

Green hills. Autumn leaves. Ben & Jerry's.

Half an hour later, I pulled off the Dolphin Expressway onto Twelfth Avenue and parked my thirty-year-old convertible, canvas top up, in an open lot.

I walked to the jail, a hot rain falling, as it did practically every day in the summer. But as the fat drops pelted me, I could smell the dewy grass of a manicured playing field on a cool September morning.

-5-

Nadia and the Feds (Part Two)

One week before the Gorev shooting . . .

Office of the United States Attorney for the Southern District of Florida

In Re: Investigation of South Beach Champagne Clubs
and one "John Doe"

File No. 2014-73-B

Statement of Nadia Delova (Continuation)

July 7, 2014

(CONFIDENTIAL)

Q: [By AUSA Deborah Scolino] I understand your reluctance to
become involved, Ms. Delova, but you may not appreciate the
precariousness of your position.

A: [By Nadia Delova] I do not understand this word, *precar*...

Q: You admit signing the ESTA form marked as Exhibit A?

A: Yes.

Q: In order to gain admittance to the United States?

A: Is great country.

Q: And you swore you had no criminal convictions involving moral turpitude despite being jailed in Latvia and Estonia?

A: I was only Bar girl. No turpitude.

Q: You swore you would not work in the United States.

A: Nicolai Gorev told me to say that or they would not let me in.

Q: And you swore you would leave within ninety days?

A: That, too, he told me to say.

Q: You are a coconspirator with Mr. Gorev in a wire fraud and money laundering scheme. Probably racketeering, too.

A: I do not know your laws.

Q: After illegally entering the country and illegally working, you stole a watch from a customer at Club Anastasia.

A: *Nikogda!* Not true. The man gave me as gift.

Q: Nonetheless, the Miami Beach police arrested you and set this wheel in motion.

A: I feel like wheel is running over my feet.

Q: You are facing prison time and then deportation, but I am offering you immunity. I would like you to reconsider my proposition concerning Nicolai Gorev.

A: I am afraid. Will you give me agent to come along? Maybe someone who speaks Russian, and we will say he is my cousin.

Q: Spanish speaking, I've got. But not Russian. And it's really not a good idea to take anyone along. It will raise Gorev's suspicions.

A: I am not sure I can do this. I am not a professional actress.

Q: But Ms. Delova, that's exactly what you are.

A: I do not understand.

Q: How much money do you make at Club Anastasia in one night?

A: Twenty percent of customer's tab. On some nights, I make two or three thousand dollars.

Q: See what I mean?

A: But those were stupid Americans. Salesmen. Dentists. Ordinary men with credit cards.

Q: So?

A: Nicolai Gorev is a killer.

-6-

Interred with Their Bones

If there is a more dispiriting place in Miami than the county jail, I haven't found it . . . and I've spent a lot of time at the morgue. Approaching the jail, you can hear the anguished shouts of inmates on the upper floors, yelling through the barred windows at their wives, girlfriends, and homies below. Inside, you've got that institutional smell, as if a harsh cleanser has been laced with urine. Buzzers blare and lights flash. Steel crashes against steel as doors bang shut with the finality of a coffin closing.

Sitting in the lawyer visitation room at the county jail, I said hello to Victoria Lord and nodded at Steve Solomon. I pulled a legal pad from my briefcase, wrote "State vs. Solomon" on the first page, and gave my new customer a stern look. "First rule. You have to tell me the truth."

"Jesus, Lassiter. I'm a professional. You don't have to tell me that."

"So we're agreed. The straight story."

"Hell, yes. Like I tell my clients, 'Lie to your spouse, your priest, and the IRS, but always tell your lawyer the truth.'"

"Lie to your spouse?" Victoria gave him a pained look.

"Just an expression, Vic."

"Second rule," I said. "Tell me everything. Even stuff that doesn't make you look good. Clients sometimes tell little lies they think don't hurt the case, because they're embarrassed about something. It always comes back to haunt them."

"We're on the same page, Lassiter. A client who lies to his lawyer is like a husband who cheats on his wife. It seldom happens once."

"Why all this talk about cheating on spouses?" Victoria asked.

Solomon waved off the question with the two-handed football official's signal: incomplete pass.

"C'mon, Lassiter. How about I just tell you what happened?" Solomon spoke quickly, keeping his eyes on me. He seemed more willing to talk about murder than infidelity.

"Third rule," I said, ignoring his request. "In trial, don't lean over and whisper in my ear."

"Why the hell not?"

"You'll distract me. Plus I won't be able to hear the testimony."

Solomon let out a long, exasperated breath. "You've got two ears."

"I had multiple concussions playing ball."

"Maybe you played too long without a helmet."

"I've got tinnitus and some hearing loss."

Solomon turned to Victoria. "You brought me a deaf lawyer?"

"Plus I'm bone tired of clients who try to tell me what to do."

"A deaf, punch-drunk, burnout lawyer."

"When you want me to ask a question on cross, or you need a recess to take a piss, you'll write a note on a legal pad in legible block letters."

"What is this? Fifth grade?"

"I'll read your note and decide what to do."

Solomon reached across the table, grabbed my legal pad and pen, and scribbled something. Then he shoved the pad back at me: *SCREW YOU, LASSITER!*

"I think you've got the hang of it," I said.

"Now, are we done with your rules?"

"We're not done, but if you want to talk, I'm here to listen."

"Great. I'll speak loudly so you can hear and slowly so you can understand. First, what's the chance you can get me out on bail?"

"State Attorney is seeking an indictment for first-degree murder. He usually gets what he wants, so the answer is none."

"I'm sorry, Steve," Victoria said.

"It's okay, hon. Been here for contempt. Lots of times, in fact." He turned to me, smiling. "Does that shock you, Lassiter?"

"Not that you've been held in contempt. Only that you consider it a merit badge."

"A lawyer who's afraid of jail is like a surgeon who's afraid of blood."

"Glad you're comfortable here. If we lose, life at Raiford won't seem so bad."

Solomon looked as if he wanted to do to me what the state said he did to the Russian. "Lassiter, you have a remarkable ability not to inspire confidence in a client."

"Why don't you tell me your story and see if you can inspire my belief in your innocence?" I said.

"Before I do, promise you won't get on that white horse of yours and start making moral judgments."

"I'm a lawyer. I make legal judgments."

"Good. Because you're no more a pillar of the Bar than I am. I remember when you were charged with killing your banker."

Yet more proof, I thought, *that our past clings to us like mud on rusty cleats.* Pamela Baylins was my banker and my lover. Client funds went missing from my trust accounts. She accused me; I accused her. She ended up dead, and I was indicted.

"Bum rap," I said.

"So's this!" Solomon chewed his lower lip, then turned to Victoria, his dark eyes lighting up. "I get it now. You hired Lassiter because he's been wrongfully charged, and you think he can relate to me in some band-of-brothers, soldiers-in-the-foxhole way."

"I think his unique experiences might be useful," Victoria said evenly. "I think you two have more in common than either of you may realize."

"Doubt it," I said.

"Agree with that," Solomon said.

"You both piss people off, just in different ways."

I shrugged. So did Solomon.

"If you were criminals—"

"Which I'm not," we both sang in unison.

"Steve would be a smooth-talking con man and Jake would be a strong-arm robber."

"What?" I protested. "I'm not smooth talking?"

"You were both athletes in your younger days," Victoria said. "Famous locally in odd sorts of ways."

Solomon showed a crooked little grin. "You gotta be talking about Wrong Way Lassiter. Scored a touchdown for the other team."

"Scored a safety," I corrected him.

"It's the only reason anyone even remembers you played for the Dolphins."

"Shakespeare said only our bad deeds live after us," Victoria, the smart one, said. "The good is oft interred with their bones."

"Wrong Way Lassiter," Solomon repeated, pouring dirt on my bones.

Life is unfair. In my last season before being cut, I made a hard-as-hell tackle on a kickoff against the Jets. So hard my helmet cracked down the middle and the ball came loose. Somehow, I scooped up the fumble. So far so good, but I'd suffered a concussion on the tackle and was already dizzy. I got turned around and ran to the wrong end zone. Where roughly eleven New York Jets happily landed on me. Two points for the Jets, Dolphins lose by one, and my name lives in infamy.

I had so far resisted, but now I gave in. "Glad you enjoy that old story so much . . . Last Out Solomon."

"I knew you'd bring that up!" he shot back.

"I used to take my nephew Kip to the UM games on Sunday afternoons. It was years after your time on campus, but everyone still talked about that day in Omaha."

"Screw that. I was a damn good college baseball player. Full scholarship."

"Solomon, you couldn't hit your weight and you were damn skinny. In the field—shortstop, as I recall—you were only average."

"Yeah? Keep going."

"You could run like hell. Amazing speed."

"State champion sprinter out of Beach High, thank you very much."

"At UM, I remember you scored from first on a single against Florida State."

"Did it a couple times. Stole a helluva lot of bases in four years."

"And still haven't returned them, I bet."

"So, go ahead, Lassiter. You're dying to talk about the championship game against Texas." Solomon closed his eyes and his jaw muscles clenched, a man awaiting the firing squad.

"Not much to say. Bottom of the ninth, Texas up by a run. You draw a walk, steal second and third."

"Go on—you're loving this."

"I admire what you did next."

"Bullshit." Solomon eyed me suspiciously.

"I mean it."

Victoria broke in. "What is it you admire, Jake?"

"Your partner's courage. His absolute confidence in himself. I admire what he *tried* to do, even if it didn't work out."

"I don't believe what I'm hearing," Solomon said.

"You had the pitcher rattled after those stolen bases. So you took that big lead. I figure you were angling for a wild pitch so you could score. Or hoping the pitcher would try to pick you off, and he'd throw the ball into the dugout."

Solomon's voice was barely a whisper. "He caught me leaning the wrong way and picked me off. Game over."

"You were leaning the wrong way because the pitcher never stepped toward third. His motion was toward home plate, but he threw to the third baseman. It was a balk that wasn't called. You were robbed."

Solomon beamed at me. For a moment, I could see the charm that had knocked Victoria off her feet.

"Right on the money, Lassiter. I don't like to whine about the balk that wasn't called because it sounds like I'm making excuses."

"I admire that, too."

"No matter what I say, no matter the truth, I'll still be Last Out Solomon."

"There's a lesson in this," I said.

"That you can't trust umpires?"

"Actually, that's not far off. The ump was too chickenshit to call the balk in a championship game. Just like some judges are afraid to take a case from the jury and grant a judgment of acquittal, no matter how pathetic the state's evidence."

"I get you, Lassiter. Society's rules don't always work. They're limited by human frailty."

"Exactly. Take the justice system. Lousy judges. Lazy lawyers. Sleeping jurors. Sometimes the innocent go to jail and the guilty go free."

"I'm with you on this, Lassiter." He sounded positively delighted. "Your job is to do everything you can to win, even if you have to break some dishes . . . or some ethical rules."

"Only the small ones," I said. "I won't bribe a cop or lie to a judge, and I don't use perjured testimony."

"You won't need to, Counselor."

"Okay, then. Tell me what happened that morning at Club Anastasia."

For the next several minutes, Solomon described how a Russian Bar girl named Nadia Delova came to his office, asking for help in getting back pay and her passport from Nicolai Gorev. Victoria kept nodding, an indication she'd already heard the story, and nothing jumped out at her that contradicted his earlier version. Then Solomon got to the juicy part.

-7-

Club Anastasia

*N*adia knocks on the door in the corridor behind the bar and says something in Russian Solomon does not understand. There is movement from inside, the sound of a bolt sliding, and the door opens.

Nicolai Gorev lets them into his office, then rebolts the door. "So, gerla, who is this?"

Solomon extends a hand, which Gorev doesn't take. "Steve Solomon. I'm a lawyer."

Gorev scowls. He is a heavyset man in a black suit with a bloodred silk shirt open at the neck. Black curly hair on his chest, a shaved head. Diamond rings on each pinky, a diamond-encrusted watch, and two diamond earrings. Diamonds seem to be the order of the day.

"We don't need no stinking lawyer." Gorev plops into a cushy chair behind a cluttered desk. Red velvet drapes cover the rear wall, except for an open space that holds a kitschy black velvet painting of Lenin's tomb. Solomon and Nadia take seats in front of the desk.

"Nice artwork," Solomon says, gesturing toward the velvet painting.

"Is joke, idiot!" Pronouncing it ee-dee-oat! "I hate Lenin. And Stalin. Putin is okay. Knows how to make a buck."

"Nicolai's personal heroes are both Americans," Nadia said.

Gorev nodded. "Donald Trump and Bernie Madoff. True capitalists!"

A speaker plays a distinctive jazz tune. It only takes a few seconds of the sax for Solomon to recognize Dave Brubeck's "Take Five." Somehow, the song seems out of place here.

"Solomon is very big man in Miami," Nadia says. "On the television."

"Who gives a dump? Why are you here, gerla?"

"I want my passport and my back pay."

"Why? You are not going back to Russia."

"I am leaving club. Getting married."

Gorev's laugh sounds like a bulldog sneezing. He even slobbers a little. "Who is the lucky son of bitch?"

"Not your business."

Wiping his mouth on the sleeve of his suit coat, Gorev turns to Solomon. "You, lawyer. Are you marrying my best B-girl?"

"No. I have a girlfriend."

"So? Maybe you keep girlfriend as mistress." Gorev laughs again, this time without the moisture.

"You do not know the man I am marrying," Nadia says.

"Of course not because there is no such man. You just want to quit."

As he listens to them argue, Solomon nods in tune to the drum solo.

"You know this music?" Gorev asks.

"Everyone knows 'Take Five.'"

"And the five-four meter? Do you know where Brubeck learned it?"

Solomon shakes his head.

"From street musicians in Turkey. Americans are very smart that way. You call it American jazz, but you steal from your black slaves and from Eurasians and everyone you can."

Solomon shrugs. "I just like the music."

"But this is why I love America. World's greatest thieves!" He turns to Nadia. "Are you going to work for that bastard Bebchuk in Brooklyn?"

"I am not going to work. My husband will support me."

"Such bullshit."

Just as the repetitious two-chord piano vamp beats into Solomon's brain, he puts on his lawyer's voice and says, "Mr. Gorev, you are wrongfully holding my client's passport. We could get a writ of replevin to force you to return it. Then there is the matter of withheld wages."

"I wipe my ass with your writ." He turns back to Nadia. "Tell me, you little shlyukha, what is going on?"

"I'm not a whore, you svoloch bastard!"

"Tell that to the police in Riga. You just weren't very good at it."

"I leave because I will not be part of your wire fraud and money laundering anymore. Or the racketeering."

Gorev freezes. "Where did you learn these words?"

"Nowhere." Panic crosses her face.

"You, lawyer! Did you teach this stupid girl those words?"

"If I did, I wouldn't tell you. And don't talk to her like that."

"Or what? You will sue me." Gorev opens a desk drawer and comes out with a Beretta semiautomatic. Aiming at Nadia, he says, "Take off your dress."

"I have taken off my clothes for you for the last time."

"I am not going to screw you. I am looking for wire."

"I would never—"

"Are you working for the government or for the jeweler?"

"I work for you only."

Gorev swings the Beretta toward Solomon. "What about you, lawyer? Are you wearing a wire?"

"I never work for the government. And I have no idea who the jeweler is."

"Nadia, my little Nadia. Why make me do this?" Gorev sounds truly sad, as if he has to put down a beloved old dog.

"I will go. Forget everything."

She starts to stand, but Gorev shouts, "Nyet! Sit!"

She sinks back into the chair.

"*Do you know my brother Alex used to fly helicopters in the army?*" Gorev says.

"*Of course. It is all Alex talks about. That and the hockey.*"

"*Alex loved dropping captured Chechens out of the helicopter and watching them hit. Splat! He was very happy when I asked him to help me with a girl who betrayed me in Russia. He took her up in a helicopter and dropped her into a giant pit. Six hundred meters deep. Nadia, you know the place. The jeweler knows the place. But Alex was so disappointed. The fall was so far and the pit so deep, he could not see her hit the ground.*"

"*Just so we're clear,*" Solomon says. "*You have committed a variety of felonies under Florida law. Reckless display of a firearm. Assault. Terroristic threats.*"

Gorev makes a snorting sound and dismisses Solomon with a wave of the gun. "*Gerla, you have been talking to government.*"

"*No. I swear.*"

"*Did they ask you about Aeroflot 100?*"

"*They ask nothing. I say nothing. I know nothing.*"

"*If either of you is wearing a wire, I will kill you both,*" Gorev says matter-of-factly. He points the gun at Solomon. "*I have a feeling it is you. Lawyer, your clothes.*"

"*I have nothing to hide.*"

Solomon starts unbuttoning his shirt. He senses movement in Nadia's chair. Forces himself not to look in her direction. Keeps a steady gaze on Gorev, but still, from the corner of his eye, he sees:

Nadia reaching into her purse.

Pulling out a handgun!

Gorev sees or senses something. He swings the gun back toward Nadia. Half a second late.

The gunshot hits him squarely in the forehead, snapping his head back, and then forward again. He topples face-first onto his desk, blood oozing from his ears and over those diamond earrings. Steve is frozen in his chair.

Nadia leaps up, dashes to the rear wall of the office behind Gorev's desk. Pulls at the Lenin's tomb painting, which is on a hinge and swings away from the wall. A combination safe is behind the painting. She expertly twirls the dial, this way and that, and within seconds, the door is open. She reaches in and digs around, flipping through a dozen foreign passports. Finds the one she wants, tosses it into her purse. Then pulls a gallon-size freezer bag from the safe and puts that into her purse, too.

Steve's ears are ringing from the gunshot, but now he hears shouting outside the office door. Gorev's name is being called. More shouts in Russian. Banging on the door, but it's bolted from the inside.

"Nadia, we need to call the police," Solomon says. "Right now."

"No police!"

"It was self-defense. I can't be your lawyer, but I'm a helluva good eyewitness."

Nadia rifles through Gorev's desk drawers, finds something. A key. Then she slips Gorev's Beretta into her purse.

"No!" Solomon yells. "Don't touch that. Gorev's prints are on it. We need it."

She points her own gun—a Glock nine millimeter—at Solomon. "I am sorry. You should have had gun."

Still holding the Glock on him, Nadia takes the key and slides open the red drapes behind the desk, exposing a hidden door. She unlocks the door and tosses the Glock at Solomon. "You may need this," she says as she exits into a rear alley.

Steve catches the gun, goes to the drapes, and tries the door. Locked! More angry shouts in Russian from inside the club.

Then the gunfire starts from the corridor. Bullets thudding into the outside of the thick wooden door they had entered. Instinctively, Solomon raises the Glock and fires two rounds into his side of the door. That *stops the incoming gunfire long enough for him to grab his cell phone and dial 9-1-1.*

As the phone rings, he looks down at the Glock. He has no idea how many rounds are left in the magazine. But he knows two bullets are now in the door. One is in Gorev's brain. And the gun is in his hand.

"I am in deep shit," Steve Solomon says aloud.

-8-

Where Is Nadia?

guess there's no sense in my telling you how reckless you were," I said.

"None," Solomon said.

"Steve knows," Victoria agreed.

We were still in the claustrophobic confines of the jail's lawyer visitation room. Chairs and a metal table were bolted to the floor. Victoria made notes in neat block printing on a legal pad. I preferred working without notes, studying Solomon, looking for any trace of prevarication. So far, nothing. He told the story with apparent sincerity. Hell, it was such a bad story, if he were lying, he'd have a better one.

"Wandering clueless into the cave of the Russian bear," I continued. "Gorev was probably *Bratva*. Russian Mafia."

"I guess," Solomon said.

"I mean, taking a big lead off third base is one thing, but this . . ."

"I thought you weren't going to bust my chops, Lassiter."

"You're right. Let's just sum it up. The cops find you in a locked room with a dead man. Your fingerprints are on the gun used to kill him, and gunpowder residue is on your right hand."

"Nadia was wearing those Holly Golightly gloves or her prints would have been on the gun," Solomon said in his own defense.

"But Nadia can't back you up because she's disappeared," Victoria said. "And even though she has a strong self-defense claim, which you could corroborate, she's unlikely to show up voluntarily."

"Because even though she's likely innocent of murder," I chipped in, "she's probably guilty of robbery. Any idea what was in that freezer baggie she took?"

"None."

"Cash?"

"Don't know."

"Drugs maybe?"

"Like I said, no clue."

"What was that bit about her wearing a wire? Is she a government informant? And if so, whose?"

Steve shrugged and threw up his hands.

I looked at Victoria's legal pad. She had printed in neat block letters: *WHERE IS NADIA?*

My question exactly. We needed her to win the case.

I was enjoying working with Victoria. Enjoying her company, too. I made a mental note not to get too damn enamored of the lady lawyer.

"I read the arrest report and asked George Barrios about the wire," I said. "He claims not to know anything. Says for sure it wasn't a city investigation."

"You already talked to the chief of Beach homicide?" Solomon asked.

"On the way over here."

"You guys are pals?"

"Actually he arrested me once. When I was cleared, he apologized."

"Tell him he's gonna have to send me roses and chocolates."

"Let's win first; then I'll tell him."

"Barrios is an asshole." Solomon sounded frustrated.

"He'll give you a fair shake," I said. "He's smart and honest, and lots of cops are neither."

"I suppose you're friends with State Attorney Pincher, too."

"Over the years, I've found it helps to be on good terms with the chief prosecutor."

"Why—so you can plead your guy out and go fishing?"

"If we had the time, I'd explain the finer points of lawyering to you, Solomon."

"I got nothing but time."

"Consider me a rocky island in the middle of a raging river. You're a capsized soul floundering in the water, headed for Niagara Falls. Now, you can reach out and try to grab hold of me, or you can try to swim against the current. Entirely up to you."

"I want a warrior, not an island. I'd always heard you were a tough guy, Lassiter, but frankly, I don't see it."

"You'd be surprised. They don't call me a shark for my ability to swim."

"A shark without teeth is just a mermaid."

"Boys!" Victoria wrinkled her forehead and pointed a finger at Solomon, then at me. She could have been an elementary school teacher with two unruly students. "Just when you were working so well together."

She was right. We needed to get back on track. "What about Gorev's brother dropping a woman down a pit six hundred meters deep?" I said. "What the hell was that about? And saying that Nadia and the jeweler know the place. What place? What jeweler? And Aeroflot 100? What's the big deal about that flight?"

"You got me," Solomon said.

On her legal pad, Victoria wrote, *WHO IS THE JEWELER? WHAT ABOUT AEROFLOT 100?*

So many questions. It was still early in the case, but not too early to be worried. I felt as if I were boxing blindfolded and with one hand tied behind my back.

"You know the weakness of the state's case," Solomon said.

"Not yet."

"C'mon, Lassiter. Motive! Why would I kill the guy?"

Solomon was both right and wrong. Technically, the state doesn't have to prove motive in a murder case. It has to prove the who and the how . . . but not the why. But the jury wants to know motive. Just why would Steve Solomon plug a total stranger?

"Because you're in love with Nadia," I said.

"What!"

"Barrios's theory."

"That's so insulting," Victoria said. A lover's response rather than a lawyer's.

"You were so smitten you agreed to help her rob Gorev," I went on. "Barrios is looking for evidence you've been sneaking over to the Beach for a quickie now and then."

"He won't be finding any, because it isn't true." Solomon's eyes flashed with anger. To me, he sure looked as if he was telling the truth.

"When that fails, he'll go to the femme fatale option," I said. "Nadia really did come to your office to hire you. Told you how Gorev is always shortchanging her, and how he keeps cash in an office safe. So, you two were just going over to get her passport and collect what was owed, and she would show her B-girl gratitude with some tricks she learned in the motherland."

"So sex is the underpinning of the case?" Victoria's voice was part astonishment and part anger.

"Jurors love sex," I said. "Keeps them awake."

"This is ludicrous," Solomon said.

"Anyway, things go south. Gorev tells you to kiss your shyster ass, maybe threatens to turn Nadia over to INS or ICE. You shoot him. Nadia takes what she's owed and everything else in the safe and leaves you holding the smoking gun."

"Felony murder under Section 782.04, subsection one-A, two-D," said Victoria, Ms. Smarty Pants. "The unlawful killing of a human being while committing robbery. It's treated as first-degree murder when the robbery victim is killed."

"No way they go for the death penalty where the victim is a Russian gangster," I said. "But under the statute, there's only one other possible sentence."

"Life without parole." Victoria let out a long, slow breath.

"This is bullshit!" Solomon said. "All I did was go to the club to help Nadia get her passport and back pay. I didn't shoot anybody."

We were all silent a moment. Out of the corner of my eye, I saw Victoria scribbling on her legal pad. This time, the letters were smaller. I don't think the note was for the case, but rather for her to ponder. Feeling as if I were a Peeping Tom, I turned away but not before I saw the painful words: *WAS STEVE SCREWING NADIA?*

-9-

Stand Your Ground Solomon

Victoria and I were on our way out of the godforsaken jail and headed for our cars. The earlier rain had stopped, but now storm clouds had gathered over the Everglades to the west and were headed our way. One of those bifurcated skies. To the east, over the ocean, pure blue with a few puffy white clouds. To the west, barreling toward us, a churning black sky with bursts of lightning, like the coming of aliens in a sci-fi movie.

"Do you know the irony here?" I asked.

"Not really," Victoria said.

"Your boyfriend would have a better story if he'd told the cops *he* shot Gorev."

"Hmm."

She wasn't listening. I thought I knew why.

"Listen, Victoria, if we were playing baseball, this would be the big leagues."

"Meaning what?"

"If you're batting and the state is pitching, get ready to hit the dirt. They'll be throwing at your head."

"You're talking about Detective Barrios."

"And he's the nicest guy we're gonna deal with. Barrios knew I'd tell you the state's so-called theory. The theme of their case. Solomon's lust of the Bar girl. But it's crap. They may not even go with it at trial. He's just trying to distract us and drive a wedge between you and Solomon."

"Okay," she said, pursing her lips.

"Say it like you mean it. I need you to be strong. So does Solomon."

"Okay!"

"And get ready for more crap. Next, Barrios will have some snitch in the jail telling Solomon you and I were spotted necking over cocktails at LIV."

"Necking? You're kind of a throwback, aren't you?"

"I don't tweet or blog or order pizza with arugula on top. So, yeah, call me old school. All I'm saying, expect the state to play rough."

"By spreading rumors about you and me?"

"For starters."

She smiled. "That'll give Steve a good laugh."

I gave her a sour look. "Thanks a lot."

We reached the parking lot. The sky had grown even darker, and the wind had kicked up. Paper bags from a fast-food joint swirled across the pavement.

"I mean, seriously, Jake. What are you, like fifty?"

"Forty-eight, okay? I don't put my teeth in a jar and I still drive at night."

"I'm thirty-three."

"So? I've dated younger women for years."

"You mean Dolphin cheerleaders?"

"Ex-cheerleaders."

"And South Beach models. Your reputation is replete with inappropriate women."

"Other than women who've jumped bail, I didn't know any were inappropriate."

"Really, I heard you were one of those serial seducers."

"Only in my misspent youth. I hung out with the wrong crowd."

"Football players?"

"Cops and firemen."

"And now?"

"Now, I help little old ladies cross the street . . . and sometimes tall young ones."

We reached Victoria's car and the raindrops started to fall. It was that time of year. Sun. Clouds. Rain. Sun. Clouds. More rain.

Victoria opened the driver's door and ducked inside. I stood there, getting wet.

"What did you mean before? Steve would have a better story if he told the cops he'd shot Gorev."

I thought I'd show off. "Section 776.032 of the Florida Statutes."

"Stand Your Ground law."

"Exactly. Florida's protection for scaredy-cats with guns. Total immunity. The jury never gets to hear the case if the judge buys the defendant's story."

"But the defendant must show he reasonably believes the shooting was necessary to prevent death or serious injury. And we would need the missing gun for that. Gorev's gun."

"You would think so. But do you know *State versus Mobley?*"

"The two-hundred-and-eighty-five-pound guy who killed two men because one had hit his friend."

"Two *unarmed* men. One had thrown a punch. That's it."

"That case is on appeal."

"Nope. Florida Supreme Court denied cert this week. Third District opinion stands."

"You surprise me, Lassiter. You pretend to be a cowboy, banging your way through the saloon doors. But you still read appellate cases, like a young associate trying to make partner."

"I learned a long time ago it's best to be underestimated."

"The *Mobley* case . . ." Victoria was thinking about it. It's what lawyers do. Read precedent. Noodle a bit. Try to apply facts from other situations to your own, hoping the legal principles help your case.

Mobley surprised a lot of people even more than the verdict in the George Zimmerman shooting of Trayvon Martin did. Here's what happened. There's an argument between a man named Chico and two abrasive young men inside a restaurant. Chico's friend is the 285-pound guy, Mobley, who sees the argument and gets worried. He goes to his car and gets his .45 caliber Glock. When his pal Chico leaves the restaurant, one of the young men punches him, hard, in the eye. The second man approaches Mobley and seems to be reaching under his shirt. Bang! Actually five bangs. Mobley fires five shots, killing both unarmed men. That's right. There was no weapon under the second guy's shirt.

The judge held an immunity hearing and found the big guy's fear was unreasonable and ordered a trial. A jury would still have the chance to disagree with the judge and find the shooting justified under Stand Your Ground. But here's where it gets interesting. The appellate court in Miami reversed the trial judge. Mobley's fear was reasonable. Shooting the two unarmed men was justified.

Immunity granted. Charges dismissed. The jury never got to hear the state's case.

"So you're saying that we don't need Gorev's gun if he was threatening Steve in some other way," Victoria said. "Throwing a punch or even a stapler."

"Hey, it's Florida. Toss a beach ball at me, I'll empty my .45 into you and be home in time for Jimmy Kimmel."

"But it's all hypothetical, anyway." Victoria frowned. "Steve didn't fire the shot. If anyone has immunity under Stand Your Ground, it's Nadia."

"Which means . . ."

"If we can find Nadia and convince her to come back and every piece falls into place . . ."

"If she only took from the safe what belonged to her," I said. "And if she'll testify that Gorev had a gun, which Solomon will corroborate."

"And if she admits the shooting, out of fear for her life, she gets immunity and everyone goes home."

It was a lot to hope for, like the Miami Dolphins winning the Super Bowl, instead of finishing eight-eight every year. But trial lawyers, like athletes, relish a tough fight.

We exchanged see-you-laters. Victoria backed out of her parking spot, and I stood there a moment, watching her through the windshield, the wipers clacking back and forth. We were working well together, thinking along the same lines. I headed for my car, feeling invigorated. It was a challenging case, but we had a client who swore he was innocent, and he might just be.

I got into my Eldo, turned the ignition, and felt the old V-8 rumble to life. I sat there, my mind reviewing the past hour or so. Introspection has never been my strong suit, but I had a sudden realization. That invigoration? That pleasant little buzz? Sure, some of it had to do with the case. But what I really liked was being with Victoria. A second thought then, an itchy little one in the back of my brain, as scary as the pop when a ligament tears.

Why isn't Victoria Lord my partner . . . in law and in life?

-10-

True Confession

Steve Solomon wanted to bang his head against the steel toilet. Jail cell model. No lid and no seat.

He was mad as hell. At himself.

Victoria seemed to believe his every word. Lassiter, too. Of course, he had shaved the facts like a whittler with a sharp knife and a piece of pine.

He had considered telling them the truth, the whole truth, and nothing but the truth. But he'd boxed himself in by talking to the police at the crime scene.

And damn it, I know better!

When there's a dead body in the room, you never, ever answer cops' questions without your lawyer present. Which is to say, your lawyer answers the questions by saying, "We have nothing to say at this time."

Find out what the cops know before you tell them your version. And always call your lawyer!

But he had never asked for Victoria. Even after being read his Miranda warnings—which he knew by heart anyway—he'd just blurted it all out.

Nadia.
The passport.
The guns. Two of them!
The safe.
Nadia firing in self-defense.

He could not resist the powerful human impulse to talk, to explain, to profess his honesty and innocence. When you call 9-1-1 and the cops find you in a locked room with a dead man and a gun in your hand, who has the self-discipline to clam up? Of all his many talents, staying quiet was not one of them.

Solomon felt new empathy for his blabbermouth clients, the ones who always make everything worse by talking to the investigating officers instead of calling him.

Here's the problem. Once you tell Story A to the cops, you're stuck with it. Flip to Story B at trial, and the prosecutor will impeach your sorry ass in front of judge and jury. *"Were you lying then or are you lying now?"*

That timeless ditty is the courtroom equivalent of "Have you stopped beating your wife?"

So once he told the cops Story A, he repeated it to Victoria and then to Lassiter. Not that it was a complete fabrication.

Nadia had talked about wire fraud and racketeering, just like he'd said. Gorev had spoken ominously of dropping her into a deep pit and had mysteriously mentioned the jeweler, wearing a wire, and Aeroflot 100. And, yes, Nadia had opened the safe and taken off with its contents.

There was just that other little thing he couldn't bring himself to say to the cops, his lover, or his lawyer. Really, just an itsy-bitsy, teeny-weeny little detail.

I'm the one who killed Nicolai Gorev.

-11-

A Damn Fool or a Damn Murderer

Granny, I may have caught a rare bird," I said.

"A three-legged egret?" Granny Lassiter said.

"An innocent client."

"Hallelujah!"

We were in the kitchen of my coral rock house in Coconut Grove. The aroma of fresh-baked cornbread rose in waves from the oven. Granny was sizzling butter in an iron skillet on the gas range, and I was working the chicken-fried steak assembly line. I had just dropped a slab of meat into a bowl of flour, turning it over to coat both sides. Then I dipped the meat into a bowl of milk and eggs, letting the steak swim a bit. Finally, I put it back into the flour.

That's how you bread steak, and I'd been doing it since I was twelve years old, with Granny Lassiter barking instructions. Then. And now.

"Not too wet, Jake!" Granny scowled while she waited for my prep work. "How many times do I have to tell you?"

Granny had been old for about thirty years, but her appearance hadn't changed in all that time. Still had black hair with a white streak down the middle, but if you ever called her "Skunky," she'd brain you with a rolling pin. A short woman, she wore baggy shorts and a T-shirt with an outline of the map of Florida and the saying "Tourists! Go the Hell Home."

Granny was not really my grandmother. Probably a great-aunt, but who knows? We'd never really talked about the Lassiter lineage of Florida Keys trailer trash. She raised me after my father was killed in a bar fight outside Islamorada and my mother took off with a roughneck from Louisiana or Oklahoma or some such place. That star-crossed couple had a daughter—my half sister, Janet, who at age seventeen gave birth to my nephew, Kip, father unknown.

Now Granny helps me raise Kip, while Janet lives in tents and roams the countryside in search of department stores with lax security guards. I'd call her a gypsy, but that would be an insult to the Romani people. Let's just say she's a serial shoplifter and drug abuser with the parenting skills of a wilted rhododendron.

I dropped three pieces of meat into the iron skillet where the butter sizzled and puffs of fragrant smoke rose above the stove. "I think your fire is too hot," I said.

"Ah been making chicken-fried steak since you were still peeing your pants, so hush up."

I did as instructed and watched Granny poke at the burning meat with a wooden spatula. Without comment, she turned down the heat on the range. *Ha!*

"So, if you've got an innocent client," she said, "you can quit all your bellyaching. 'Oh, poor me. Ah'm so tired of all these scumbags and their dirty money.'"

"Actually, I never said that, Granny."

"What, then?"

"Said I always wanted a cause that was just, a client I liked, and a check that didn't bounce."

She harrumphed. "You were lucky to get one out of three, and that's if the check cleared."

"This time maybe I hit the trifecta."

"So you must like Solomon?"

"He's a total pain in the ass. But so was I when I was his age."

"I ain't seen much change."

"Solomon is smart and ballsy, and he'll learn to turn down the volume."

"Unless you mess up and he goes to Raiford."

"There's always that chance. It's a helluva lot tougher to defend an innocent client. More pressure to win."

"Now, don't that take all? You don't like 'em guilty, and you're a nervous Nellie when they're innocent." She flipped the steaks with her spatula. "Maybe you should go coach football at that pantywaist school in Vermont. But don't expect me to come along and shovel snow from the porch."

"With a guilty client, you just wash your hands and walk away. But an innocent client. That's a different—"

"Kettle of snapper," she helped out.

"If I lose, it's my fault."

Granny poked at the edges of the meat, which had turned golden brown, then took the steaks from the frying pan and dropped them onto a plate lined with paper towels. That left the pan with a half-inch-thick layer of grease, the secret of Granny's famous cardiac arrest gravy. The Lassiters will never be mistaken for vegans or health nuts. Granny sprinkled flour into the grease and whisked the goo into a paste. The secret to chicken-fried gravy is a mixture that's neither too greasy nor too pasty.

While Granny was fiddling with the ingredients, adding a pinch more flour, then some milk, I told her some more about my meeting with Solomon and Lord. Yeah, technically, I was violating principles of attorney–client, but I'd long ago deputized Granny, and it's really to the client's advantage. Like a good juror, she's got common sense, so I run cases by her, including the various accounts of my clients.

"Men are such damn fools, ain't they?" Granny said when I had finished.

"Can you be more specific?"

"Well, first you got them male tourists, spending thousands on pissy champagne and then not even getting their peckers wet. Why not just hire one of them ladies of the night?"

"That's the brilliance of the Bar girl business, Granny. A lot of men would never hire a hooker. But if they think they're charming this exotic beauty out of her thong, well, that's different. And if it costs ten times more than your Collins Avenue professional, well, it must be worth it to their egos. Problem is, the men get so drunk, they're pretty much useless, and apparently the women have no plans to go through with it, anyway."

"Hussies," Granny said. "As for stupid men, you've also got your client. If his story is true, he's a damn fool. If it's false, he's a damn murderer."

"We're going for the damn fool defense."

"Tell me more about Solomon's law partner."

"Victoria Lord. Like I said, very classy, very pretty, very smart. We'll make a good team."

Granny gave me a look.

"In court, I mean."

"Don't you be sniffing after a client's woman," she warned.

"Ah, jeez, Granny. Give me some credit."

"You think I don't remember that Gina Florio. And her mobster husband you were representing."

"That was different. I knew Gina before Nicky Florio did."

"So what?"

"Under the law, I was grandfathered in."

"Hogwash! It nearly got you killed."

"With Victoria and me, it's all business." No way would I confess to Granny that a part of me was jealous that my client had landed such a woman.

"Seems to me you got yourself an interesting conflict," Granny said.

"You mean a conflict of interest?"

"If Solomon goes to prison, you got a clean shot at this gal, who sounds a damn sight more suitable than your usual trashy girlfriends."

"Ancient history, Granny. I've evolved."

"About damn time."

Granny was right. In my younger days, my sly grin and my bucket of blarney unbuttoned the blouses of numerous barmaids, wannabe actresses, and aspiring models just off the bus from Apalachicola. My emotional maturity was nil. Nothing mattered outside the scope of my own pleasure. But now, after so many wastrel years, I was not in a relationship and I sensed what I had missed . . . the mutual commitment, the total involvement with the needs of the other person. As I am pushing middle age—oh hell, I'm in it—the smile has gone all crinkly-eyed, the hair is flecked with gray, and I am left with the empty feeling that I may have lost out. Do I even deserve a woman like Victoria Lord? A smart, capable, accomplished woman who still manages the seductive purr of a she-lion.

"Any other advice, Granny?"

"Nothing you haven't figured out. You gotta find that missing Russian gal of ill repute."

"Top priority. She never went back to the house where she lived with the other B-girls. They told the cops they don't know where she is, and my investigator can't get near them."

"So get off your lazy butt and do your own legwork," Granny said. "Just like the old days."

I'd already sent Sam Pressler, my investigator, to Anastasia, but he couldn't get past the thug in a black suit at the velvet rope. "Private club," the guy had said. Meaning you had to come in with one of the girls who secretly worked there. Pressler was a retired cop who wore perma-press short-sleeved white shirts and baggy pants. He had as much chance of being picked up by a Bar girl as I did of becoming Miss Universe. Before leaving, Pressler did a "trash pull" from the Dumpster behind the joint, looking for any leads, but came up empty, except for his own stained trousers and a stink he carried into my office.

I'd also spent twenty seconds researching Aeroflot Flight 100 because of what Gorev had said to Nadia, moments before he was killed:

"Did they ask you about Aeroflot 100?"

"They ask nothing. I say nothing. I know nothing."

Aeroflot 100 was a daily nonstop flight from Moscow to New York. Leaves at 10:15 a.m., Moscow time, gets into JFK just before noon, eastern time. I figured that was Nadia's route to the US but didn't know what it had to do with any criminal investigation.

"I have an idea for getting inside the club without too much muss and fuss," I told Granny.

"Don't be busting no heads. The state Bar's warned you about that."

Granny was right. I've been given "private reprimands," a kind of double-secret probation, which is better than having the Florida Supreme Court deliver a "public reprimand" while you stand, head bowed, in front of the bench in Tallahassee.

I'm embarrassed about some of the things I've done in the practice of law. Realizing that, I've probably been too hard on Solomon. He's still young, and if he's not spending life in prison, he'll mature, just as I have. So who am I to preach about rectitude? When I was a young lawyer, I was always being held in contempt. In one of my first trials, a judge warned me:

"Keep going, Mr. Lassiter, and I'll send you to a place you've never been."

"Already been to jail, Your Honor."

"Not talking about jail. I'm gonna send you to law school!"

These days, I try to act with integrity, but I'm a trial lawyer, damn it. In the legal system, not everything is black-and-white. I make my living in the gray.

There's an inherent conflict in trial lawyers' jobs. The Ethical Rules state: "As an advocate, the lawyer zealously asserts the client's position under the rules of the adversary system."

Zealously!

But where do you draw the line between zealousness and chicanery? Go ask some law professor. All I know, when you have an innocent client, it's easier to slide into that gray area without falling into the quicksand of self-loathing. So I was prepared to chop-block the state, to hit the prosecutor once from the blind side and twice upside the head in pursuit of Solomon's acquittal.

I was thinking these thoughts when I heard metal cleats clacking against the Mexican tile floor of the living room, and my nephew Kip came clomping into the kitchen.

"Not chicken-fried steak again." Whining. I've warned him about that. Lassiter men don't whine.

"Hush up, wash up, and clean up that mud you drug in," Granny ordered.

Kip was in eleventh grade now and working his tail off to make the football team at Biscayne-Tuttle, a private school on the shores of Biscayne Bay. Unlike his block-of-granite uncle, Kip was gangly and loose-limbed. He had decent speed but only average athletic skills, and currently he was a third-team cornerback.

"How'd practice go, champ?" I asked.

"Two pass breakups and a couple tackles."

"Good job."

"Plus I got torched on three long passes."

"It happens. Always clear your mind after a bad play. Learn from your mistakes, but don't dwell on them."

"I know, Uncle Jake. You've told me a zillion times."

"Hurry up now," Granny said. "Dinner will get cold."

"We expecting company?" Kip asked.

"No, why?" I said.

"'Cause there's a guy on the porch. Sitting in the rocker."

"A guy?"

"A soldier," Kip said. "Three stripes. That's a sergeant, isn't it?"

-12-

Reporting for Duty

I opened the front door and stepped onto the porch, scattering several green lizards. It was a hot, moist night with the scent of jasmine in the air. The jacaranda tree in the driveway was shedding the last of its purple flowers, succumbing to the summer heat.

And there was Manuel Dominguez sitting in Granny's rocking chair on the porch. Buzz cut, square jaw, just the beginning of a double chin. He wore a US Army dress blue uniform. A brass disk with crossed rifles on his collar identified him as a member of the infantry. Gold-braided chevrons on each shoulder marked him as a sergeant. Four gold overseas service bars on his right sleeve indicated he'd served in several combat zones. A fruit salad of colorful ribbons was pinned to his chest. If I had to guess, I'd say they were for various acts of distinguished service and valor. Perhaps in Desert Storm or Afghanistan or maybe the Battle of Gettysburg, for all I knew.

Because none of it was real.

Manuel Dominguez wasn't really a sergeant. Had never been in the Boy Scouts, much less the army.

He was a former client. A small-time grifter and con man I'd walked out of the courthouse a couple of times and left behind once or twice, too. But his crimes were always nonviolent and his sentences always short. Most recently, I'd gotten him probation for a lottery scam called advance fee fraud.

"Hey, Manuel," I said. "What's the charge this time?"

"Nada, jefe."

"So why you here? You want some chicken-fried steak?"

"Already ate."

"Lemme guess, The Forge."

He snapped off a crisp salute. "Scallops ceviche, the bone-in porterhouse with a side of Parmesan truffle fries. Rose Marie went for the caviar and Dover sole. We split a butterscotch soufflé for dessert."

"You get the Johnnie Walker sauce with that?"

"Is there any other way to go?"

"And who paid?"

"An orthodontist from Topeka. Here on a convention. I limped in, using my cane. And of course Rose Marie had her pregnancy pack under her dress. Looks about eight months, I'd say. The orthodontist sent us a bottle of Cristal, then came over to the table to shake my hand and give me the 'thanks for your service' speech. I told him how I dismantled IEDs in Iraq, and about the one I didn't quite dismantle. Of course, he insisted on paying the dinner tab. Then his wife took a selfie with us to show the folks back home."

"No photos, Manuel. I've told you about creating evidence."

"Hey, what's the harm?"

"Actually, wearing those medals is a federal crime."

"Tell that to John Wayne. I got a standing ovation when I limped out of there."

Dominguez was basically a professional moocher, running his hungry soldier scam all over town. Tuesday night was The Forge, Thursday was Joe's Stone Crab during the season, and Katsuya for sushi during the summer. I couldn't remember the rest of his schedule.

"And how is the lovely Rose Marie?" I asked.

"Great. Due any year now."

"So if you haven't been busted, why the hell are you lurking on my porch?"

He wrinkled his forehead and scrunched up his mouth. Looked embarrassed, if that's possible for a career con artist. "When I was on probation, I had to take some classes."

"If you took cooking, you wouldn't have to prey on unsuspecting orthodontists."

"Actually, I studied for the PI exam. Passed and got my license."

"Congratulations. I guess they did away with the good character requirement."

"I used an alias, but I got the badge just the same. I'm a private dick now."

"So you lied to get some semihonest work. I'm proud of you."

"Well here's the thing, Jake. I got a client who knows me and you are tight."

"Thick as thieves," I agreed. "You're my favorite lowlife. So who's your client?"

"Call him Mr. X."

"Okay, that's creative."

"Mr. X hires me to find this Russian girl. Natasha . . . something."

"Nadia Delova."

"That's her."

Now we were getting somewhere, I thought. You pick up leads anywhere you can, even from a phony sergeant. "Why's Mr. X want to find her?"

"Ah, jeez, Jake. I can't tell you that. Ethics and all."

"Let me take a wild guess. Mr. X has a proposal for me."

"How'd you know?"

"Because, Manuel, you couldn't find a beet in a cup of borscht."

"Huh?"

"Mr. X didn't hire you to find Nadia. He hired you to bribe me."

"Bribe? No way, José. He wants to do a joint adventure."

"Joint venture?"

"*Exactamente.* And if you find her, there's fifty large in it for you."

Manuel grinned at me and rocked back and forth in Granny's chair. From somewhere down the block came a screeching sound weirdly like a woman's scream, but I knew it was just a peacock in mating mode.

"Just *find* her?" I said.

"Well, bring her to Mr. X before the police get to her. Otherwise, no deal."

"Aw, Sergeant Dominguez. I can't do that."

"Why not?"

"Because Mr. Y has already offered me a hundred thousand."

"Who the hell is Mr. Y?"

It took less than a second to come up with the answer. If I'd hesitated, Manuel would have seen the indecision. It's tough to con a con man. "Didn't he tell you, Sarge? Mr. Y is Mr. X's brother."

"Benny has a brother?"

Benny. One horse had crossed the line. Let's go for the perfecta. All I needed was the last name. But I couldn't ask for it without tipping Dominguez that I was just fishing for information.

"Benny's brother Max," I said.

Benny and *Max* sounded good together, I thought.

"Benny never mentioned him. Is he in the same racket?"

"Well," I said, "they're into so much."

Manuel seemed to think about it before a scowl crossed his face. "Wait a second, Jake! You're pulling one over on me."

I yanked the rocking chair backward, then shoved it hard forward. Manuel scrambled to stand up, wobbling unsteadily as he got his feet under him. Too much butterscotch soufflé. "Give Benny my regards, Manuel. And get the hell off my porch."

-13-

What a Hunk

Victoria was in bed reading her notes, which she had already begun color coding. She wore her pajamas. A present from Steve. Victoria's Secret pj's, because, as he put it, with Solomonic wisdom, "What the hell else would I buy you?"

The phone rang, and she sat up in bed.

"Sorry for calling so late," Lassiter said when she answered.

"I'm still awake, so don't worry about it."

He told her about the visit from Manuel Dominguez and asked if she was going to see Steve in the morning. Sure, she'd ask if the name Benny meant anything to him. Maybe Nadia or Gorev mentioned the name. And if not, did Steve have any idea who Benny might be?

She wanted to ask Lassiter something, but it was difficult, and she hesitated a moment before blurting it out. "You believe Steve, don't you, Jake? That he didn't shoot Gorev."

"I do."

"Great. Steve always says he presumes his clients are guilty because it saves time."

Lassiter laughed. "I like that. I just might steal it."

"Like I said, you guys are more alike than either one of you wants to admit."

"Nah. He's luckier than I am."

"How do you mean?"

There was a pause, just the electrical hum of the line. "Well, Steve has you."

She froze a second and didn't respond. Then Lassiter added, "In his corner, I mean."

But that's not what she thought he meant. He had not complimented her lawyering, but rather her womanhood. Lying there in her pink daisy tank pajamas, she was sure of it. Then he'd become embarrassed and tried to backpedal. Maybe that's what gave her the courage to ask a question of her own.

"Jake, what about the rest of what Steve said?"

"What do you mean?"

"Do you believe in your heart he wasn't involved with Nadia?"

"That again? Jeez, Victoria, I already told you. Barrios is stuck for a motive and that's all he could come up with. I'm not even sure he believes it."

"What if it were you?"

"How do you mean?"

"This beautiful young woman comes to your office and asks you to have a sit-down with a gangster who's allegedly holding her property. You don't know the territory. You haven't checked her out. Or him. Would you just hop in your car and go?"

"How beautiful did you say she was?"

She let out an exasperated sigh. "I'm serious, Jake. What did you call it the other day? 'Wandering clueless into the cave of the Russian bear.' Would you have done it?"

"A beautiful woman in distress is a powerful intoxicant."

"So men are basically weak. Is that what you're saying?"

"Actually, the opposite. There's something deep in men that makes us the protectors. It's probably been engraved in our DNA since the time we were still swinging on vines. We're the hunters and the rescuers. It's even part of our mythology. We rescue damsels in distress from the dragons . . . or the Russian *Bratva*."

"In order to get laid," she said.

"Not necessarily. A man doesn't have to be sleeping with the damsel or even want to. He just saddles up and rides into danger because that's what a man does. So to answer your question, yeah, I probably would have done the same thing as Solomon. At least, I would have when I was his age. These days, I might have done some research, popped a couple anti-inflammatories for my knees, and taken along backup."

"You're not that creaky, Jake. You know what my secretary said when I told her we were hiring you?"

"Nope."

"She's seen you in the gym. And she said, 'Ay, Lassiter. *¡Qué bueno está!* Roughly translated, 'What a hunk!'"

"Ex-hunk is more like it. But all those years pumping iron. It's a habit I can't break. And every year, I do less weight and fewer reps. Not because I want to, but because of the aging process and my fear of tearing some tendons I didn't know I had."

There was something in his voice that troubled her. In their first phone call, all that angst about losing cases and now the talk about aging. Was Lassiter over-the-hill?

"Jake, I have to ask you something else, and I hope you won't be offended."

"Shoot."

"Back in the jail, Steve called you a burnout."

"Actually, he called me a 'deaf, punch-drunk burnout.'"

She smiled to herself. At least Lassiter's memory still worked. "Well, what about it? Are you going through some personal crisis?

Have you lost that swagger, the legendary Lassiter cockiness? Is there anything bothering you we should know about?"

"Have no fear, Victoria. Once we're in trial, the adrenaline starts pumping, and I come out swinging from the opening bell."

She hoped it was true. That was, after all, the Jake Lassiter everyone talked about.

"I've just become more thoughtful as I've matured. I'm more open about my feelings. And maybe I just talk too much."

"No! It's good. I wish Steve did that."

"Like I say about a lot of things, give him time."

With that, she said good night and hung up.

Victoria spent the next twenty minutes trying to will herself to sleep. But her mind was too active. Thoughts of Steve, locked in that jail cell. They'd come so far together since they met as opponents in criminal court. A rookie prosecutor, she had been hoodwinked by Steve in that stupid talking bird case. Well, technically, an illegal importation of wildlife case. Defending the smuggler, Steve tried to call a white cockatoo named Mr. Ruffles to testify. As precedent, he cited *The Case of the Perjured Parrot*, a Perry Mason novel involving a bird that had witnessed a murder.

Of course, the judge denied Steve's motion. But then Solomon the Sneak tricked *her* into getting the bird to talk. The judge declared a mistrial and held them both in contempt for bickering.

"When I checked my calendar this morning," the judge said, "the case was State versus Pedrosa, *not* Solomon versus Lord.*"*

To make matters worse, Mr. Ruffles pooped on her Armani jacket, and State Attorney Ray Pincher fired her. The same guy who would now be prosecuting Steve.

She and Steve then spent a couple of hours in adjacent holding cells behind the courtroom. She was furious. He was flirting. What was it he had said that was so damn infuriating? Oh, yeah . . .

"Cell mates today, soul mates tomorrow."

How did he know?

As she became drowsy, her thoughts surprisingly drifted to Lassiter. A good man. A complicated man. And something else. *¡Qué bueno está!*

·14·

Fed Talk

I hung up the phone with Victoria and realized, *I do talk too much!*
And what about the rest of it?

"Steve's luckier than I am. He has you."

How ass-puckeringly embarrassing. I blame the Jack Daniel's. Three fingers after shooing Manuel Dominguez off the porch, and another three fingers before calling Victoria. Let's see: three plus three equals . . . hammered.

Jeez, I should listen to Granny. *"Don't be sniffing after a client's woman."*

At least I was proud of myself for telling the truth. She'd fed me this lob: Was Steve screwing Nadia? I had every chance in the world to toss a grenade into their relationship. But I did the right thing. I told the truth.

Then, at the end, she'd said she wished Steve were more like me. Okay, not exactly. But she wished he opened up a little more. Showed his pain. Like me. The wounded boar.

Just then, the phone rang.

Holy shit! It had to be Victoria calling back.

She must not be able to sleep. Wanted to talk some more. Or maybe needed me to come over and share my Jack Daniel's. I was on Poinciana. She was on Kumquat. I could jog up Solana and be there in three minutes.

I picked up the phone, calmed my voice, and said, "Hello again."

"Again?" A man's voice.

"Who's this?"

"George Barrios."

Just why was the Miami Beach chief of homicide calling me after midnight?

"Who'd you think was calling, Jake?" Detectives have an insatiable curiosity.

"One of your ex-wives, George."

"Better you than me."

"Whoever got killed tonight, I assure you I have an alibi."

"You always do. Listen, Jake, we gotta talk."

"Now?"

"First thing in the morning."

"Okay, how about a preview?"

"There are some things I gotta tell you about Nadia Delova."

* * *

I didn't sleep well. Up at sunrise, I found a tiny frog hopping across the Mexican tile in the kitchen. A cockroach—we euphemistically call them palmetto bugs—was flat on its back, its legs wiggling helplessly. Nearby, a green lizard—call him Mr. Gecko—watched, deciding what part to eat first. Hey, it's not my fault. Or Granny's. We keep a clean house. It's just summer in Miami.

At 6:00 a.m., wearing my Penn State boxers—tasteful little Nittany Lions on a blue background—and nothing else, I picked up the *Miami Herald* from under the jacaranda tree in the driveway. I intended to skim the paper and have one cup of coffee before meeting Detective Barrios.

It was already hot and humid enough to give a guy jock itch. By the time I got back to my front door, several mosquitoes had dive-bombed my ankles for breakfast.

The *Herald*'s lead story reported that the pink flamingos at Hialeah Park had begun laying eggs again. This may not seem like front-page news, but the flamingos had gone five years without sex before a recent orgy. This gave me hope.

Thirty minutes later, I was dressed in faded jeans and a T-shirt from the Quarterdeck Lounge, a favorite watering hole and fish joint. Twenty minutes after that, I was aiming my old Caddy across the MacArthur Causeway toward Miami Beach. The car is a cream-colored 1984 Biarritz Eldorado with red velour upholstery and a personalized license plate: "JUSTICE?" Yeah, I think it's a good question.

In its day, the car would have been considered a pimpmobile, but it was actually owned by Strings Hendricks, a Key West piano tuner and occasional marijuana smuggler. I walked him out of criminal court because of a faulty search, and the car was my fee. I saw no reason to upgrade to a Lexus or Mercedes or any of the other showy wheels my fellow trial lawyers seem to favor.

Traffic was its usual mess on Dixie Highway. It hadn't started raining yet. Of course, at 3:17 p.m., give or take ten minutes, it would pour. It does nearly every day in the summer.

Once on the causeway, I passed the mansions of Palm and Star Islands on my left and admired the gleaming cruise ships lined up in Government Cut to my right. The ships were poised for their Friday departures to the Caribbean. Fun-filled, prepackaged, all-you-can-eat floating hotels, complete with evening entertainment from bands and comedians too lame to make it in Vegas.

Detective Barrios had told me to meet him at a Cuban café on Sixth Street between Meridian and Washington on South Beach.

He didn't want me in the city cop shop. Maybe he was afraid I would spread my defense lawyer cooties. Or maybe he was just more comfortable not having his colleagues see him consorting with the enemy.

Of course, I'd get to question him under oath, both at a pretrial deposition and at trial. But then, he'd have the state attorney protecting him from my insidiously clever questions, which usually start: "Then what happened?"

Barrios and I had a decent relationship both before and after I'd been wrongfully accused of killing Pamela Baylins, a serial seductress and looter of my trust accounts. This was something I intended to teach Solomon. Make friends with cops, or at least try not to give them the burning desire to shoot you in the kneecap.

Solomon. So damn brash. So much like my earlier self.

I found Barrios sitting at a two-person table in a corner of the café drinking an espresso and nibbling a guava pastelito. His back was to the wall so he could see all the patrons enter and, if necessary, plug anyone who jumped the café con leche line. He was a burly man nearing retirement age, with suntanned, muscular arms poking out of an orange polo shirt. His shaved head looked as if it had been stained a dark walnut. I eased into the chair facing him and ordered an American coffee.

"*Que pasa*, George? Why'd you drag me over here?"

"In my opinion, we both want the same thing."

"Justice in an imperfect world. Not to mention the love of a fine woman."

"We both want to find Nadia Delova."

"Ah, yes."

"If the state finds her, she'll testify that your guy pulled the trigger, and it's lights out for Solomon."

"That's one possibility. Or maybe she'll testify she pulled the trigger standing her ground, then hightailed it with Gorev's gun. As my guy says."

"Why should she do that? She'll risk being prosecuted for the robbery."

I laughed my big-time know-it-all trial lawyer laugh. "Meaning that if she testifies for the prosecution, it's only because the state gives her immunity for both the shooting *and* the robbery. Which is fine with me. I love cross-examining immunized witnesses. 'Isn't it true you robbed the safe, Ms. Delova, and that the state agreed to drop those charges if you would identify my client as the gunman?'"

"What I really called you for is this. State Attorney Pincher wants you to know there's a rumor around town that someone's put out a hit on Nadia."

"Why tell me?"

Barrios was silent.

"You saying Pincher thinks I'm behind it? What bullshit!"

Barrios shrugged. "I told him that was crap. But he thinks you don't want to find her and you *really* don't want us to find her. That you're afraid she'll torpedo your defense . . . if she's alive to do it. He wanted to warn you to keep clear of that sort of thing."

"If Ray Pincher wasn't such an asshole, I'd be insulted."

"I told him that wasn't your style, Jake. But you know . . ."

Yeah, I did. Pincher had that disease prevalent among prosecutors. He thought defense lawyers were pond scum.

"Appreciate the warning, George, and I got something for you in return."

"I'm listening."

"Some guy named Benny is looking for Nadia. Maybe he's your man."

"Benny? That's all you've got."

"Hey, this ain't *NCIS*. In real life, evidence comes in dribs and drabs. Whoever he is, Benny's offering fifty thousand to whoever can deliver Nadia."

That raised Barrios's eyebrows. He took out his little cop notebook and wrote, *BENNY*. Then he polished off his guava pastelito, which made me hungry, so I ordered one of my own, along with a beef empanada that had just come out of the oven; the aroma of the pastry filled the small café. Pastry and meat. Breakfast of champions.

"In return, George, I got a couple questions for you."

"Ah, what you shysters call a quid pro quo."

"What can you tell me about the gun used to shoot Gorev?"

"File your discovery papers with Pincher's office. He'll tell you all about it."

"You just did, George. If the gun had any connection to Solomon, you'd be dancing on the table."

He shrugged. "It's a Glock 17, older-model nine-millimeter semiautomatic. Solomon could have concealed it inside his suit coat."

"Or his purse," I said. "Oh, wait. That would be Nadia's purse."

"The Glock was purchased lawfully from a shop in Houston by a guy from South Orange, New Jersey. Name of Littlejohn. Guy owns a courier business. No criminal record. Told us one of his drivers lost the gun on a trip to Kentucky."

"Like I said, you can't tie the gun to Solomon."

"Solomon had it in his hand when the cops broke in, and he admits shooting into the door with it. His prints are on it. I'm pretty happy with the connection."

"We'll fight about that in court."

"You said you had two questions."

"Right. I subpoenaed the city for all police records on Nadia Delova, and I haven't gotten a document of any kind. Not even a parking ticket or a reply that you don't have anything."

"City's written reply is being vetted by Pincher's office."

"Bad sign. C'mon, George. You can't stonewall on discovery."

He reached into a slim briefcase and took out a single piece of paper, which he slid across the table.

A booking photo of Nadia Delova.

Date of birth, January 16, 1986, Saint Petersburg, Russia.

Charge: grand larceny, to wit, one Rolex Submariner, black matte limited edition. The photo showed a very attractive, very pouty brunette. Lots of hair and lots of lips. No smile, but for a mug shot, it was striking. The date of the arrest was five weeks before the shooting.

"Another charge you can immunize her for," I said. "So where's the rest of the file?"

"That's the thing."

"Oh, boy. Let's hear it."

"There's no file. It's missing."

"On the computer, then?"

"*Nada.*"

"George, this stinks, and you know it. You talk to the arresting officer?"

Barrios motioned for another espresso, which he took straight. The only Cuban-American in Miami not to pour a cup of sugar into his morning brew.

"Scott Kornspan. One year out of the Academy. Clean record. Took a complaint from a middle-aged guy staying at the Delano. The Russian girl picked him up at the bar in the lobby, took him to Club Anastasia, got him drunk, and had him sign for a few thousand in champagne on his AmEx card. Then when he passed out, she took his Rolex. Kornspan arrested the girl, who claimed the guy gave her the watch as a gift. She bailed herself out with a cash bond. Four thousand dollars."

"And Kornspan's written report?"

"Says he filed it. No explanation for what happened."

"It's gotta be on the computer. Everything's on the computer."

"Not there. Apparently deleted in a slick way that can't be undone."

"I'm guessing you have an idea what happened to it, George."

He shrugged his old cop shoulders. "I start with the proposition that Solomon claims Gorev accused Nadia Delova of wearing a wire."

"And you know for sure she wasn't an informant for the City of Miami Beach?"

Barrios nodded. "I checked. No investigations she's involved in."

"And I'm guessing Pincher says the state wasn't handling her."

"So he says."

"And the language Nadia used that spooked Gorev. 'Wire fraud.' 'Money laundering.' 'Racketeering.'"

"Fed talk. FBI US Attorney. Justice Department."

"But the feds can't just walk into your building and expunge a file. You have a liaison with the US Attorney?"

"I have a chief of police."

"So? What's he say?"

"Says he was advised by the powers that be that he can't talk about it."

"The 'powers that be?' That's all he said?"

"That. And, 'the Patriot Act is a bitch.'"

"You ever read the so-called Patriot Act, George?"

"No. Why would I?"

"I tried. It's nearly four hundred pages. Basically, it gives the feds the right to come into my house and perform a rectal exam if they don't like the cut of my jib."

"You haven't become one of those antigovernment nut jobs, have you Jake?"

"No way. I love the military. I love the government inspecting slaughterhouses so I don't get poisoned by my rib eye. I don't even mind paying taxes for your salary. I just wonder what's left of the Bill of Rights."

"Everyone's got their pet peeves," Barrios said. "With me, it's murder."

That shut me up a second.

"So what do you glean from the chief's comment, Jake?"

"Doesn't take a rocket scientist. The feds were handling Nadia Delova. Someone in the US Attorney's office was running an investigation of Gorev's operation." I tapped a finger on Nadia Delova's mug shot. "And that someone sends this naive waif of a B-girl into harm's way, wearing a wire."

"The feds would never have given her a gun," Barrios said. "Meaning Solomon brought it and used it."

"Not so fast. It's equally likely that Nadia brought it without either her handler's knowledge or Solomon's. And it was the fed's responsibility. They're the ones who apparently wired her and sent her on her mission. Meaning that someone in the employ of the United States government screwed the pooch. If Nadia testifies for the state or the defense, that screwup will be on the front page of the *Herald.*" I took the last bite of my empanada and drained my coffee. "You know what I'm thinking, George?"

"I have a pretty good idea."

"You want Nadia Delova to testify and so do I," I said. "But the federal government sure as hell doesn't."

Nadia and the Feds (Part Three)

One week before the Gorev shooting . . .

Office of the United States Attorney for the Southern District of Florida

In Re: Investigation of South Beach Champagne Clubs and one "John Doe"

File No. 2014-73-B

Statement of Nadia Delova (Continuation)

July 7, 2014

(CONFIDENTIAL)

Q: [By AUSA Deborah Scolino] So it's agreed then? You will work with us.

A: [By Nadia Delova] Do I have a choice? You will send me to jail otherwise.

Q: Can you come up with a reason to meet with Nicolai Gorev in private?

A: He has been shortchanging my pay. But he does that to everyone, and we talk about it all the time.

Q: Anything else, then?

A: He is holding my passport. I will say I need to go home. Mother is sick.

Q: Will he believe that?

A: Maybe not. He knows I hate my mother. I will think of something.

Q: Can you get him to discuss the business?

A: Yes. Business is all he ever discusses.

Q: Do you have any questions for me?

A: When this is done, can you keep me from being deported?

Q: I promise to use my best efforts. But I have to be honest. It won't be easy.

A: What if I was married to an American?

Q: A sham marriage won't help.

A: No sham. A man has asked me to marry him.

Q: Congratulations.

A: *Spasibo.*

Q: Just play your role, Ms. Delova, and I'll do everything possible to help you.

A: I am afraid of Gorev.

Q: Just act naturally. Give him no reason to suspect you.

A: He has instincts. Like a rat. Maybe I should take a gun.

Q: No. We cannot approve that. Do you understand?

A: [No response]

Q: Ms. Delova. I'm serious. No gun.

A: I understand. Now, show me this wire you want me to wear.

-16-

Giving Men Hope

Three days after my breakfast with Detective Barrios, I was headed back to Miami Beach. It was just after 9:00 p.m. as the old Eldo rumbled east on the Julia Tuttle Causeway, the high-arcing bridge that connects midtown Miami with the Beach. I had a dandy view of the mansions of Sunset Islands as I reached the Beach side; then I swung onto Arthur Godfrey Road and headed toward the ocean.

Since my investigator Sam Pressler had failed, the job of getting into Club Anastasia had fallen to me. A cleaned-up, dressed-up version of me. With luck, I'd get in. With skill, I might strike up a conversation with a B-girl who was a friend of Nadia's. With both luck and skill, maybe I could get a clue to her whereabouts.

I was tuned to the sports radio station, where callers wailed and moaned over LeBron James's decision to leave the Miami Heat for the Cleveland Cavaliers. Honestly, some of these people sounded positively suicidal. Then about ten minutes of commercials for a nudie bar they called a "gentleman's club," a shooting range that featured machine guns, and a mail-order firm selling male enhancement pills. The station clearly knew its demographics.

I know I should listen to NPR and get a twenty-minute feature about a Rumanian viola player who performs Hoffmeister's etudes backward . . . and, by the way, send us some money. But I've been listening to sports talk radio—the septic tank of broadcasting—since my playing days.

Now the radio callers were complaining about the Dolphins, and my thoughts drifted back to broiling Sunday afternoons in what I still call Joe Robbie Stadium. As a pro, I made up for my lack of skill and speed with effort and sweat. I was never late for a meeting, I worked harder than the guy next to me, and I played hurt. Same thing at the University of Miami Law School, night division. I never cut class. I studied harder than the guy next to me, and I played poker with the smart scholarship kids.

As a lawyer, I break as few rules as possible, and just as in football, I play the game without fear. My college coach, Joe Paterno at Penn State, once told me to stop thinking so much. "Buckle your chin strap and hit somebody. Play fast and hard, and something good will happen. Don't be afraid to lose."

My pro coach, Don Shula, had lots of advice, too. One August scorcher during two-a-days, I was on my knees puking up my guts after wind sprints, and Shula shouted, "Lassiter, get off my field! Go die somewhere else."

I twirled the dial and caught a bit of the Foggy Bottom Boys singing "I Am a Man of Constant Sorrow." That's when my cell rang.

"Why are you doing this without me?" Victoria Lord asked.

"Because a B-girl is unlikely to pick me up when I'm with a woman more beautiful than she is."

"Don't try to flatter your way out of this. I should be there. Maybe not sitting with you, but somewhere in the bar. As backup."

I laughed. "You gonna protect my chastity?"

"Oh, damn it, Jake. I'm feeling useless."

"You're not. When we get to court, I'll be leaning on you a lot. But in the street, you gotta trust me."

"The Fontainebleau is not exactly the street. Did you remember what Steve said?"

"Dress nicely and wear an expensive watch. Just like Nadia told him. Catnip for the B-girls."

"Well, did you?"

"My suit is my one and only Armani. Linen and silk, a dark blue."

"Perfect."

"Birthday present from my granny. Forty-six long, and they had to let out the butt and thighs. Those Italians got legs like spaghetti."

"And the watch?"

"Audemars Piguet Royal Oak."

"Oh, my God. In eighteen-karat gold?"

"That's what it says."

"Exquisite. Where'd you get it?"

"A client."

"Fee or a present?"

"As I recall, I put him in a headlock and ripped it off his wrist. Must have been a fee."

She laughed, told me to be careful, and hung up.

I hadn't exactly lied to my cocounsel. The watch said eighteen-karat gold, and it sure as hell looked like the Royal Oak. And I did get it from a client, José Villalobos, a guy who sold knockoff goods out of a warehouse on Bird Road near the turnpike. But instead of a $25,000 Piguet, it was a ninety-dollar Villalobos. In the dark, I didn't think a Bar girl could tell the difference.

Victoria and I had talked several times in the last couple days. She had told me that Steve had no idea who Benny was. The name had never come up with Nadia and wasn't mentioned in the confrontation with Gorev. I told Victoria about my conversation with

Detective Barrios and how we were both convinced that Nadia had been working with the feds. Yesterday, my process server had delivered subpoenas to both the FBI's and the US Attorney's offices downtown, demanding all documents related to "Russian nationals named Nadia Delova and Nicolai Gorev, regarding any and all investigations of wire fraud, money laundering, racketeering, and any other federal crimes."

It only took twenty-four hours for the responses. Identical boilerplate motions to quash the subpoenas on grounds that "said documents would compromise an ongoing investigation and endanger national security, and that further, production of said documents would violate Public Law 107-56, 115 Stat. 272 (2001), commonly referred to as the Patriot Act. This is not to be construed as an admission that any such documents exist or ever existed."

I just love bureaucratic jibber-jabber.

The government's response pretty much confirmed that Nadia had been working with the feds, and it did something else, too. It corroborated Solomon's story about Gorev accusing Nadia of wearing a wire. Every little tidbit of Solomon's account that proved true was helpful to our case. His other, more important claims—that Gorev pulled a gun and Nadia shot him—were bolstered by his veracity on the wire accusation.

I turned my Caddy over to the valet in the driveway of the Fontainebleau. The hotel has been renovated a couple of times since James Bond and Goldfinger played gin rummy there in the 1960s. As I recall, Goldfinger cheated.

There's no more Boom-Boom Room. No Sinatra or Hope or Gleason playing one of the lounges. It's now a "luxury resort" with a swimming pool the size of Massachusetts and several bars where conventioneers are likely to gather, the bait to attract the Russian sharks.

On Miami Beach these days, you've got Mansion and Cameo and Mynt and a dozen other clubs where party animals—yeah,

I know the term is as dated as I am—go to, well . . . party. I'm long gone from that scene. In my playing days, like a lot of jocks, I hung out at places like the Booby Trap and Cheetah and other strip joints. Booze and breasts and wasted nights. Maybe getting older and presumably wiser ain't such a bad deal.

I wandered into the lobby's Bleau Bar, whose primary characteristics are blue lighting, blue seating, and blue cocktails. It was crowded, and I made my way toward the window that overlooks the pool. You can reserve a table there for 350 bucks . . . drinks not included. There were well-dressed couples that had Midwest written all over them. I mean that as a compliment. Well groomed, well dressed, a little starry-eyed. Not the tattooed, lip- and eyelid-pierced young crowd you find south of Lincoln Road.

There were a few single women in the place. A business suit here, a nice dress there, a convention badge yonder. The women gave me the once-over and didn't faint from overheating. A woman once told me I was damn sexy if you like overstuffed upholstery. Now that I think about it, she might have said "garage sale overstuffed upholstery." I don't know what she meant, except I'm a little on the large side. Another woman said I wasn't bad-looking if you like craggy-faced men with broken noses. Well, some women do, damn it. And hadn't Victoria called me a hunk? That was still floating around in my mind.

I don't pay a lot of attention to my looks. I don't go for body lotions or self-tanners or manscaping. Back in *Miami Vice* days, I didn't wear pastel linen jackets with the sleeves pushed up to my elbows. With my oak tree forearms, I couldn't roll up the sleeves if I wanted to.

Basically, I'm a throwback. I have old habits, old friends, and old values. I'm so unhip that I could soon become trendy, like skinny ties and suit pants that stop at the ankles.

From the Bleau Bar, I walked over to LIV, the nightclub where Miami Heat players like to guzzle champagne and sing off-key after winning a championship. The place was closed for a private event. It could have been a real estate developer celebrating a new skyscraper that might topple in a category-five hurricane. Or a fancy bar mitzvah or *quinceañera* party. Or Donald Trump throwing a party for himself, since no one else would do it. Whatever it was, I couldn't get in.

I strolled downstairs to the pool where the Glow Bar was just getting ready to close. Nonetheless, the handsome young bartender offered me a Glow Cocktail, which he described as a mixture of soda, elderflower liqueur, passion fruit puree, fresh pear, and some vodka. I was guessing not much vodka, but you get to keep the souvenir glass. Twenty bucks if you're interested, which I wasn't. There were a few people hanging around in swim and resort wear, but this clearly wasn't the place to get picked up by a Russian B-girl.

I took an elevator to the conference room level. A convention of insurance salesmen seemed to be the big event. The panels and speeches were over for the day, but the registration desk was still there, and a few name badges lay on the table in alphabetical order. No-shows.

I chose Gus J. Gustafson of Duluth, Minnesota. There was a gold star on the badge, which may have meant Gus sold more whole life insurance than the guys with the silver stars, but not as much as the platinum stars. A stretchy lanyard of bright-red fabric was attached to the badge, so I hung the thing around my neck. Now, I thought, the evening was ready to begin.

I paid a hefty ransom to the valet for my Eldo, which was far older than the kid who drove it from the garage. He gave me a smile intended to extract a ten-buck tip. I handed him a five and headed south down Collins Avenue toward the next stop.

My cell phone rang. Victoria again.

"Anything happening?" she asked.

"Let it go, Victoria. It's my party tonight."

"I'm sorry. I just left the jail. Steve's pretty excited. Says you're doing exactly what he would do."

"Then maybe I should rethink it."

"Oh, stop! You two are going to be great friends when this is over."

Not if I'm visiting him at Raiford, I thought.

"You bet," I said. "We'll play squash every Tuesday."

"So what's happening?"

"Fontainebleau was dead. I'm headed to a couple more places."

"If you need me . . ."

"Good night, Victoria. You're a great partner, and when we get to court—"

"I know, I know. You'll lean on me."

"I mean it."

"Good luck, Jake, and call me whatever happens."

Sailing down Collins, I could have stopped at the Soho Beach House or the Palms. The Setai or the Shore Club, the Raleigh or the SLS Hotel. But instead, I followed a hunch and headed for the still-trendy Delano, turning into its almost hidden driveway at Seventeenth Street.

The hotel was built in the 1940s and then updated—to put it mildly—about twenty years ago. Its open, high-ceilinged lobby, with ocean breezes swirling through the billowing white linen curtains, is iconic, if not a little clichéd by now. There's the big white piano in the lobby along with the Rose Bar with its upholstered rose-colored walls. Upstairs are those all-white $1,800-a-night rooms.

The Rose Bar is a scene and a place to be seen. Tourists flock there for overpriced drinks, hoping to spot Mick Jagger or Rihanna, but settling for Gloria Estefan or Dwyane Wade.

Tonight, it was hard to pin labels on the people in the bar. A few middle-aged locals celebrating birthdays. Some rockers from the local music scene, some local glitterati B-listers who might have had a season on a reality show, and a guy I pegged as a real estate mogul entertaining a woman thirty years his junior. The best-looking women in the place were a couple of drag queens whose hair and makeup must have taken hours.

I took a seat at the bar, glanced at the menu of seventeen-dollar drinks, featuring fruit-spiked sparkling wine, and ordered a Jack Daniel's, straight up.

It only took a few minutes.

Two perfumed women, one blonde and one brunette, sandwiched me like a slice of salami between two halves of a fragrant croissant. The blonde wore a silky electric-blue minidress with a plunging neckline, the brunette a blazing red leather miniskirt with a white blouse unbuttoned from here to Hialeah. Both had long, bouncy shampoo commercial hair. They were in their late twenties, I guessed, but in the dim lighting and under all the makeup, it was hard to tell.

The blonde aimed her décolletage at me, grabbed my left wrist, and looked at my watch. I hoped she liked the knockoff Piguet. "What time you got, mister?"

I gave her my best crinkly-eyed grin. "What time do you want it to be?"

She smiled and her eyes danced. "Funny man! I love man with humorous sense."

"We're tourists from Moscow." The brunette now. Both had Eastern European accents.

"Out for fun," the blonde said.

I pointed at my badge. "I'm from Minnesota myself."

"Ooh," they both oozed, as if this were an exciting development.

"Do you have Indians in Minnie's Soda?" The blonde again.

"You betcha. Got the Chippewa up in Grand Portage and the Ojibwa over at Leech Lake."

Their eyes went wide at this news. I'd had a teammate on the Dolphins who was part Chippewa, part Sioux, and I knew quite a bit about our Native Americans, including how to lose my wages at their casinos.

"What do you do, handsome funny man?" the blonde asked.

"My game's insurance." I pointed to my plastic badge. "Say, do you girls own or rent?"

"We visit."

"'Cause I got a heckuva deal on homeowner's liability. No charge for a jewelry rider."

I was about to begin extolling the virtue of double indemnity life insurance when the brunette started running her fingers through my hair. I had used some of my nephew Kip's polisher to give my mop a sleeker look and hoped she wasn't getting greasy fingers.

"Nice hair, big man," she purred.

The blonde slipped a hand inside my Armani jacket and was letting her lacquered fingernails tickle my chest. "Strong man, too."

We exchanged names. The brunette was Marina, the blonde Elena. I told them to call me Gus and gave them my best, "Pleased to meetcha."

"Gus, do you like caviar?" Elena said.

"Yah. Haven't had it since cousin Sven's wedding over in Hibbing. Gotta say I prefer it to lutefisk. Any fish you gotta soak in lye, Gus J. Gustafson can do without."

"We know a place with great caviar," Marina said, just as I hoped she would.

"And champagne," Elena added.

"Tickles my nose. But heck, ain't that what life's all about?"

My bookend beauties each slung an arm through one of mine. The gesture reminded me of a couple of cops escorting a client toward the slammer. But these two leaned into me so I could feel their breasts against my upper arms. The feeling was not unpleasant. I knew they did not intend to bed me down on fleece pillows. They merely intended to fleece me. Their smiles, their touches, were as smooth as a Ray Allen jump shot from the corner. Giving men hope. That's what they did for a living. And they were damn good at it.

"Let's go, Gus," Marina said. "Tonight, we show you time of your life."

· 17 ·

The Night Has a Thousand Eyes

Club Anastasia was just off Washington Avenue between Seventh and Eighth Streets on South Beach. "Off" Washington, because the entrance was in an alley.

A dark alley with Dumpsters, mud puddles, and a clanging of a Jamaican steel band coming from a nearby apartment building with open windows.

A red velvet rope in front of a narrow door looked out of place. Like a festive ribbon wrapped around a garbage pail. Standing at the rope was your typical no-neck bouncer in a black suit, white shirt, and black tie. The sign above the door said simply, PRIVATE CLUB. The bouncer eyed Marina and Elena as if they were strangers and said, "Password?"

Marina muttered something in Russian. The bouncer nodded gravely and opened the velvet rope to paradise.

"You gals know your way around this burg," I said as we climbed a scarred wooden staircase to the second floor. Music poured out of an open door at the top of the stairs. Not Russian music. American jazz. I could swear it was "In a Sentimental Mood," a Duke Ellington composition with John Coltrane on sax. The club might be run by racketeers and mobsters, but their taste in music wasn't bad.

Inside it was dark. Marina led us to a sofa behind a translucent curtain that gave the impression of privacy. The sofa was just large enough for three very close friends. We squeezed into it, me in the middle again. A pot of artificial ferns sat on each end of the sofa. I could make out several other mini-sofas, populated by threesomes. Men in the middle, hot women flanking them. More potted plants off to the side.

I could see the bar through the flimsy curtain. A three-hundred-pound bartender was staring into a mirror behind the bar, talking into a cell phone. A blue neon light above the mirror spelled out "Club Anastasia."

"Champagne!" Elena shouted.

"Perrier-Jouët!" Marina chimed in.

A cocktail waitress waltzed through the curtains. She wore a French maid's outfit you might see in a porno film. Black lacy mini with a white apron the size of a napkin and a white rhinestone collar. In five-inch platform heels, she appeared to be the height of an NBA forward. "A magnum?" she suggested helpfully.

"Da!" my two friends cried in unison.

"But first, vodka shots?" The waitress, too, had an Eastern European accent. Russia or the Baltic states. They sound alike to me. "Best Russian vodka, not available in stores."

"Da!" Elena and Marina agreed.

The vodka arrived a microsecond later, courtesy of another cocktail waitress in an identical orgy outfit. The idea was to get me drunk quickly. The B-girl scam wasn't invented by the Russians, but they were pretty good at it.

The drinks arrived in tumblers, not shot glasses. Icy cold. I tossed mine down. So did my two new best friends. It was cheap vodka, as raw on the throat as a rusty blade. Theirs, I was sure, was one-hundred-proof tap water.

"Another round!" Marina called out.

By now, "The Night Has a Thousand Eyes" was coming from the speakers. Not the pop version by Bobby Vee. The earlier number with fine trumpet and sax riffs, as well as haunting lyrics:

"The night has a thousand eyes,
And it knows a truthful heart from one that lies."

By the time the third vodka arrived—or was it the fourth?—I told the ladies I had to pee and carried my drink to a dingy restroom down a dark corridor. I wasn't lying. I took my time pissing into a urinal filled with ice, melting about a quart of cubes. I washed my hands, splashed cold water on my face, and checked the walls and ceilings for cameras, finding none. Then I poured out the tumbler of rotgut vodka and filled it with water.

By the time I got back to our love sofa, a 1.5-liter bottle that claimed to be Perrier-Jouët was sitting in a champagne bucket roughly the size of an oil drum. The bottle had been opened in my absence and the girls had already poured three flutes of bubbly.

"Vashe zdorovye!" Marina toasted me.

"Tvoye zdorovye!" Elena said. "To your health."

"And our fun!" I joined in.

I took a sip. It was the real thing. While I was guzzling, I glanced at Marina, who tossed her drink into the potted ferns with a quick flick of the wrist. Then she leaned in and nuzzled my ear with her lips. As I turned toward her, I could see Elena pour her drink into the plant at her end of the sofa. The girls were working. No time to get tipsy. I'm the mark who is supposed to be blubbering by the time the check comes.

"Drink!" Elena ordered.

By now, Marina was running her fingers inside my suit coat, headed southward in the general direction of my crotch. I could feel her breath in my ear as she whispered, "Do you like threesome?"

"You betcha."

"We are fun girls with many tricks."

Now she was running her hand over the outside of my pants. I was on assignment with a clearly defined goal, but there is a part of every man that doesn't necessarily follow instructions. We can't help it any more than the ape in the zoo. I was becoming aroused. I rationalized this on the grounds that it was in keeping with my horny tourist persona.

"Oh, *big* man," Marina cooed in my ear. I was sure she said this to each and every male of the species who wandered into this den of spiders.

The women kept pouring, and I had no choice but to keep guzzling as they sluiced their drinks into the plastic ferns. Fortunately, I can hold my booze, but even so, I was beginning to feel a little groggy. One of the cocktail waitresses delivered the second magnum even before we'd finished the first. She also brought a check on a little silver tray.

"Time to start tab, mister. Need credit card."

I had tucked my Gus J. Gustafson badge inside my jacket pocket as we were coming up the rickety stairs. No need to confuse the waitress, especially since my credit card read, "Timothy R. Dugan." Yeah, this was one of those gray areas in the practice of law. When José Villalobos gave me the Piguet knockoff watch, he also handed me the Timothy Dugan credit card. Not that it was phony . . . strictly speaking. Villalobos had several cards in several different mythical names. But here's the thing: he always paid the bills.

It's just better, he reasoned, not to be paying for the equipment, electricity, and water for his marijuana grow-house in his own name. Okay, maybe his lawyer gave him that advice. So sue me, I think the marijuana laws are bullshit.

Anyway, Villalobos had placed a restriction on the Timothy Dugan card, just for me. Any charge over $1,000, and he would get an automated text message notifying him. The charge would initially go through, but the alert would give him five minutes to call in and complain that he hadn't used the card or authorized its use. If he made the fraud alert call, the company would immediately grant him a "charge-back" and notify the merchant that the charge, originally paid, was now being debited against that merchant's account.

So I had five minutes from the time my card went through the Anastasia terminal. As the waitress handed me the pen to sign the slip, both Elena and Marina moved into high gear. Marina unzipped my fly and had one hand inside my pants. *Oh, what I do for clients!* Elena was massaging my neck. It felt good and made me a little sleepy, as was intended.

I gave the bill a quick glance without studying it. They'd charged for twelve rounds of vodka at ninety-nine dollars a shot, and the first magnum of champagne was a whopping $5,500. Altogether, with 9 percent sales tax the club never paid to the city, county, or state, and a convenient 20 percent service charge, the bill came to $8,627.52. And there was still that second magnum to be billed.

I signed the slip with a nearly indecipherable "Timothy Dugan." Neither Elena nor Marina watched me sign. I'm sure they were trained that way: don't draw attention to the bill itself. While Marina worked a hand under my boxers and onto Mr. Wonderful, Elena was nibbling one earlobe.

The cocktail waitress took off and handed my card and the charge slip to the bartender, who took less than ten seconds running it through the terminal. Then he smiled, gave a thumbs-up to the waitress, and went about his business.

Now the clock was really ticking. I had five minutes to work. "You know, I think I had a colleague come here a couple weeks ago," I said.

"What?" Elena's teeth let go of my ear.

"A friend from Saint Paul. Lester. Was down here for a flood insurance meeting. Told me he went to a Russian place, drank some champagne. Expensive as hell, but said it was worth it. You know why?"

"Why?"

"He met this girl named Nadia. Dark-haired tall gal with fair skin and blue eyes. Had a helluva night."

"Nadia?" Marina's hand shot out of my pants as if she'd touched an acetylene torch.

The women exchanged looks. No more stroking, no more nibbling. Everyone was quiet a moment. Just the sound of a jazzy piano and bass coming from the speakers, then a trumpet joining in. It could have been the Miles Davis version of "So What."

"I thought you might know this Nadia," I said. "I figure you girls are all friends."

"Why do you want to meet her when you have us?" Marina's voice overflowed with suspicion.

"Well, it's gonna sound crazy, but my friend Lester, the flood insurance guy. He wants to send her a present. Jewelry, I think."

"Is bullshit," Elena said.

"What do you want?" Marina said.

I dropped the flat vowels of my Minnesota accent and looked hard at Elena. "I think Nadia's in trouble and I want to help her."

Marina's eyes narrowed into slits. "Who are you, big bastard?"

"My name's Lassiter. I'm the lawyer for the man accused of killing Nicolai Gorev. Lots of people are looking for Nadia and maybe want to hurt her. I need her to tell me the truth about what happened."

Marina and Elena looked at each other, and I zipped up my pants. They said something to each other in Russian. Just then, the bartender barged through the curtain, waving a slip of paper in his meaty hand.

"Card bounced, Mr. Dugan. You got another one?"

"Is not Dugan!" Marina cried out.

"Who then?" the bartender asked.

Elena chattered a few angry sentences in Russian.

Marina did the same.

The bartender motioned to one of the waitresses. "Get Alex. Now! *Seychas!*"

Alex had to be Nicolai's brother, the guy who liked to drop women from his helicopter.

The bartender pointed at me with a fat finger. "You! Up!"

-18-

The Pit and the Jeweler

Everything happened very quickly. Both women leapt off the sofa and moved several feet away. The bouncer from downstairs tore through the curtain. At the same time, a third man emerged from a corridor in the back. Judging from Solomon's story, the corridor led to the office where Nicolai Gorev had been killed. The office had likely been inherited by his brother Alex, the guy now approaching me with balled fists.

Alex wore a charcoal silk suit, Italian cut, not the right style for his burly frame. He had dark eyes and a bushy black mustache. His salt-and-pepper hair was receding. I pegged him at about forty. From the body language of the others, Alex was the boss. The new boss.

"What the hell do you want?" he said.

A bebop saxophone was playing "Yardbird Suite," and it was all I could do not to tap my toes. "Just making friendly conversation," I said.

"He's been asking the girls about Nadia," the bartender said.

"Why do you care about that *shlyukha*?" Alex demanded.

"Why do you care that I care?"

"Who are you? FBI asshole?"

"No, lawyer asshole. I represent the man wrongfully accused of killing your brother."

"Wrongfully?"

"Your brother pulled a gun, and Nadia shot him in self-defense."

"Crap lie! Police found no gun. You know what I'd like to do with you?"

"Drop me out of a helicopter into a pit six hundred meters deep?"

That stopped him a second, and all we could hear was Charlie Bird Parker's saxophone.

"What do you know about it?" His eyes were wary. I had just gone from a man with too many questions to a man who already knew too much.

"That you liked to drop Chechens out of your army helicopter."

"Screw the Chechens."

"And once in a while, drop a woman who was giving your brother a hard time."

"Do you know who invented the helicopter, lawyer asshole?"

The bartender and the bouncer took positions on either side of me. If they grabbed my arms, Alex would have a clean shot at my face or gut.

"Leonardo da Vinci," I said.

"Invented! Not drew picture. Igor Sikorsky. Russian."

I decided not to say Sikorsky did the work in the United States and became quite wealthy without employing Bar girls.

"What's your point?" I asked.

"I love helicopters. But I don't have one to drop you out of."

"Pity."

"I have boat to drop you in Gulf Stream."

I had no smart-ass reply to that.

"What do you know about that deep pit?" Alex said.

In reality, nothing. But I'd touched a nerve and wanted to probe like a dentist testing a tender tooth.

"I know enough," I lied.

Alex Gorev moved closer, invading my personal space. "You can tell me now or I can have the shit beat out of you."

I remembered something Solomon heard Nicolai Gorev say about that deep pit: *"Nadia, you know the place. The jeweler knows the place."*

"I know as much about the pit as the jeweler," I said.

Gorev's dark eyes went wide. I had surprised him, and he did not like surprises. He glanced around the bar. A couple of the other tourist marks were looking this way. Maybe getting edgy about the place.

"We need a more private place to talk." Gorev turned to the bouncer and said something quickly in Russian. Then he turned back to me. "My car is downstairs. We go now."

Before I could say *nyet*, the bouncer grabbed my left arm above the elbow while the bartender took my right arm. They started pushing me toward the door. I gave no resistance. I figured we had a staircase to go down, then the alley, before they shoved me into the backseat . . . or the trunk. I would much rather take my chances in the alley than in this confined space.

With my good-natured cooperation, there was no reason for the bouncer to latch on to my left wrist and hoist it into a hammerlock over my shoulder blade. I'd separated the shoulder three times. Then there was the rotator cuff surgery with its requisite scar tissue. So, I didn't much care for the pain shooting through the joint.

That's why I stomped hard on the bouncer's instep. How hard? Two hundred forty-five pounds hard. I thought I heard his talus bone *cra-ack*. I know I heard him scream something in Russian.

With my left hand free, I pivoted and threw a short hook into the bartender's huge gut. I caught a slab of his ribs instead of his solar plexus, but he still let go of my right arm. I threw my right elbow at his throat and smashed his Adam's apple. He gagged and crumpled forward. But Alex came up from behind me and tossed a punch or a karate chop—I never saw it—at the back of my neck. It is a thick neck attached to a thick skull.

Still, I saw stars and staggered two steps forward. Joining in the fun were Marina and Elena. Marina leapt onto my back, wrapped an arm around my neck, and raked my cheek with her lacquered nails. Elena had removed her shoes and pounded a stiletto heel into my chest, which only a few minutes ago, she was lovingly stroking. Then she reached inside my suit coat, no doubt trying to pick my pocket. Fortunately, that's not where I keep my wallet. But maybe that was a diversion, because I immediately noticed that my watch was gone. One of the women was now the proud owner of a knock-off Piguet.

Nearing the top of the staircase, I shook off both the women, turned, and ducked as Gorev threw a sloppy roundhouse right at my chin. His punch sailed high, and I did the manly thing. I kneed him in the groin because I hate hitting people in the face. I have missed the face so many times, slugging the skull instead and breaking knuckles.

Gorev squealed something in a Russian falsetto and doubled over. The bartender moved toward me and threw a big paw toward my face. I stepped backward . . .

Right off the top stair.

Arms windmilling, I caught the bartender's wrist and pulled him toward me. I shifted my hips like a sneaky little wide receiver and pulled him around me like a dance partner.

We both tumbled down the stairs, but he was a three-hundred-pound pillow of lard that helped cushion the roll. The only downside, his breath smelled of beer and garlic as we bounced to the bottom.

I stumbled to my feet. The bartender stayed down.

I staggered outside, hearing rapid footsteps on the stairs behind me. Alex and the bouncer. Followed by Marina and Elena.

I didn't have my sea legs, and as I wobbled away, the gimpy bouncer easily caught up, then used both hands to smash me into the side of a nearby Dumpster. A garbage can sat alongside. If this were the 1950s, the can would be metal, and I could have grabbed the lid and brained the bouncer, just the way Sonny Corleone beat up his lousy brother-in-law in *The Godfather*. But this was 2014 and the can was blue rubber—recyclables on Thursday—and there was nothing to grab but maybe some Styrofoam peanuts inside.

The bouncer came at me with his fists, in a stand-up prizefighter stance. I covered up, bringing my elbows in to protect my gut and my fists up to shield my pretty face. He took a few swings, hitting me with short punches, my forearms taking the abuse. I would be black-and-blue tomorrow. When he paused to take a breath, I snapped a short left jab that hit him squarely on the nose, which spouted a Trevi Fountain of blood.

He brought up his hands to his face, so I pivoted and put all my weight into a right hook that dug deep into his solar plexus. That dropped his hands, giving me the time for a big whirling uppercut, the bolo punch. I've taught the punch to Kip on the heavy bag that hangs from a live oak tree in the backyard. With enough behind it, the bolo dents the bag, rattles the tree, and snaps the twigs on some orchids growing out of the limbs. But that's against a bag. Against a man, it takes too long to deliver . . . unless you have the hands of Sugar Ray Leonard, or your opponent is already bloodied and hurting. I brought the punch up from below my waist, and it met no resistance until it landed squarely on the bouncer's chin. The impact lifted him off his feet. Then he crumpled to the ground and pitched forward on his knees, vomiting, just missing my dress shoes. Nobody said fighting was pretty.

I turned and saw Gorev moving toward me, something in his right hand. A switchblade. Click. The blade popped out.

Lord, how I hate a knife.

"We haven't finished our talk, big mouth," he said.

That's when I heard the car tires squealing in the alley behind me. A Miami Beach police cruiser braked to a stop. A uniformed officer sat at the wheel. Detective George Barrios leapt out of the passenger door and surveyed the scene. The bloody, vomitous bouncer by the Dumpster. The porcine bartender facedown in the doorway. The two B-girls, now both barefoot and holding their shoes, their bouncy hair messy and tangled. Gorev, watching me with a murderous glare, his knife and hand back in his pocket. And, of course, little old me. Disheveled and beaten, scratched face bleeding, suit coat shredded, and quite possibly drunk.

"You look like shit, Jake," Barrios said.

"Whadaya mean? This is my best suit."

"How about I give you a ride home?"

"My car's a block away."

"Not a good idea. There's a DUI checkpoint at the entrance to the MacArthur, and you'll never make it through."

"Okay, you're on."

I was about to open the back door of the police cruiser when Gorev shouted at me. "We will talk again, lawyer asshole."

"Make an appointment. Have your B-girl call my B-girl."

"I promise you will tell me everything you know about Benny the Jeweler."

"Benny the Jeweler?"

"Who the hell else we been talking about?"

I was groggy so it took me a moment to process the information. The jeweler who knew all about the pit in Russia was named Benny. The guy who hired Miguel Dominguez to find Nadia was also Benny. I never won the Fields Medal for mathematics, but I could put two and two together. They were the same guy. Just a shred of evidence, but still, maybe something that would help lead me to Nadia Delova.

"I'll tell Benny you said hello!" I yelled to Gorev, ducking into the rear of the police car.

When we were a block away, Detective Barrios said, "You shouldn't mess with the Russians, Jake. They're as ruthless as the Colombians back in the eighties."

"Thanks for covering my back. Who called the cops, anyway?"

"No one. We been watching you ever since you got to the Fontainebleau."

"To protect me?"

"Hell, no. To let you do shit we can't. And maybe pick up a scrap of evidence here and there."

"Either way, I appreciate the help."

"You're getting too old for this shit, Jake."

"You're telling me." My head was throbbing, and I knew the rest of my body would start feeling the pain as soon as the adrenaline ebbed. "George, there's this burg in Vermont with a prep school. I'll bet they've got a little police force with a kindly chief like Andy Griffith."

"What are you talking about?"

"A New England Mayberry. Maybe the chief is about to retire just like the football coach at the prep school. We could have lunch every day at the local diner. Meatloaf and mashed potatoes."

Barrios looked at me sideways. Maybe wondering if I'd left some of my brain cells back at Anastasia.

"When you go on pension, George, think about it. Vermont. You and me. Best pals."

"Did you get a concussion, Jake? Vermont? Don't you have a murder case to try?"

"You're right. For now, I need to start putting the clues together. But when this is over, who knows?"

"What'd you find out from the Russians?"

"Nothing you didn't hear."

"I heard 'Benny the Jeweler.' You been looking for a guy named Benny who might want to kill Nadia Delova. Now you know he's a jeweler with some connection to the Gorev brothers."

"That's about it."

"So what's Benny the Jeweler's involvement in the shooting?"

"Not a clue."

I straightened out my Armani suit coat, which had three tears. Granny would be pissed. Checked to make sure I still had my wallet, which I did. No more watch, of course. My Ray-Bans were gone. No cell phone, but I remembered leaving it in my car. I patted my suit pockets, reached into one, and came out with a folded napkin with the Club Anastasia logo. A phone number was written on it, 786 area code. A South Florida number.

Elena hadn't been trying to pick my pocket. She'd slipped me the phone number in all the commotion.

"George, don't drive me home. Take me to my car."

"I told you. The DUI checkpoint."

"I'm not impaired. Besides, I'll stay off the MacArthur."

"What's going on, Jake?"

"I can't tell you."

"Why the hell not?"

"I'm grateful and all. But at the end of the day, George, you're a homicide detective and I'm a defense lawyer. You want to put my guy away, and I want to walk him."

He gave a little harrumph. "And here I thought we were both after the same thing. Justice."

He said it earnestly. No sarcasm intended. So I responded the same way, with deadly honesty. "George, you know how I always piss and moan about the system not working?"

"Yeah, you bore the shit out of me with it."

"It's real. I mean, it's the way I feel. You know that, right?"

"If you say so, Counselor."

"It's the way I think. Call it my philosophy."

"I know. The so-called justice system."

"There ought to be a better way. Maybe we should abolish the adversary system altogether. Maybe we should have three investigating judges hop in a car and go out into the night to find the truth. And whatever they say—innocent or guilty—goes."

"But that's not the way it is."

"Exactly. We're gladiators, you and I. We go into an arena where there's a winner and a loser."

"I just sharpen the sword of the state attorney. He's the gladiator."

"Either way, blood will be shed. The strong will win. Not necessarily the one with the just cause or pure heart."

"And you're not about to change the system. Is that your point?"

"Not tonight. I'm too damn tired."

"Then good luck, Jake. And *vaya con Dios*. To you and your client."

"That's the other thing, George. Solomon didn't hire me to do justice. He hired me to win."

-19-

The Other B-Girl

Five minutes after the cops dropped me at my car, I headed north on Alton Road, pulling into an all-night gas station. Traffic in the southbound lane was gridlocked all the way from Fifth Street to Lincoln Road, thanks to the DUI checkpoint on the MacArthur Causeway and the construction on Alton. The city had torn up the street to install a water drainage system. It was about time. When a full moon coincides with high tide, the stores haul out the sandbags, and you could surf down the street. Global warming and rising seas are causing Miami Beach—equal parts mangrove, barrier island, sandbar, and man-made fill—to sink into the ocean.

Horns were blaring and drivers—drunk and sober—were pissed off. Some stood outside their cars, yelling at each other or just cursing at nothing in particular.

I parked next to the air hose machine and kept the car running, just for the AC. I grabbed my cell from the glove compartment and called the number on the Club Anastasia napkin.

"Allo?"

"It's Lassiter. Can you talk?"

"Da."

"You're the blonde, right?"

"Elena Turcina. Friend of Nadia."

"You know where she is, don't you?"

"Da. She is a good person. Sweet. Maybe too—what is the word?—naive."

"Will you tell me where she is?"

"How do I know I can trust you?"

"I have a feeling she's in big trouble with the federal government."

"She told me that, yes."

"I know people in the US Attorney's office. I can help."

That was at least half true. I knew people. But I left out the part that the US Attorney, his assistants, and his investigators pretty much hated me. The FBI and US Marshals Service weren't crazy about me, either. That's what happens when you win a case or two in federal court. The feds are zealots, and they're not happy winning 97 percent of their trials. So, if you happen to nail them with an illegal search and seizure and get the evidence suppressed, they treat you like a public enemy. I know one guy in the Justice Department who, if he could, would order a drone strike on my little coral rock house just as I walked outside to get the morning paper.

Sure, I would help Nadia, if I could. But what I really wanted was for her to help Solomon.

"I will meet you in one hour," Elena said.

"Where?"

"Not on the Beach. Do you know the Russian Orthodox Church?"

I'd been thinking an all-night diner, but church was fine.

"I can find it."

"Saint Vladimir's. Just off Flagler Street. There we can talk."

"One hour," I said. "I'll be there."

Yes! This was the best news since I'd agreed to represent Solomon. Nadia held the key to his acquittal. Elena had access to the key. I was going to church and maybe I'd even say a little prayer and a "thank you" to the Big Guy.

I pulled out of the gas station and headed north on Alton. Smart guys stuck on the other side of the street were pulling U-turns and heading for the Venetian Causeway, which crosses several man-made islands on the way to the mainland. The Venetian is pocked with dangerous potholes, but when it's not closed for repairs, it will bring you out on Fifteenth Street next to what used to be the *Miami Herald*. That bayside building—like so much in Miami—has recently been torn down. The newspaper, to the extent it continues to exist, is now located somewhere on the edge of the Everglades.

Problem was, the backup on the MacArthur caused the Venetian to be clogged, too, so I headed farther north on Alton, passing the golf course and hanging a left onto the Julia Tuttle Causeway. I noticed a gray Range Rover behind me. There'd been one two pumps over at the gas station. It probably meant nothing—a lot of Range Rovers in Miami—but I kept an eye on my rearview mirror.

Traffic was blessedly clear on the Julia Tuttle. Sailing over Biscayne Bay, I dialed a number on my cell that I now knew by heart. I was calling Victoria Lord.

-20-

Lassiter, Solomon & Lord

Victoria simply could not fall asleep.

She'd been lying there all night. Fearful. For Jake.

He was out there somewhere in the dark, trying to scam the Bar girls, who were maybe the best scammers on the planet. Likely, he would come up empty. Or he could somehow make things worse. She was worried about the case but even more worried about Jake. What would happen to him if he got inside Club Anastasia and started shooting off his big mouth?

Jake had a ton of confidence in himself, but she wondered if he fully appreciated just how dangerous Russian mobsters were. Obviously, Steve hadn't.

I was right when I said the two of them didn't know how alike they are.

Maybe when this was over, if it ended well, the three of them could hang out together. Get grilled snapper sandwiches at Scotty's Landing on the bay before they tore the old fish joint down to build another shopping center. Maybe even team up to try a case together, if it was big enough and the money wasn't too thin. Wouldn't that be something?

Lassiter, Solomon & Lord.

Wouldn't look bad on a shingle, either. Steve would have to get used to second billing, but Jake had seniority.

With those thoughts, she drifted off to sleep. Dreaming. A sweet, sexy dream. A Caribbean island, hotel room on the beach, windows open, breeze swirling diaphanous curtains across the bed. Locked in passionate, rhythmic lovemaking with Steve. Her breaths coming faster, harder, feeling that hot stirring below.

The ringing phone jolted her awake with a startling revelation. The dream!

It wasn't Steve. It was Jake.

Lassiter! Oh God.

Well, it meant nothing, she told herself. Just the brain playing nighttime tricks.

The LED lights on the night stand clock read 4:12 a.m.

The phone was still ringing. When she finally answered, she heard Lassiter's voice, a bit slurred, "Howdy, pardner."

"Jake, where are you? What's happened?"

"I'm on the Tuttle, headed toward the mainland. Do you know how beautiful the city looks at night?"

"Jesus, have you been drinking?"

"All those buildings on the bay, the lights twinkling like Christmas trees. And the downtown office skyscrapers. I wouldn't want to work there, but there's something so peaceful at night."

"How *much* have you been drinking?"

"There's no traffic. I'll be at your place in fifteen minutes."

"Why?"

"Are you dressed?"

"It's four in the morning! I'm in my Victoria's Secrets."

"Make that ten minutes."

"C'mon, Jake. What's happened?"

"I need a woman."

"Go home!"

"No, not for that. Well, for that, too. But I need help with one of the B-girls, and you've got that feminine thing."

"What thing?"

"You know. That empathy shit."

"And you have such a way with words."

"Elena. That's the B-girl. She doesn't entirely trust me, so we'll tag team her. Good cop, bad cop. You're the good cop, by the way."

"No kidding."

"Okay, I'm almost at the I-95 flyover, and I'm cruising. I love the night, don't you?"

"I can't wait to hear about yours."

"Gotta warn you, I don't look tip-top."

"Why? What happened?"

"When I broke this guy's nose, his blood spurted all over my suit. Shirt, too. My shoulder's throbbing, both forearms ache, my knuckles are flaring up, and I might have tweaked an ankle rolling down a set of stairs."

"Oh, Jesus. Should you go to the hospital?"

"No way! I never felt better. I can sense it when a case turns, Victoria. I can feel it. The blood pumps a little faster and there's a buzz in the air."

Must have been a hell of a night, she thought. Something had lit a fire under Lassiter. She remembered their first phone call when he was drowning in angst about all the injustice and all the losing. Now, at four o'clock in the morning, he was invigorated.

"Gotta get dressed now, Jake."

"Say, that Victoria's Secret you're wearing. We talking a baby doll or teddy, maybe something see-through?"

"I'll have coffee brewing, Jake."

·21·
Saint Vladimir

When I headed south on I-95, I could no longer see the gray Range Rover in the rearview mirror, so I put it out of my mind. A few minutes later, Victoria met me at the front door of her house—the Solomon-Lord house—a cup of black coffee in her hand. She was wearing jeans, rope sandals, and a denim shirt tied at the waist, exposing just a flash of bare, flat midriff.

She took one look at me and nearly fainted. "Oh, my God, Jake."

"You ought to see the other guy. Three guys, actually. Plus two women, which explains the scratches on my face."

"Are you sure you don't want to see a doctor?"

"Honestly, it's no worse than playing the Oakland Raiders. They used to bite and claw a lot. Spit, too."

She looked at me with concern. "You should never wear your best trousers when you go out to fight for freedom and truth."

"Huh?"

"Ibsen. *An Enemy of the People.*"

"Right."

"You don't know much about theater, do you?"

"Not true. At Penn State, I played Big Jule in a student production of *Guys and Dolls*."

"The large, dim-witted gangster?"

"They needed someone who could lift Nathan Detroit off the stage with one hand." I lowered my voice into my big-oaf baritone. "I used to be bad when I was a kid, but since then, I've gone straight. Thirty-three arrests and no convictions."

I took a slug of the coffee, and Victoria said, "Now tell me about your night."

I gave Victoria a quick summary, making myself sound more heroic and less clumsy than I had actually been. I told her that "Benny" and "the jeweler" were the same guy, but I still didn't know what that meant or his connection to the shooting. Basically, we needed Elena to answer our questions. Especially the big one: where's Nadia?

Ten minutes later, we were cruising north on an empty LeJeune Road. I turned down the volume on the country station, quieting Johnny Cash, who was claiming he walked the line. A left turn on Flagler Street, then a quick right turn on Forty-Sixth Avenue and we were there. Saint Vladimir Russian Orthodox Church. We parked the Eldo, then walked underneath a wooden archway with three blue onion domes on top. The church was a modest one-story building with six golden crosses on a pair of red wooden doors topped by a stained glass window. I tried one of the doors. Open.

Inside, in the dim light, a single woman kneeled in front of a pew. Elena still had on her electric-blue minidress, and her blonde hair was a rat's nest. Victoria and I walked in quietly and sat in a pew directly across the aisle from her. Elena cast a quick glance our way, then continued praying. Maybe she was praying for Nadia, maybe she was asking forgiveness for stealing my watch, or maybe she had just lured us here so Alex Gorev could leap out of the shadows and chop us to ribbons with an AK-47.

After a moment, Elena crossed herself three times, slid gracefully onto the pew, and turned toward us. "Saint Vladimir was the first Christian ruler of Russia. Did you know that?"

I allowed as how I did not.

"A thousand years ago. Before then, all pagans. Now . . . pagans again." She looked at Victoria. "Who is the woman?"

"I'm Victoria Lord. Steve Solomon, the man accused of killing Nicolai Gorev, is my partner. Law partner and life partner."

I didn't care for that "life partner" bit. "Boyfriend" would have been better, but I didn't have a vote on the matter.

Elena turned to me. "You told Alex you were lawyer for Solomon."

"It's true."

"He looked you up after you left with the police. Jake Lassiter."

I nodded.

"He would like to kill you. And Nadia."

"That's why we're here. To help her."

"No, you are here to help Solomon."

"We can do both," Victoria said.

"Elena, we all know the trouble Nadia is in," I said. "Alex Gorev isn't the only one after her. So are the feds. She blew up their investigation of his brother, and they'd like to bury her so deep in a federal prison, she won't see the light of day, much less a courtroom where she can talk."

I wasn't at all sure that's what the feds would do, but it sounded pretty threatening.

"Can they do that, in this land of the free?"

"These days, they can do pretty much anything. Someone in the Justice Department screwed the pooch and they gotta keep it quiet."

"Someone had sex with a dog?"

"In a manner of speaking. The way I figure it, they offered Nadia immunity for whatever they had on her. But she's blown the deal and fled, so she still has the federal charges. Plus the state of

Florida is looking for her as a material witness in the Gorev shooting and who knows for what else? Then there's the grand larceny charge on Miami Beach for stealing a watch, which I take it is sort of a hobby with you girls."

"Yours was big fake! I checked it."

"Sorry."

"Makes me think you are big fake, too."

"Finally, we've got Benny the Jeweler," I said, testing the waters.

"What about him?"

"What's his last name?"

She shrugged her bare shoulders. "Only Benny the Jeweler. He shows up once in a while at the club, pinches the girls, and goes into Nicolai's office to talk business. Or he did. I haven't seen him since the shooting."

"Benny has hired some half-assed investigator to find Nadia," I said. "The guy tried to bribe me into giving her up. I'm pretty sure Benny wants to do her harm."

Elena shook her head, her blonde mess of hair untangling. Looking at Victoria, she said, "Your friend is a good fighter but very stupid."

"Like so many men," Victoria said.

"*Da!* Exactly." Elena slid to the end of the pew and extended an arm, showing off the lacquered fingernails of her left hand. She had rings on every finger except her thumb. She wiggled her pinky and said, "This one."

Victoria smiled. "It's real. A princess-cut diamond. I'd say about three carats, maybe more."

"Three point five! From Benny, who taught me the four Cs. Carat. Clarity. Color. Cut. Very fine diamond. Nearly flawless. He gave one to Nadia that's even larger. She wears as pendant."

"Do all the girls get a diamond from Benny?"

"All the girls get one. But the girls Benny really likes get the best ones," Elena said proudly.

"Why?" I asked. "Why the expensive presents for everybody?"

"You don't know, do you, lawyer?"

"How would I?"

"How do you intend to protect Nadia? You think Benny wants to harm her? He loves her. Not man–woman love. But like a father."

This wasn't going well. I had lost control of the conversation and the situation. "Look, Elena, I may not know all the details, but I know Nadia is in trouble. You know where she is. If anything happens to her, that's on you. Her blood will be on your hands."

Elena's eyes went cold, and her angelic features hardened. I had gone too far. She turned toward Victoria. "How do you work with such a man? He is, what is the word? Rude?"

"And boorish," Victoria agreed.

"*Da.* Very good sound. Boor-ish. I will use it with the bouncer who always grabs my tits. 'Sergei, you are rude and boor-ish.'"

They both laughed. Either at me or Sergei, or both.

"Lawyer, go have smoke. Me and Victoria talk."

I shrugged, got up, and walked out the big red doors. I have enough bad habits, but smoking isn't one of them. I sat down on a bench in the church courtyard and waited, glad I had brought Victoria along.

·22·

The Women Talk

The two women sat in the church pew, talking. Victoria realized that the atmosphere had become more relaxed as soon as Lassiter left. At least he'd had the good sense to bring her along.

"You are very pretty," Elena said.

"Thank you."

"You could be Bar girl. Small on top, but push-up bra would fix that."

Victoria tried out her Russian. *"Spasibo."*

"But you are too smart for B-girl."

"I was lucky to get an education."

"Me? Not so lucky. I worked in strip club in Riga when I was seventeen. You know Riga?"

"Latvia."

"Then Tallinn in Estonia. But no money there. So I went to Luxembourg."

"Really?"

"Lots of money in Luxembourg. That's when the Gorevs went from strip clubs to champagne clubs and I became B-girl."

"So you've worked for the Gorevs a long time."

"Since I was kid. I have been around more than Nadia. She is like child in many ways. That is why she is in trouble. And you?"

"College. Law school. I was a prosecutor for a while. I had a case against Steve that got me fired. And it brought us together."

"Do you love him?"

Victoria smiled, thinking about the complicated man she was crazy about. "On the surface, we have little in common. It's hard to explain, our dynamic. He drives me nuts. But life is better with him than without. And, yes, I love him."

"When I first saw you a few minutes ago, I thought you were with Lassiter."

"Only professionally."

"But he would like more."

"I'm not sure about that."

"I know men, more than you, lady lawyer. He has it for you."

Victoria shook her head. This was not a discussion she intended to have. At the same time, she wanted to talk freely with Elena and gain her trust. After all, that's why she was here.

"In his eyes, I can see it," Elena said. "He hurts for you."

"I really don't think so."

"Does not matter. You love someone else. Which also explains Nadia."

"How?"

"Everything she has done. The trouble she is in. Is for a man. Poor, sweet Nadia is in love."

"Really?"

"True love. She wants to marry the man and start over with clean life."

Victoria measured her words. "I'm not sure that's possible unless she tidies up the mess she's left behind."

"If you have plan for this tidy up, I will tell Nadia and see what she says."

-23-
Code Yellow

So, Victoria, you saying Nadia fell for a customer?" I said. "Won't they toss her out of the B-girls' union for that?"

Victoria nibbled at a croissant. Two hundred sixty calories and nine grams of saturated fat, according to the little card. Starbucks on Calle Ocho. It seemed like a crime. We should be at Versailles, the iconic Cuban restaurant with the French name and succulent *pastelitos de guayaba*. But it was only 6:15 a.m., and Versailles opens at eight o'clock.

"Nadia wanted to leave the club to be with her new boyfriend, but Gorev wouldn't let her. He'd kept her passport and withheld a portion of her wages. Claimed she couldn't quit until she worked there a year."

"Could be a motive for robbery and murder."

"Jeez, Jake, we'll never get her back by saying that."

"I'm just thinking out loud."

"Our pitch is, 'You fired in self-defense. No jury would ever convict you. No jury would even hear the case if the judge granted you immunity under Stand Your Ground.'"

"It's a good pitch. Let's see if she swings at it."

I chomped into the bacon-and-gouda breakfast sandwich. Three hundred fifty calories, seven grams of saturated fat.

"And she's with this man who asked her to marry him?" I asked.

"Apparently."

"But Elena won't say where they are?"

"Not directly. But she implied it's in another state. He was a tourist Nadia picked up and brought to the club. Then, instead of disappearing at the end of the night, she stayed with him all weekend and love blossomed."

"I'm touched." I took a hit of my coffee. Verona dark roast. Black and strong. "Any clues as to what he does, any convention he might have been attending?"

"Only that he owns his own business and maybe it's not doing so well."

"Don't tell me the B-girl got conned by a mark. The seductress falls for a flimflam artist."

"You're being a tad cynical, Jake."

"You're a hot woman, but you've been in a relationship for several years, so maybe you don't know how many phonies are out there."

She gave me a look and went back to rabbit-nibbling her croissant.

"What?" I said.

"I have to give you a Code Yellow."

"The hell is that?"

"You've been flirting with me."

"Have not."

"I've been fending off men since I was fifteen, so I know."

"Oh, brother. You think you're gonna have to go all Charlton Heston on me?"

She didn't get the reference, but then she was too young.

"*Planet of the Apes*," I said. "Take your stinking paws off me, you damn dirty ape!"

"You sound like a man who's heard it before."

"What did I do besides say you were hot?"

"That was quite enough."

"Okay, I take it back. You're not hot. You're not even lukewarm."

"Good. So it's agreed. You're not hitting on me?"

"Draw up a contract if you want."

"I'll take your word for it. You're not attracted to me."

I did my best to sound convincing. "Not even on a rainy Monday night. Sorry, kiddo, but you're not my type."

"Which is?"

"I don't know. The barista over there making the caramel Frappuccinos."

"The Goth teenage girl with tattoos on her neck?"

"Sure. And biker chicks with big boobs and muffin tops spilling over their short-shorts. And women who wear stretch tights to the supermarket, showing their camel toes in the frozen food section."

"Really?"

"And women under indictment who jump bail. Anything but an Ivy League lawyer who's . . ."

"Who's what, Jake?"

I let out a long, deep sigh. My shoulder ached. I couldn't close my right fist. I was dog-ass tired, and I'd been nailed by this sassy woman who I couldn't get out of my mind. She was so damn smart. Intuitive, too. Women, I have long believed, are the more evolved of the species and have attained some higher level of being. Men act as if we just crawled from the swamp, our webbed feet dripping brackish water as we waddle ashore, seeking to mate with a female or, lacking that, a warm patch of mud.

"Look, I'm not hitting on a woman who's in a committed relationship with my client," I said. "I'm not the least bit attracted to a woman who is totally unavailable. That would be stupid and self-defeating. You have nothing to worry about. Now, are we okay?"

"Thank you, Jake. Now, you should go home and get some sleep."

"Too late for that." I drained my Verona roast. "What kind of coffee does Solomon like?"

"Dark, just like you. Why?"

"Let's get one of those overpriced big ones to go. Plus a couple of scones, a slice of banana bread, and a sticky bun. Jail breakfast sucks. I've had it."

"That's very thoughtful, but it's not summer camp. We can't bring Steve a care package."

"I know the corrections officer who has the early shift at the front desk."

"He'll let us bring food?"

"*She.* And the answer is yes."

Victoria gave me a wicked smile. "Did you used to date her?"

"I always liked the way she frisked me. But it didn't work out."

"But she still does you favors. Speaks well of you, Jake."

"Aw, it's no big deal."

She seemed to think it over a moment and said, "You know what I like about you?"

"Nothing comes to mind."

"You're a better man than you think you are, Jake Lassiter."

Nadia and the Feds (Part Four)

One week before the Gorev shooting . . .

Office of the United States Attorney for the Southern District of Florida

In Re: Investigation of South Beach Champagne Clubs and one "John Doe"

File No. 2014-73-B

Statement of Nadia Delova (Continuation)

July 7, 2014

(CONFIDENTIAL)

Q: [By AUSA Deborah Scolino] A technician will show you how the wire and recorder work, but first I have a few more questions.

A: [By Nadia Delova] Why am I not surprised?

Q: How did you get to the United States?

A: By airplane to New York.

Q: Aeroflot 100? Moscow to JFK.

A: I suppose, yes.

Q: Why that flight? Why not fly Transaero nonstop to Miami?

A: Nicolai Gorev books all the flights. I can ask him if important to you.

Q: Ms. Delova, I think you know the answer.

A: *Nyet.*

Q: All right. Let's keep going. Every Bar girl takes that same flight, correct?

A: Is nice plane. Leaves in morning, ten hours later, get in around noon New York time.

Q: Always two Bar girls on the same flight, but you never sit together. Why is that?

A: Again, Gorev would know.

Q: But you do not?

A: Is the way he arranges it.

Q: And when you get to New York, you don't take a connecting flight to Miami, do you?

A: Gorev has two men with van waiting outside Customs. We drive straight to Florida. No stops except for gas and food. Not even Disney World.

Q: Why drive? You're already at JFK. Wouldn't a connecting flight be much easier?

A: You ask me so many things I do not know.

Q: No, Ms. Delova. I ask you so many things you do not answer.

·25·

Orange Is the New Solomon

Victoria wore a navy-blue Zanella A-line skirt with matching Prada pumps. Steve—her life partner and law partner, as she told Elena just hours ago—wore jailhouse orange.

He was pale and had lost weight, so he looked even skinnier than usual. She was glad to see him gobbling the pastries. Notwithstanding Steve's early bluster about having spent a day or two behind bars for contempt, this was different. It was getting to him. Jail was no place for a civilian, and her heart ached for the man she loved.

"Thanks, Vic." He chomped into the banana bread. "Great surprise."

"You should thank Jake. It was his idea, and his pull got the contraband in."

Steve sipped his coffee, savoring it. Then he looked at Jake and said, "Hard night, Counselor?"

"I've had worse," Lassiter said.

The three of them sat at a metal table in the claustrophobic lawyer's visitation room. Walls painted puke green, the air super chilled, and, of course, that smell. Disinfectant so harsh you could taste it after it burned the inside of your nostrils and throat.

"Jake could have been killed," Victoria said.

She was still waiting for Steve to say, "Thank you, Jake." But nothing. No gratitude. Not for risking his life or even for bringing the coffee. *Sometimes Steve can be such a jerk*, she thought.

"Jake really did have a hard night," she said.

"Okay, I get it," Steve said, finally. "Lassiter is noble and brave and can take a punch. Where does that leave me this morning?"

Victoria let Jake do most of the talking, even though he was barely awake. He told Steve about being picked up by the B-girls, then all hell breaking loose when he mentioned Nadia's name at Club Anastasia. He finished with a shorthand version of his bouncing down the stairs and breaking the bouncer's nose and maybe his jaw, too. Then the revelation that "the jeweler" mentioned by Nicolai Gorev just before he was shot was "Benny" who had hired a PI to find Nadia. Steve listened quietly, frowning when Jake mentioned picking Victoria up at the house at 4:30 a.m.

Victoria took over then, telling Steve about the meeting at the church. Elena had promised to reach out to Nadia about coming in from the cold and helping them. If Nadia came back, Victoria would try to fix her legal problems so she could dash away on a honeymoon with her American lover.

Everyone was quiet a moment. Somewhere, a buzzer rang, an angry discordant sound. Then a steel door clanged shut.

"So bottom line," Steve said, "Elena never told you where Nadia is."

"Not yet," Victoria said.

"Or how Benny the Jeweler fits into the whole deal."

"Says she doesn't know, except that he gives each B-girl one diamond. And that the Gorevs treat Benny like he's the boss. The girls think he might be the true owner of the club. That's something to file away for later, right, Jake?"

"It could be useful."

Solomon was frowning. "Don't see how it's significant, one way or the other."

"That's why we gather facts one at a time," Lassiter said. "It might take fact number five to make fact number two meaningful."

"Thanks for the arithmetic lesson, big guy."

Steve seems more irritable than usual today, Victoria thought.

"Did Elena say exactly what the feds are investigating?" Steve asked. "Why did they wire Nadia?"

"No. Only Nadia could tell us that," Victoria said.

"I'll bet she knows squat," Solomon said. "The agent who was handling her would only have told her what she needed to get from Gorev. Not the big picture."

"Even so, like Jake said, we gather the facts and put the puzzle together later."

"What it sounds like to me," Steve said, "is that you two kids had a fun night on the town without much to show for it."

"That's not fair, Steve."

"Wasn't all that much fun," Lassiter said.

Steve gave a sly grin. "Jake and Vic's big adventure."

Oh, how the man she loved exasperated her. Usually charming and witty and giving, he could be so damn irritating when he was off his game. Now he seemed jealous about their "night on the town." Did he suspect something between them when there was nothing? Well, nothing other than her raising the Code Yellow. And the dream she would never, ever disclose to Steve.

Lassiter said, "Solomon, I'm sure you know that a lawyer builds a case the same way a brick mason builds a wall."

"No, Counselor. Tell me."

"One brick at a time. Place the brick exactly in line with the one next to it. Smooth the mortar to the same depth each time. It takes a while to build a wall."

"Thanks for the lesson. I'll call you if we need a handyman."

"Steve, you're pissing me off," Victoria said. "You could show Jake a little gratitude."

"No," Lassiter said. "It's okay. It's the Jailhouse Blues, and I don't mean the Lightning Johnson song. Look, I see it all the time. A guy sits in here 24-7, and the frustration builds into resentment and the resentment into anger. He strikes out at the people closest to him, the people trying to help him. I'm not taking it personally."

"You're a prince, Lassiter." Steve gave it as much sarcasm as he could muster, and sarcasm was mother's milk to him. "But frankly, I don't see much in the way of results."

"We work differently, Solomon. To you, I'm just a plodder."

"Plow horse, I was thinking."

"To me, you're a showboater. You spike the ball after a six-yard run. You don't even wait to score." Lassiter got up from his chair. "Look, I'm doing the best I can, but if you have any ideas, let's hear them."

"Easy. Stop looking for Nadia."

"Why?" Victoria asked.

"Put yourself in her slingbacks. She shot Gorev."

"In self-defense. Under Stand Your Ground, she might not even have to go to trial."

"Who has the burden of proof in a Stand Your Ground immunity hearing?"

"The defendant, of course. But only by a preponderance of the evidence."

"She's probably ditched Gorev's gun. Even if she still has it and can bring it in, how does she prove Gorev was wielding it?"

"With her testimony and yours."

"I see it differently, Vic. If Nadia comes back, it's to point the finger at me. I'm the one who's charged. The government gives her immunity on whatever crap they have that led her to wear a wire in the first place. She nails me and walks. Am I right, Lassiter?"

"It's possible," he said. "But there's no way to tell."

"Why should she stick her neck out for me?"

"A chance to start over," Victoria said. "She's in love with an American she wants to marry. She wants to leave the B-girl world behind. What better way to begin a new life than to save an innocent man from a murder conviction?"

"Sweet. Very sweet, Vic. But this is the real world. The woman is a scam artist. Lassiter, you know the street. Tell my honey the facts. Her theory, her psychology of the woman starting over. It's a long shot, right?"

"All life is a long shot."

"So you think you can turn this Nadia around?"

Lassiter took a moment to answer. A look crossed his face that Victoria couldn't decipher, but he was processing information. "It's not like we're gonna drag her straight off the street into the courtroom and run the risk she'll nail you. We'll talk to her. If she backs your story, we use her. If not, we give her a first-class ticket to wherever she wants." Lassiter paused and looked at Victoria. "As long as that's not obstruction of justice."

"More likely, you'll do all this work and inadvertently lead her straight into the state's hands," Steve said. "They can't find her, but you two will."

Again, quiet settled over the stinky little room. Finally, Victoria said, "Sorry, Steve. This is Jake's call, and you can't steamroll him. That's why I hired him."

Lassiter paced around the room. It took him three steps to get from one side to the other.

"Well, Jake . . . ?" Victoria said.

Lassiter leaned back against the concrete wall and closed his eyes. Victoria could see the exhaustion wearing on him. He should have been home in bed. The look on his face told Victoria she wouldn't like what he was going to say. "We'll do it Solomon's way.

We stop looking for Nadia. If Elena calls, tell her we don't need her friend's testimony."

Now she was truly confused. Why was Lassiter backtracking? "What are you saying, Jake?"

"We go with the empty chair defense. They've got their forensics, the gun, the fingerprints. We've got Steve who can explain the shooting. Nadia wore gloves, shot Gorev, robbed the safe, took Gorev's gun, and fled. I spend closing argument pointing at an invisible Nadia, sitting in the empty chair. And let the chips fall."

Victoria was stunned. Last night, Lassiter had nearly gotten himself killed trying to find the woman, and now he rolled over because his depressed and irritable client told him to. "What's going on, Jake?"

"A lawyer should listen to his client as intensely as he listens to his lover. Hey, Solomon, maybe you can make that one of your rules."

"Please be more specific, Jake," Victoria said.

"You're too close to this to be objective. That's why it was a good idea to hire me. Or anybody, for that matter. I hear what Solomon is saying, but you don't."

"Go on."

"Forget putting Nadia on the stand. Solomon doesn't want us even to talk to her because he knows what she's going to say."

"All we want is the truth."

"Sometimes the truth will not set you free. Sometimes it will send you away for life."

"Jake, you're not saying . . ."

"Like they say, love is blind. Or at least nearsighted. There can only be one reason Solomon is so sure Nadia won't help us. She didn't shoot Nicolai Gorev. He did."

"No, he didn't! He told us . . ." Victoria whipped around and glared at Steve, but he was looking at Lassiter. Expressionless.

"Steve, tell me the truth," she ordered.

Steve didn't speak.

Neither did Lassiter.

The two men were locked on to each other. Neither blinked. A sense of understanding seemed to be growing, along with the silence, between them.

"Steve! Who shot Gorev?" Victoria said.

"Don't answer, Solomon," Lassiter said. "You're doing swell."

Victoria was speechless. She felt as if her head was filled with sand.

Lassiter kept his eyes on Steve. "At our first meeting, you told me you didn't shoot Gorev. Nadia did. Thankfully, you told the same story to the cops. I'll put you on the stand to say the same thing under oath. If you have a sudden change of heart, keep it to yourself. I can't ethically offer testimony I know to be false. It's one of those damn little rules I adhere to."

"Works for me," Steve said. "What else you got?"

Victoria felt dizzy. It was all she could do to listen to Lassiter, who seemed completely at ease with learning that his client was guilty of murder.

"Like I said, we go with the empty chair. The state didn't even try to bring Nadia to court. I'll contrast that with the lengths we went to. On cross, I'll get Barrios to admit I got busted up trying to find her. Hell, he wiped the blood off my shirt."

"You got my vote," Steve said.

Victoria felt her eyes filling with tears. The two men in her life were bonding over perjury. Only Lassiter had to pretend he didn't know that it was.

"You want to hear my closing argument?" Lassiter asked, pacing again.

"Sure," Steve said. "Give it a whirl."

"Where is the one witness who could contradict my client's story?" Lassiter boomed in his best baritone. He paused and pointed at the chair he had vacated. "There! What? You can't see her? Of course not. The state never brought her to you. Why? With all their resources, they could have found her, if she was just an innocent witness to a crime. There can only be one reason for that empty chair. She fled because she's the killer. She won't get anywhere near this courthouse because she pulled the trigger, killing Nicolai Gorev and framing my client for the murder. You saw Steve Solomon stand up, put his hand on the Bible, and swear to tell the truth and nothing but the truth. You heard him testify and open himself to vicious cross-examination, but you have not heard one word from any witness who can contradict him."

"I like it," Steve said.

"Great, we're gonna go with what we've got. We've got a shot."

"After everything you've said to me about justice, you're really okay with this, Jake?" Victoria asked.

"Hell, yes. I think I might win this case. I might walk a killer out of court. Then I'll wash my hands, and polish off some Jack Daniel's, and move to Vermont."

That's when Victoria began to cry a flood of tears.

-26-

She Wears Short-Shorts

Victoria said she'd get home from the jail by taking one of those new car services—uberX or Lyft—so I said good-bye to the lovebirds and drove to my little coral rock house on Poinciana.

Granny was waiting for me in the kitchen, slicing fresh kernels of corn off the cob into a pot of steaming grits. A chunk of Reggiano cheese was waiting to be grated, and some green onions would go into the pot, too. Granny had become fancier in her cooking lately.

She took a look at my face and said, "You try to kiss a bobcat last night?"

"Something like that, Granny."

"I got some witch hazel to put on those scratches. Ain't even gonna ask what you look like under your clothes."

"Sorry about the suit, Granny."

"Always knew it was a waste of money. Like putting britches on a mule."

I reached for the coffeepot, and she swatted my hand away. "You need some sleep."

I didn't disagree. I just ate my grits with some buttermilk biscuits that oozed with butter. I thanked Granny, went to my bedroom, and sacked out fully clothed until midafternoon. When I woke up, I felt worse than when I went to bed. Everything hurt.

I downed six aspirin with coconut water, showered, and put on a pair of faded Penn State running shorts and an old T-shirt with the saying "I May Be Old, but I Got to See All the Cool Bands." I was alone in the quiet house, the only noise the quiet whir of the ceiling fans. Kip was at summer football camp. Granny had either gone grocery shopping on her bicycle or fishing in the Coral Gables Waterway. She had her own spot under the bridge that connects LeJeune Road with Cocoplum Circle, and she'd likely bring back a snapper or two.

I turned on the television and found the country music station on the satellite. Listened to Patsy Cline sing "Crazy" with that tremulous little hitch in her voice that makes you want to put your arms around her and protect her from the big, cruel world.

I hobbled into the backyard and toppled into the hammock that hangs between two palm trees. Cloudy and steamy hot. Palm fronds hung limply like wet laundry on a line. Humid as a jock strap after an August practice. Thunder boomed in the distance.

I grew drowsy again. I must have fallen asleep because I dreamed of a fine snow falling on a Vermont football field. I jogged across the field in a sweat suit, a whistle around my neck, shouting at my pale prep schoolers, all skinny arms and pipe stem legs.

"Hustle! Hustle! Hustle! And for God's sake, hit somebody!"

Then I heard my name called.

"Jake. Jake. Are you awake?"

I blinked my eyes open. Victoria sat in a wooden rocking chair on the porch, ten feet from my hammock. Next to her, on a table— an old wooden wire spool Granny had sanded and painted—was a bottle of Jack Daniel's and two tumblers. The bottle was full, so she must have brought it.

"Hey," I said, using up all my witty conversation.

"How you feeling?"

"Tip-top."

She gestured toward the booze. "Ice?"

"Straight up is fine."

She poured us two tumblers, half-full. I didn't peg Victoria for a sour mash whiskey gal. Maybe a cosmo or a margarita. Maybe a mojito with fresh-squeezed cane juice and pulverized mint leaves. But she took a long pull on the Jack Daniel's, so I had some catching up to do. The first taste was golden heat in the throat, soothing to body and soul.

She was wearing short white shorts. Very short shorts. Her long legs were crossed at the ankles. On her feet were platform sandals with those crossing straps that go halfway up the calf and make a woman look like a Roman gladiator. Except on Victoria, they just accentuated her floor-to-ceiling legs with nicely developed calves. Pilates or weights, I imagined. She wore a stretchy pink tank top, which showed her well-formed delts and small, perky breasts. To sum it up, it looked as if a high-fashion model had just decided to plop down in my backyard for an after-work drink.

"I love Steve and I admire you," she said between drinks.

"I hear a 'but' coming."

"But you both infuriate me. Steve lied to me! How can I deal with that?"

"That's between you two. Leave me out of it."

"Really? Then let's talk about your strategy, which just happens to be based on Steve's phony story."

"What would you have me do? Withdraw because my client might be guilty?"

"*Might* be guilty? You said he was a murderer!"

131

"No. I said he was a killer. Not every killer is a murderer or even committed a criminal act."

She polished off her whiskey. "You're talking about self-defense."

"One possibility."

"Or defense of another. In this case, Nadia."

"Possibility number two."

"Stand Your Ground."

"That's three."

"And there's always accident."

"Unlikely but yes."

"Or insanity."

"I forgot about that one," I admitted.

"Instead of telling Steve to shut up, why don't you get the whole story and defend him based on what he did?"

"We've been over this, Victoria. Two reasons. First, we have to defend him based on what he told the cops. Otherwise, he gets skewered on cross based on prior inconsistent statements and we lose. Second, if he tells me he shot Gorev and has no defenses, I can't put him on the stand to say otherwise."

"I know. I know. The one ethical rule you cling to."

"Like a drowning man with a Styrofoam cooler."

"I hate this game we have to play. And I thought you hated it, too."

"I do, but I don't make the rules. I just try to do my job and not hit anybody after the whistle."

"Do you remember what you said the day I retained you?"

"I think I mentioned the retainer had to be paid up front."

"You asked me, 'Does it ever get you down? That nearly everyone is guilty.'"

"And you told me it comes with the territory. You were right. I was just venting. All these years banging my head against the courthouse door gets to a guy. But the truth is, if I only represented the innocent, I'd starve to death."

"Today, in the jail, you seemed to relish it. That Steve may be guilty and you have a way to get him off. As if half-assed lawyers can get an innocent client acquitted . . ."

"Actually, they can't."

"But it takes the great Jake Lassiter to get a big fat NG for a guilty man."

I hoisted myself out of the hammock, lurched to the porch, and eased my aching body into the chair next to Victoria's rocker. It was getting dark, and in the distance, lightning flashed against a backdrop of silver clouds.

"You're starting to worry me, Victoria. Are you able to sit second chair and help me win this thing?"

For the second time today, I saw tears fill her eyes. "I don't know."

"You started this conversation by saying you love Steve. That's the touchstone. The starting point and the finish line. If you focus on that, you'll be fine."

A single teardrop tracked down her cheek. "I think Steve was screwing Nadia."

"He tell you that?"

"Of course not."

"Elena tell you that?"

"No."

"So what's going through your mind? Why would Steve cheat on you?"

"Because he's a man, and men are assholes."

"Okay, I'll grant you that. But have you ever suspected him of anything? Ever caught him?"

She wiped the back of a hand across her eyes. "No. But before we met, he was one of those commitment-phobic bachelors who went from woman to woman."

"Statute of limitations has expired on that." As we talked, I was fighting an internal battle. Part of me wanted to torpedo their relationship, but the better part compelled me to say exactly what I believed. "So basically this is just some woman's intuition thing."

She refilled her glass. "Don't be condescending."

"All I'm saying, you have no proof. Victoria, it's been a really long couple of days. You need to step back, get some sleep, then start going through those color-coded files of yours."

She took a sip and closed her eyes, enjoying the taste of the whiskey. "You've been in committed relationships, right?"

I thought I knew where she was going, and I wanted no part of it. I'm protective of my private life, especially the embarrassing parts. "Sure. I've been involved with a couple women who should have been committed."

"C'mon, Jake. Be serious."

"Yeah, I've had relationships. What about it?"

"You ever cheat?"

"When there was a problem in a relationship, and I was young and stupid, instead of working on the problem . . . yeah, I stepped out."

"Proves my point. Before all this happened, Steve and I had been arguing a lot. Some of our closeness had been lost."

"Happens to everybody. Then you know what? If you've bonded and you love each other, like you two do, it all comes back together."

"Maybe it's too late."

"Jeez, Victoria, you're adding two and two and getting five. Steve didn't cheat on you with a B-girl."

"How can you be so sure?"

I didn't want to answer, but it just came out. "Because I wouldn't have."

"What?"

"You're the one who said how much alike we are. Solomon and me. Frankly, I didn't see it, but maybe you're right. And I wouldn't have cheated on you with a B-girl or anyone else, and neither would Solomon."

She took a long drink. Too long, if you ask me. "I'm lifting the Code Yellow," she said.

"Meaning what?"

"Code Green, Lassiter."

"Does that mean what I think it does?"

"You're not half bad looking."

"And you're beautiful and you know it. So what? Where does that get us?"

"You want to make out?"

I laughed because it was . . . well, damn funny, coming from this gorgeous, smart, tipsy young woman who happened to be in love with my client. "Just where will we do this making out? The local drive-in movie?"

"My place. The male inhabitant is indisposed."

"And after we make out, what then, Counselor?"

"Why don't we take it one step at a time? See what happens. We're both adults."

"No, we're not. You're a sixteen-year-old girl who's flirting with the captain of the football team because you think the guy you really like just kissed a cheerleader under the bleachers."

"You're rejecting me? No man has ever . . ." Her eyes welled with tears.

"There was a time when I wouldn't have been man enough to say no. But those days are gone, and I'm not taking part in get-even sex. We're not going to wake up tomorrow hating ourselves and each other."

"I already hate you for turning me down."

"Tomorrow, you'll thank me. Look, I need you. Steve really needs you. And when this is over, you and I will have a drink—preferably coffee—and laugh about tonight."

She pushed the tumbler of Jack Daniel's away, apparently realizing there was no more need to loosen her inhibitions. "So we're going back to work?"

"First thing tomorrow."

"I want to find Nadia."

"Why? So you can ask about Steve and her?"

She shook her head. "Purely professional. It's always been our strategy to find her."

"Haven't you been listening? Our strategy has changed. No Nadia."

She got out of the rocker, pulled her short-shorts down a bit from where they had been riding up into her crotch. "Elena called me. She wants to meet us tomorrow night after work. Said she thinks Nadia might talk to us on the phone."

"Not interested."

"Suit yourself. I'll go alone."

"You're letting your personal feelings interfere with your judgment."

"You do your thing, I'll do mine."

"Damn it, Victoria. It doesn't work that way. The case has one boss. Me. We have one strategy. Mine."

"If you change your mind, I'm meeting her on Tenth Street Beach."

"In the middle of the night."

"When she gets off work, four a.m."

"It's just a few blocks from Anastasia. Alex Gorev has to know that Elena and Nadia are friends. He could have Elena followed."

"I'll let you know what I find out."

"I won't be there to protect you," I said.

"I don't need you."

And with that, Victoria Lord hopped off my back porch, wobbled just a bit on those long legs, turned at the corner of the house, and was gone.

-27-

The Cemetery and General Custer

By 7:00 a.m., I'd had my coffee—actually Café Bustelo espresso—and was jogging south on LeJeune Road, thinking about Victoria Lord, about Steve Solomon, about the mysterious Elena, and about the missing Nadia. Today's problem was simple. I should be working on getting discovery from the state attorney. Instead, I was worried about Victoria and trying to decide what to do tonight.

If Solomon was a problem client—and he was—Victoria was an unreliable cocounsel. Refusing to take orders. Going off on her own mission. What she planned could be dangerous for her . . . and the case. Right now, breathing hard, my running shoes thudding against the pavement, I was worried more about her than *State v. Solomon*.

Jeez, what does that say about me? As a lawyer and a man?

I decided to push her out of my thoughts and concentrate on my strained breathing and aching body. I was wearing a nylon swelter sweat suit with elastic cuffs at the wrists and ankles to increase my body heat. I was trying to sweat out the champagne and vodka and the general toxins of my life.

Let me make it clear: only a madman does this in Miami in the summer, which runs roughly from May until Halloween. Even early in the morning, the heat rises from the pavement like steam from a New York City subway grate. As Yogi Berra reportedly said, "It's not the heat, it's the *humility*."

I pounded along, passing El Prado and Hardee, then crossed the bridge over the waterway and onto Cocoplum Circle. Rivers of sweat rolled down my back into the crack of my butt.

I turned right, heading west on Sunset. A gray Range Rover followed me around the circle and slowed to match my jogging pace. I remembered a similar vehicle at the gas station and then on the Julia Tuttle the night I met Elena at the Russian church. I squinted and tried to see into the heavily tinted windows but couldn't make out the driver. It could have been a man, a woman, or a well-trained chimpanzee. Then, instead of passing me, the Range Rover squealed into a U-turn and headed east on Sunset. Staring back into the morning sun, I couldn't make out its license plate. The driver could have been one of Gorev's thugs following me, hoping I'd lead them to Nadia. Or maybe one of State Attorney Pincher's investigators, trying to spook me. Whatever, there was nothing I could do about it.

I kept plodding along, passing Almansa and Mindello, then hanging a left on Erwin Road, and there it was.

The Pinewood Cemetery. It's where I go to think.

One of the great little secrets of South Florida: Miami and its surrounding towns are young. We don't celebrate much in the way of history. There aren't any three-hundred-year-old churches or quaint houses dating from the Revolutionary War. But we have the Pinewood Cemetery, which holds the remains of our pioneers from the mid-nineteenth century.

It's not a cemetery of manicured lawns. It's a natural forest of scrubby palms, casuarina pines, and gumbo limbo trees with their twisted trunks and limbs. As a result, the place is almost entirely in the shade, and on windy days—which this one was not—a good breeze would whistle through the trees.

I padded across the floor of pine needles and sprawled out on a wooden bench in front of the grave of a veteran of the Spanish-American War.

Thinking.

Regardless what I told Victoria—*"I won't be there to protect you"*— how could I not be? Generally, the beach is safe. Still, at night, there are robbers and rapists and the occasional Miami Beach cop who gets drunk and runs over sleeping (or screwing) tourists in a four-wheel ATV. Really. It happened not long ago.

I should have been thinking about the case. Figuring how and why Nadia snookered Solomon into riding shotgun. Was it her plan to rob Gorev all along? Did Solomon know? And if she brought the gun, how did Solomon end up shooting Gorev?

To hell with it. I don't know the answers and on this sweaty morning, I don't care.

I eased up from the bench and prepared to jog back home and take a cold shower. Or, at least, cool. Our tap water doesn't really get cold. Before leaving this peaceful place for the real world, I passed a couple of old headstones, one a Confederate soldier from Tennessee and one a Union soldier from Massachusetts. Then the tiny gravestones of infants, "Baby Girl Mary" and "Baby Boy James." So common in those days and so damn sad.

A troubling thought came to me. Maybe it was the cemetery. Maybe it was my having been thrashed the night before last. Or even my feelings for Victoria, which I had yet to explore, much less express, even to myself.

Why am I so worried about Victoria? Why is she in the forefront of my mind instead of the case?

Okay, let's look at this logically. Nothing is more important in the practice of law than this: the client comes first.

In theory and in practice, that's always the way I've behaved. Many years ago, I stood in the central courtroom of the old federal courthouse, a place of gilded chandeliers, marble pilasters, wooden wainscoting, and a ceiling of stars. The words *ornate* and *stately* don't begin to describe the place. On that day, I took the oath of admission to the Florida Bar promising to support the Constitution.

I took the words seriously. Still do. The Sixth Amendment right to counsel means—in my opinion—*damn good* counsel. A lawyer who will take a punch for his client and maybe dish out a couple, too. In this regard, Solomon and I are alike. He's proud to have been held in contempt for his clashes with prosecutors, judges, and witnesses. What was it he said to me that first day?

"A lawyer who's afraid of jail is like a surgeon who's afraid of blood."

I criticized him then. Maybe it was his brash and boastful manner, but certainly not his theory of the practice, with which I agree. But now, here I was thinking about his lover . . . instead of his case. Here I was, drawn to Victoria Lord in a way that violated my principles. At least I could pat myself on the back for not succumbing to her whiskey-induced come-on. Oh, the self-loathing that would have caused!

But what about tonight—so late that it would be almost dawn tomorrow—and Victoria's plan to meet Elena on the beach? How could I let her go alone?

After all these ruminations, I made a decision. I have a Florida concealed firearms permit. But then, who doesn't? We have about nine hundred thousand residents licensed to carry concealed weapons, tops in the nation. Take that, Texas!

Anyway, I own a nine-millimeter Beretta. So tonight, very late, I planned to place it in a shoulder holster inside a lightweight sport coat, saddle up my old steed, and follow Victoria to the beach.

For some reason, I thought of General George Armstrong Custer in his buckskins, riding across the Montana plains that day in 1876. In my mind, I saw the general, a Colt .45 on his hip, six hundred soldiers with rifles under his command. I imagined him thinking, *What could go wrong?*

-28-

Playing Poker with the Feds

An hour after leaving the cemetery, I traveled 138 years into the future. Which is to say, I drove the fifteen miles to my office on South Beach. I don't have fancy digs. No deep carpet or marble tile and certainly no oceanfront view. I'm on the second floor of a land-locked building above a Cuban restaurant called Havana Banana. Climbing the stairs each day, the aroma tells me what the lunch special will be. Today, carne asada, basically a skirt steak marinated in olive oil, garlic, and jalapeño. I love it.

Jorge Martinez, the owner, will send a platter up the stairs, without my even asking. Of course, I never charge him when fighting the Health Department over repeated sanitary violations. Years ago, I saved him from personal ruin with exceedingly wise advice when his first restaurant went belly-up.

"Declare bankruptcy," I told him.

"But my lifelong dream is Escargot-to-Go."

Finally realizing that fast-food snails would not launch a thousand franchises, he folded his cards and opened Havana Banana, which is reasonably profitable when not dispensing salmonella with the quesadillas.

Entering the door at the top of the stairs, I discovered my long-time secretary, Cindy, missing from her cubicle. No surprise. She often headed for the beach when I was late getting in. But I wasn't expecting to find a woman in the two-chair waiting area. She wore a business suit in charcoal gray. Solid gray. Not even a pinstripe. And sensible black pumps. A plain leather briefcase at her feet. About forty, short brown hair that didn't need much tending. I get a few walk-in clients, but my well-honed instincts told me she wasn't a felon.

"Mr. Lassiter?" It was part question, part accusation.

Fortunately, I'd worn a navy sport coat over my khakis and striped long-sleeved shirt. Some days, I come into the office in flip-flops, baggy shorts, and a T-shirt with the slogan "Officer, I Swear to Drunk I'm Not God." So sue me.

"That's me, unless you're a process server."

"I'm Deborah Scolino. Assistant US Attorney."

"Ah, I was hoping you were a bank robber or, at the very least, an embezzler."

That did not get a smile from AUSA Scolino.

"Can we talk?" she said.

I ushered her into my inner sanctum. A plain office. Desk, a leather chair for me, a set of bookshelves with never-read legal treatises, and two client chairs with stiff backs. No certificates on the wall. I keep my law school diploma on the bathroom wall at home. It covers a crack in the plaster and reminds me of the tenuous connection between the law and justice every time I pee.

I settled behind my desk. She sat primly in one of the client chairs covered in real imitation leather.

"Miami Beach police say you caused quite a ruckus at Club Anastasia the other night," she said.

"Do they now?"

"Apparently you are searching for a Bar girl named Nadia Delova."

"You mean your CI? The ill-trained young woman you wired and sent into a Russian mobster's inner sanctum?" Taking a shot at it. Who else could it be but the woman sitting across from me?

She gave me a deadpan look they must teach in federal bureaucrat school. "I can neither confirm nor deny that Ms. Delova was ever a confidential informant for the federal government."

"But the fact you're here means that the investigation didn't die with Nicolai Gorev."

"I can neither confirm nor deny any such investigation ever existed."

"Now you're looking into his brother Alex."

"I can neither—"

"And maybe Benny the Jeweler."

She opened her mouth, but nothing came out. She had stopped neither confirming nor denying, and her eyes blinked twice. I would like to play poker with this woman.

"Benny the Jeweler," I continued, my fishing line dangling in the water. "Quite a piece of work."

He may well have been. I really didn't know.

"Just how much do you know about Benny?" she asked, unable to resist.

Not a helluva lot, but your expression just told me he's a big piece of the Gorev puzzle.

I love this part of the game. AUSA Scolino thought she was asking me a question, but instead she was answering one of mine. I decided to rebait the hook.

"Benny and B-girls and diamonds. It's a helluva story."

And that was pretty much all I knew about it.

"You know about the diamonds?" If Ms. Scolino had been nonplussed before, now she seemed downright dumbfounded.

"Doesn't everybody?" I said, winging it.

"Of course not. Do you know how the diamonds get to Miami?"

"Actually, that's of very little concern to me."

I was starting to put together the pieces. Jeweler. Diamonds. Russians. And Scolino's question: *"Do you know how the diamonds get to Miami?"* That was likely the evidence she wanted Nadia to get from Nicolai Gorev.

This wasn't some penny-ante wire fraud investigation about Bar girls and credit cards. This was diamond smuggling.

I needed more information. Starting with who the hell was Benny the Jeweler and where do I find him? I went fishing again.

"Would it be okay with you if I talked to Benny the Jeweler?" I asked.

"Absolutely not."

"Not that you could stop me."

"No, you could go to his . . ."

She stopped. A thought crossed her face. *Uh-oh.* She just discovered I was holding a pair of deuces.

"You don't know who Benny the Jeweler is," she said. "You don't even know his last name."

I gave her my best grin. "I can neither confirm nor deny . . ."

"Well, I'm certainly not going to help you compromise a federal investigation."

"Certainly not," I agreed.

"If I were you, Mr. Lassiter, I would be extremely careful about doing anything that could be construed as obstruction of justice."

"I wouldn't dream of it. In fact, every day I do two things. Brush my teeth and uphold the Constitution."

"Mr. Lassiter, are you being sarcastic?"

"Why do you ask?"

"When I clerked for a federal judge, she told me I lacked a sense of humor or even the ability to determine when other people were joking."

"Then you've got the right job," I said. "Federal per-se-cutor."

"Now, that was a joke, right?"

"If you'd like it to be. Thank you for stopping by to threaten me."

"There was no threat, Mr. Lassiter."

"Then for the record, I'm not obstructing your investigation. I'm helping it."

"In heaven's name, how?"

"You haven't asked, but here's everything I know. Nadia's best friend, another B-girl, told me she has no idea where Nadia is."

Lying to a federal prosecutor always makes my day.

"That's it?"

"Your turn. What do you know?"

"Nothing I can share with you."

"You have one advantage over me, Ms. Scolino."

She looked at me dubiously.

"You've met Nadia, right? In this investigation you can neither confirm nor deny."

She shrugged, ending the charade for at least one question. "Of course."

"You've spoken to her. Gotten a handle on who she is. Her credibility. Her trustworthiness."

"Yes. All of that."

"And I'm betting you've examined and cross-examined a lot of witnesses in your time."

"Hundreds, at least."

"Without revealing any secrets of national security, what can you tell me about Nadia?"

"Nothing!"

"I'm not asking what she told you. I'm asking, did you believe what she told you?"

"Nadia said a lot of things about Nicolai Gorev that were surely true. But when it came to Benny the Jeweler, she was evasive."

"And . . . ?"

"You're a big man, Mr. Lassiter. What, two hundred and thirty pounds?"

"I wish. Closer to two hundred and forty-five these days."

"I trust Nadia Delova about as far as I can throw you. She knows things about the Gorevs and Benny the Jeweler, and if she will tell the truth, I can bring down a very significant international ring of . . ."

"Yeah?"

"Of none of your business."

"Seems to me you're walking on a tightrope, Ms. Scolino."

She waited, so I filled her in. "You're trying to rescue your own fouled-up investigation, but if Nadia shows up to testify in Solomon's case, the whole world will see the federal screwup that led to Nicolai Gorev's death. You can't let that happen, meaning you need State Attorney Pincher's help. So I'm just wondering. What are you and Pincher cooking up? What conspiracy of sovereigns is taking place in the shadows?"

"None, I assure you."

"Then you should get busy on one. Because you've given me the theme of my defense. Steve Solomon isn't responsible for Gorev's death. Neither is Nadia Delova. *You* are, Ms. Scolino. The federal government is responsible. You sent that poor girl into the lair of a Russian mobster. You either gave her a gun—"

"We did no such thing!"

"Or she felt the job you assigned her required one. She was improperly trained, improperly supervised, and totally unsuitable for the task you gave her, and a man is dead as a result."

"That's ludicrous." Pink splotches rose on her neck. I seemed to have the same effect on her as poison ivy.

"Be on the lookout for my subpoena. You're a defense witness, Ms. Scolino."

"We'll move to quash."

"My client's fair trial rights trump your need for secrecy. Motion denied."

"You have the scruples of an alley cat."

"Thank you. Feel free to give Pincher a preview of my closing argument. He's always looking to suck up to the federal government. Maybe the two of you can come up with something that won't cost you your job."

She was quiet a moment, then said softly, "What is it you want?"

"A deal I can live with. You get to keep Nadia out of the courthouse, and I get Solomon out of jail."

"That's called extortion, Mr. Lassiter."

"No, it's not. It's called lawyering."

Nadia and the Feds (Part Five)

One week before the Gorev shooting . . .

Office of the United States Attorney for the Southern District of Florida

In Re: Investigation of South Beach Champagne Clubs and one "John Doe"

File No. 2014-73-B

Statement of Nadia Delova (Continuation)

July 7, 2014

(CONFIDENTIAL)

Q: [By AUSA Deborah Scolino] Before you leave, just a few more questions.

A: [By Nadia Delova] It never ends.

Q: Do you know a man known as Benny the Jeweler?

A: *Da.* All the girls know Benny.

Q: Is he a customer?

A: Elena says he is partner of Nicolai Gorev. Maybe even big boss.

Q: So Benny owns the club?

A: Many clubs. But this is all B-girl talk.

Q: Has Benny ever given you any gifts?

A: My pendant.

Q: Indicating for the record a diamond pendant of perhaps . . . what would you say, Ms. Delova, four or five carats?

A: Not sure. Is big.

Q: Did you have sex with Benny?

A: Yes.

Q: Is that why he gave you the diamond pendant?

A: He gives diamond to all the B-girls.

Q: Why does he do that?

A: Is generous gentleman.

Q: Do you know where Benny gets his diamonds?

A: Wherever a jeweler gets them. Not my business.

Q: Are you being truthful, Ms. Delova?

A: *Da.*

Q: Because you know your immunity does not protect you from perjury.

A: You keep telling me.

Q: Have you ever heard Nicolai Gorev and Benny discussing diamonds?

A: [No response]

Q: Ms. Delova . . .

A: Always same talk. Benny says, "When are diamonds coming?" And Nicolai says, "When they come, they come."

Q: So you are aware that Gorev is in the diamond-smuggling business?

A: They never use that word. *Smuggling*. I never use that word. Only you use that word.

Q: When you wear the wire and speak to Gorev, try to get him to talk about the diamond business. Try to use the word *smuggling*.

A: He is not idiot.

Q: Meaning what, Ms. Delova?

A: Why not I just ask him to shoot me?

-30-

On the Beach

I *will not be scared.*
  I will not be scared.

If she said it enough, Victoria thought, it will work. Lassiter told her not to come here, but she wanted to know the truth, and this was the only way to get it.

She had pulled the car into an empty spot on Ocean Drive and Sixth Street. Even at 3:30 a.m., the sidewalks were crowded. Tourists, local partyers, your usual collection of young people—male and female—who looked like models or lifeguards at play. Music still poured from cafés and clubs on the west side of the street. She walked through an opening in the coral rock wall that separated the sidewalk from the beach and headed toward the water.

Ahead of her the dark ocean, the shore break a soft murmur in the night. Behind her, the lights of Ocean Drive. She angled left and started walking north toward Tenth Street, passing a children's playground; the slides and rides cast shadows across the sand.

As Victoria walked, she grew bolder and headed closer to the water, each step taking her farther into the enveloping darkness.

She wished there'd been that famous moon over Miami, creamy beams riding the inbound waves. But it was a moonless black night with only the faintest of breezes.

She thought of the two men whose lives were intertwined with her own.

Steve and Jake. You've both disappointed me.

She'd always known that Steve treated the justice system like a pinball machine. He liked to smack it within an inch of the buzzer signaling "tilt." Now she'd learned Jake was pretty much the same, though he approached the system as if it were a heavy punching bag. Slug it until sand bursts from the seams.

And me?

Silly me, I believe that sign over the judge's bench: "We Who Labor Here Seek Only the Truth."

Well, tonight, she would try to get Elena to lead her to the truth, which is to say, lead her to Nadia. Putting her on the phone with Nadia would be a good start. Then, with luck, a face-to-face meeting. With Steve's mouth clamped shut, there was no one else who could tell her what happened in Gorev's locked office.

Her thoughts turned to last night.

OMG.

Just who was that woman toting a bottle of whiskey and trying to seduce Jake? The embarrassment was nearly palpable.

I'm just thankful Jake did the right thing.

A strange thought, then.

If I wasn't involved with Steve, would I go for Jake?

She tried not to answer, but her brain wouldn't listen. There was the age difference, but now it didn't seem to matter.

Yes, I would go for him. And now I better chase that thought away.

Nearly at Tenth Street. A silhouette ahead.

A woman, thank God. Just standing there at water's edge. Barefoot, her toes in the warm fizzing shore break. Long blonde hair, tight jeans and a halter top. It was Elena Turcina, changed out of her come-screw-me uniform.

"Elena!"

The woman turned and waved, then looked around as if to make sure no one else was coming. Victoria closed the distance between them, passing the darkened lifeguard stand. In the daytime, it's a round wooden shack painted bright pink with a yellow handrail. At night, just a dark cylinder rising out of the beach.

Victoria pulled off her flats and let her toes sink into the wet sand.

"I am happy you are here," Elena said.

"Likewise. You've spoken to Nadia?"

"She is so afraid—she does not know what to do. But I told her she could trust you."

"What is it she fears?"

"She was working for government against Nicolai. Alex would kill her for that and then kill her a second time because of what happened to Nicolai."

"That's why she needs my help. A lawyer to get the government to protect her."

"She wants to go see Benny. He always looked out for her."

"That might not be a good idea. He may think Nadia informed on him, too."

"But she did not. She told me she did not talk about Benny."

"But Benny may not believe that."

"This is too confusing for me. I will put you on the phone with Nadia."

In the distance, Victoria heard an engine. At first, she thought it was a boat. But then she saw the light farther south on the beach. A four-wheel ATV, the vehicle the police used. Coming their way. No law against being on the beach at night, but cops are always on the lookout for drug dealers and underage drinkers. Victoria squinted into the night, trying to make out the figure on the ATV as it picked up speed, heading directly for them.

·31·

In the Shadows

I was hidden in the dark, leaning against the trunk of a tall, spindly palm tree twenty yards behind the pink-and-yellow lifeguard station on the Tenth Street Beach. I'd been there for forty minutes, tucked away in the shadows. The nine millimeter was in its holster under my sport coat.

Jake Lassiter, the long arm of the law. Or armed arm. Or something.

I'd seen Elena arrive first, walk to the shoreline, and dip her toes into the water.

I'd watched Victoria walk north, casting glances toward Ocean Drive. And now they were talking.

So far, so good. I heard the ATV before I saw it. Miami Beach police. No worries unless the cop was drunk and mowed them down. More likely, he would stop and try to get a phone number. Cops and firemen are, without doubt, the horniest bastards on the planet.

I kept my eyes on the ATV as it neared the two women.

-32-

"Evening, Ladies"

D id Nadia tell you about the shooting?" Victoria asked.

Elena nodded, her eyes on the oncoming ATV.

Not wanting to spook her, Victoria would take this part slowly. "Did she say whether Gorev had a gun?"

"When we get Nadia on phone, she will tell you."

Victoria took a deep breath and said, "Elena, did Nadia say who fired the gun? Who killed Gorev?"

"She will tell you story. Soon we call."

They both watched the ATV slow as it approached, a uniformed cop aboard. Dark-blue shirt, sleeves rolled up to reveal his bulging biceps. Young, wearing a helmet with its visor down, as if in the midday sun. He looked creepy, Victoria thought, like that Robocop character in the movies. The cop crept by, then stopped five yards in front of them. Turning, he said, "Evening, ladies. Or should I say morning?"

"Hello, Officer," Victoria said.

"Everything all right out here?" The question was polite, both in words and tone. But something was off, and Victoria felt a chill go up her spine.

"Fine. Just strolling."

"Excellent."

He put both feet on the sand but was still straddling the ATV, which idled in neutral.

Suddenly, he unsnapped his holster strap and pulled his pistol.

·33·

Gun-Shy

Just as I figured, the cop was making small talk with the pair of tall, gorgeous women on the beach. I couldn't blame him. Most nights, he probably runs into nothing but seaweed and flotsam from passing freighters.

My eyes had grown accustomed to the dark, but the three of them were still just silhouettes dimly lit by the lights from Ocean Drive. I don't know what it was then that made the hair stand up on the back of my neck. Maybe the way he was straddling the ATV. Both feet on the ground. Keeping his balance. Was he afraid the two women would attack him?

And then it occurred to me that it wasn't necessarily a defensive posture.

I took off at a gallop toward them just as he pulled his firearm. "Hey! Hey!" I shouted.

If any of them heard me, they didn't react. As I reached into my holster—

Three rapid gunshots.

Both women fell to the sand.

Oh God!

The driver settled back into his seat and calmly took off, headed north along the beach, then angling toward Ocean Drive. I raced toward the spot where the women fell.

Elena was on her back in the shallow water.

Victoria was facedown in the sand.

"Victoria!" I cried out.

No movement. No sound.

"Victoria!"

I was ten yards away. She rose to one knee, turned toward me. Even in the dark, I could see the panic, her features frozen.

"Where are you hit?"

She ignored me and crawled toward Elena. Rolled her over gently. Blood flowed from Elena's chest. Two wounds there. One in the middle of her sternum. Another just inches to the right. And a third entry wound, directly between her eyes, which were open and rolled back.

Two to the chest, and one to the head.

Police are taught that. But so are hit men.

I fell to my knees, wrapped my arms around Victoria, who was trembling.

"I just dived to the sand and lay there thinking I'd be dead in a second. But he never fired at me." Sobbing now. "My God. My God. Poor Elena."

"I'm sorry," I said. "I'm a shitty bodyguard."

"No. You were right. Jesus, Jake. I got her killed!"

"My fault," I said. "I should have been with you."

Damn it! I'd tried to protect them both and had failed miserably. Truth was, we both got Elena killed.

* * *

In the dawn of a Miami Beach morning, a few joggers and power walkers went by, scarcely paying attention to the crime scene. The Miami Beach cops—the real ones—took their sweet time interrogating us.

Separately.

Starting with Victoria.

By the time they got to me, the sun was already peeking over the horizon where the ocean met a blue-gray sky. We stood under a portable tent the cops had thoughtfully erected near the pink-and-yellow lifeguard stand. Crime scene tape was stretched from the coral rock wall to the water's edge, where it was attached to a metal pole jammed into the wet sand. The tide was coming in, playing havoc with the crime scene.

Photos had been taken, the sand combed for spent cartridges whose positions were marked with little flags. An assistant medical examiner had come and left with the body. A full autopsy would be performed at the morgue located, crazily enough, on Bob Hope Road.

Detective George Barrios and a younger female cop from homicide questioned me. She introduced herself as Detective Linda Vazquez, and she looked about fifteen years old. I assumed Barrios was training her. Then again, cops frequently question you in pairs. One might pick up on something the other misses. Or one can ask questions sweetly while the other hits you in the nuts with the phone book, though these days there aren't a lot of phone books around, what with the Internet and all.

Both George Barrios and Linda Vazquez were wearing blue nylon Windbreakers with "CMB Police" on the back. In about an hour, the sun would make them regret it. Barrios looked tired. Maybe thirty years of being rousted from bed was getting to him.

"Can we keep this short?" I asked. "I'm worried about Victoria."

"She's fine," Barrios said. "And if she needs a hug, we've got very handsome paramedics on the case." He gave me a sly look. "But it's commendable that you're protective of her."

"Is that a question, George?"

"No, but this is. Are you screwing her?"

"What's that have to do with anything? And the answer is no."

"Then help me get this straight. You knew Ms. Lord was coming to the beach in the middle of the night to meet this Bar girl."

"Elena Turcina. Let's give her the courtesy of a name."

"And you told Ms. Lord not to come."

"I thought it might be dangerous."

"That the only reason?"

"Why? Victoria give you another one?"

"She refused. Cited attorney–client privilege."

"Maybe I should follow her cue. She knows more law than I do."

"You know what I think, Lassiter?"

"You're counting the days to retirement and multiplying by twenty-four to figure the hours."

"The other night, at Club Anastasia, you nearly got yourself killed trying to wheedle information from this B-girl . . . Elena what's-her-name."

"Turcina. So?"

"She's your link to Nadia Delova, who you thought was gonna sail into the courtroom and win your case. But sometime between Anastasia and last night, you find out Delova isn't going to help you. Or worse, she could kill your case. You won't go to the meet. And you tell your cocounsel not to go."

"So? Or did I say that already?"

"What happened in the last forty-eight hours to change your mind?"

"Which case you working on, George? Gorev's murder or this one?"

"Jeez, Lassiter, you think I'm off base thinking the murders are related?"

Rather than answer, I just sulked a moment. Barrios had the basics right, but just where was he going with them?

"So, let's sum it up," Barrios said. "You told your girlfriend not to come over here."

"My cocounsel."

"Whatever you say. And you told her you weren't coming."

"Yeah, I did."

"But you came, anyway. Carrying."

I'd given the first cops on the scene my Beretta and my license to carry it. They'd probably hold it for six months before returning it, if they ever did.

"Your weapon hasn't been fired," Detective Linda Vazquez said. I'd almost forgotten she was there.

"Right. I started running toward the three of them just as the phony cop pulled his gun."

"Why didn't you fire?" Vazquez asked.

"On the run? At fifty yards? Into a crowd of three?" I turned to Barrios. "George, you take your rookie to the range yet?"

Vazquez didn't back off. "Once the perpetrator remounted the ATV and drove off, why not shoot at him them?"

"All I cared about was getting to Victoria and Elena. And the ATV was angling toward Ocean Drive. If I'd fired, I'd probably have shot some drunken tourists from Iowa."

Vazquez looked puzzled, as if something I said didn't add up. "You claim you were here to protect the women."

"I don't get it, Detective. Are you criticizing me for not shooting up South Beach? You want me to go all Wyatt Earp like your pals on Memorial Day a few years ago?"

"Got nothing to do with this," Barrios fired back.

Barrios didn't want to go there. Collins Avenue, Urban Beach Week 2011. Not the finest hour for Miami Beach's finest. Cops signaled a motorist to pull over on Collins Avenue. When he didn't, a dozen Hialeah and Beach officers fired 116 shots at him. Yeah, killed him, several times over. Also wounded three pedestrians.

"It just seems strange," Detective Vazquez said. "You appointed yourself the bodyguard for your lady friend—"

"Cocounsel."

"You show up with a gun, but you're at such a distance, there's not really much you could do."

"I was there in case Alex Gorev and his bouncers showed up. I would have recognized them two blocks away. I could have cut them off. A cop on an ATV didn't seem threatening."

"When the guy was approaching the women, did it occur to you that he might not be a cop?" Vazquez said.

"Why would it? He was in uniform on what looked like a police vehicle."

The two detectives exchanged looks. They seemed to be deciding who would speak next. Overhead, half a dozen white terns squawked, then landed in the wet sand, pecking away, searching for breakfast. I could have used some coffee myself.

"You don't see what this looks like to us, do you, Lassiter?" Barrios asked.

"I'm not that good at cop-think. Maybe draw me some stick figures."

"Gonna give you a clue. For whatever reason, you decided that the other B-girl, Nadia Delova, was not gonna help your case. You didn't want to be put in touch with her. So you told your very attractive cocounsel to drop it. But she wouldn't. Don't ask me why. I don't know yet. I will say she has a sterling reputation in town for ethics, which is more than I can say for either you or Solomon."

"Okay, assume everything you say is true," I said. "So what?"

"Think about it, Lassiter. C'mon. Shake off those concussions and use your noggin."

I thought about it, just as I was ordered, and, of course, there it was. Where it had been all the time. Because George Barrios, like every cop, sees evil wherever he looks.

"Aw, George, you're not serious. You think I knew someone was gonna bump off Elena?"

"Or worse." Barrios exhaled a long breath and looked at me with tired, disappointed eyes. "You knew where she was gonna be and at what time. You could have set up the whole deal. You weren't here to protect the two women. You were here to protect the assassin. Because you're thinking once Nadia Delova learns her friend had been gunned down, she'll dig deeper into whatever hole she's in."

"What bullshit."

"Just a theory. A possibility. One of many."

"Am I free to go now?"

"You don't see me getting out the cuffs, do you?"

"Is this the part where you say, 'But if I were you, Jake, I wouldn't be leaving town just now'?"

"Hell, no, Jake. I've been wishing for years that you'd leave town."

-34-

Grief and Hunger

The cops let us go around 10:30 a.m. Half an hour later, Victoria and I sat across from each other in the café at Books & Books on Lincoln Road. I figured we wouldn't run into any Russian mobsters or Miami Beach cops among the bookshelves in the art history section.

I drank my coffee and Victoria sipped her herbal tea. Both in silence.

At first, we didn't exchange words or share our grief. Instead, we were lost in our own mournful thoughts. Doubtless, Victoria blamed herself for Elena's death. I knew I blamed myself.

Finally, Victoria said, "I should have listened to you."

"And I should have gone with you. Been right there alongside you."

"Then what? You wouldn't have pulled your gun when you saw a cop coming. Or what seemed to be a cop. He probably would have shot you first."

Victoria had already told both Barrios and me that she could give virtually no physical description of the gunman. His face was hidden by the darkness and the visor. As far as she could tell, he was slightly taller than average with a weightlifter's body. No noticeable accent in the few words he spoke, except that his enunciation was so precise as to perhaps cover up an accent.

We were quiet again. Replaying what could have been, what should have been, what never would be. Both crushed under the burden of self-imposed guilt.

After a while, we realized that despite our grief, we were hungry. We'd missed breakfast again so went directly for lunch.

I ordered the grilled calamari with the mango coleslaw and Victoria had the veggie burger. Waiting for the food, Victoria said, "Right before the phony cop pulled up, Elena said Nadia would talk to me. She was going to call her."

"That was then. Now Nadia will be spooked, and who can blame her? That's the one thing that Barrios was right about. Someone was sending a message to Nadia."

"Elena also said Nadia might contact Benny the Jeweler."

"Bad idea."

"I told her."

The food arrived, and I started chomping on the calamari. A few more moments of silence as we ate, both lost in our own thoughts.

I've made many mistakes in my life. Most I've put behind me. What else can we do? But this awful murderous night would linger. This would plague me.

Victoria slid something across the table at me, breaking my concentration.

"What do you suppose this is?" she asked.

"A cell phone in a pink case with little bunny rabbits and shiny sequins."

"Do you think it's a cell phone I'd carry?"

"How would I know?"

"C'mon, Jake. You've picked juries. You can read people."

"It's not you. You'd have a Prada cell phone if they made them. So what?"

"I told the cops it was mine, and they bought it."

It took me a moment. These days, it takes longer, especially after sleepless nights. "You grabbed Elena's cell phone!"

"When I saw she was dead, I slipped it into my jeans. I'd left mine at home."

"Cops search you?"

"I was the person closest to a dead body. I'd say they had the right to look for weapons."

"They open the phone?"

"First, they asked if it was mine. I said it was."

"Lying to the cops. I've been a good influence."

"It was hard to do, believe me."

"I'm proud of you. All this time, I thought you were this uptight and upright chick."

"Chick?" She furrowed her forehead. "I had to lie, Jake. Otherwise I couldn't have refused what the cops asked next."

"Permission to look at the phone."

"I declined. Cited *Riley versus California*."

"That's my girl! Cocounsel, I mean. Jeez, that case came down just in time! Unanimous. All nine justices. Cops need a warrant to search your cell phone."

"Surprising outcome, don't you think?"

"Not at all. The justices don't have bags of cocaine in the trunks of their cars, so the drug seizure cases usually go the government's way. But every justice has a cell phone."

"That is so simplistic."

"Think so? I'll bet Justice Scalia e-mails Justice Thomas the hottest porn sites on the Internet."

I picked up the pink phone, punched the little round button, and the icons came to life. The wallpaper photo was Elena and Nadia in thong bikinis. They were smiling broadly and wearing oversize sunglasses with their undersize swimwear. The smiles were open and seemingly real. They looked so damn happy, and now the photo was indescribably sad.

I put the phone down and said, "Have you looked at the contacts?"

"Those and the recent calls."

"So you have Nadia's number."

She nodded. Almost afraid to say it aloud.

"That's a very tough phone call you're about to make," I said.

"Nadia deserves to know. And needs to know for her own protection."

"Do her this favor. Tell her the feds think she knows all about Benny the Jeweler's diamond-smuggling operation. Benny probably thinks it, too. That's why he hired that jerkoff Manuel Dominguez to find her. If Alex Gorev wasn't behind Elena's killing, Benny was. Make sure she realizes Benny is not her friend, no matter how many diamonds he gave her."

"I will. And no matter what you say, I'm still going to ask her what happened in Nicolai Gorev's office."

"Good luck with that. But if she does talk, be prepared for the worst."

"What do you mean?"

"Emotionally. If it's not what you want to hear. If it's damaging to Steve. Just steel yourself, okay?"

"I'm a big girl, Jake."

Maybe so, I thought, but right now she looked emotionally fragile, and I was worried about her.

"What are you going to do?" Victoria asked.

The truth would be: *try to come up with some razzle-dazzle to keep your boyfriend out of prison.* But that would be followed by her asking how. And I didn't have an answer just yet. But there was one thing I could do.

"Find Benny the Jeweler."

"How?"

"Same as always. Walk into a china shop and start breaking things."

·35·

Women and Love

Victoria walked several blocks east on Lincoln Road, crossed Collins Avenue, and made her way to the boardwalk that ran parallel to the ocean. She found a quiet alcove with a bench in the shade. Pulling out Elena's cell phone, she knew how hard the next several minutes would be.

A mixture of dark emotions. Grief and guilt and sorrow. But another powerful emotion, too. Her love for Steve. That's what took her to the darkened beach, and that's what propelled her now. There was such a thin thread of hope that he could stay out of prison. Nadia held that thread, but with her own life at risk, how could she be persuaded to help?

"Elena!" Nadia said when she answered the phone.

Victoria took a breath but did not speak.

"Elena?"

Victoria tried. She'd rehearsed it, but no words came.

"Elena, is that you?"

"Nadia. Ms. Delova, this is Victoria Lord. I'm—"

"I know who you are. Where is Elena?"

The beginning of fear.

"I am so sorry. Last night . . . on the beach . . . a man pretending to be a policeman . . ."

The sound of Nadia's breath catching, then great racking sobs.

"Nadia . . ."

When the sobbing subsided, Nadia said, "Were you there?"

"Yes. We were talking. About you. About how to help you."

"A policeman, you said."

"A fake policeman."

"In Riga, the Gorev brothers would hire policemen to do their dirty work. When they ran out of real policemen, they just started dressing up thugs in uniforms. Cheaper, too."

"So you think Alex Gorev is behind the murder?"

"Who else?"

Victoria took a breath before answering. On the boardwalk, two teen girls in bikinis pedaled by on rental bicycles, laughing in the innocent way of fifteen-year-olds. They left the scent of coconut oil in their wake.

"We can't rule out Benny the Jeweler," Victoria said.

"No. Benny has always been kind to me."

"Still, you know about his business, and he's under federal investigation."

"You think Benny would harm me? That is crazy."

"He's hired a PI to find you."

"To help me. To make sure I am safe."

"Please listen, Nadia. Benny knows the feds are looking for you. They need your help to indict him."

"I know nothing. Not even his full name."

Victoria didn't believe her, but what else could she say? She'd given the warning.

"Why do you even care?" Nadia asked.

"I don't want you to get hurt. Maybe I can even help you with the government."

"Or are you being nice so I will help the man you love?"

Nadia, it seemed, was a woman who believed that all life was a series of giving and getting based on quid pro quo. Maybe she was right. Maybe altruism was a philosophical ideal, a pretty notion unrelated to real life.

"Elena told you about Steve and me?"

"She liked you. I am sorry about your man. I did not mean for it to happen that way. But I know what you want, and I cannot do it. I cannot help him."

"Can we talk about that day? Can you tell me what happened?"

"I know what your man told police. It did not happen that way. I am sorry."

The words were crushing. But were they true?

"Elena told me you are in love, also," Victoria said. "I would like you to be with your lover, not on the run from Gorev's thugs and the government."

"I am with my man now, and it is heaven."

Where? Oh, how Victoria wanted to ask the question, but she was afraid of going too fast, of scaring Nadia off.

"Tell me about him. Elena said he was a customer at first."

"Funny, yes? B-girl falls for customer. He was in town for a convention about three months ago. Food products. I picked him up at Clevelander. He spent fifty-three hundred dollars at club. Shocked when bill came, but no protest. I spent night with him at hotel. Big violation of Gorev rules. The next two days, I stay away from club, except to reverse charge for him on credit card terminal. Otherwise, only with him. Now I am at his home. He wants to marry me."

Nadia sounded proud. And why not? A man wanted her for something more than just her body. Nadia's tone had softened. Now it was just two women speaking about love. Victoria thought it was time to dig deeper. "Maybe I could come see you, and we could talk face-to-face."

Victoria heard Nadia sigh, and then: "Why don't you just ask me directly what you want to know?"

"Did Nicolai Gorev have a gun?"

"Many guns. But that day? In his hand, no."

Victoria felt as if she'd just been punched in the gut. She had been so sure that Steve had told the truth about that part. Gorev's gun. The threat. But if Gorev was unarmed, whoever fired would not have acted in self-defense. The shooter—either Steve or Nadia—was not entitled to immunity under Stand Your Ground. Without being threatened with death or great bodily harm—the touchstones of self-defense laws—one of them had simply pulled the trigger and killed Gorev.

Victoria got to her feet and paced in circles on the boardwalk.

"If Gorev had no gun, why was he shot? What happened?"

"Are you sure you want to know?"

"Yes! The truth. Someone shot Gorev with a Glock nine millimeter. I need to know who! I need to know why!"

"The Glock was mine. I brought it in my purse."

Victoria stopped breathing. That's what Steve had said. Could there be a glimmer of hope? "Did you shoot Gorev?"

"Your man told the police I did."

"But is it true?"

"I have said too much already."

"Nadia, please!"

"Your man does not always tell the truth. That is all I can say."

Victoria felt her slipping away. "Let me come see you. We can talk. No one has to know."

"I am long way from Miami."

"I don't care."

"Too dangerous. I am sorry. I wish I could help your man, but I cannot. I am now going to pray for Elena's soul. Please do not call me again."

The phone clicked dead, and Victoria's hopes faded under the glare of the midday sun.

Tomahawk Steak for Two

I found Manuel Dominguez in the library room with its stained glass windows at The Forge on Arthur Godfrey Road. A few years ago, Shareef Malnik, the owner, gave the fancy old joint a major face-lift. It is still opulent, ornate, and a tad over-the-top. There are still gilt-framed mirrors and exposed brick. But the old mahogany has been replaced with blond woods. There are modern crystal chandeliers, and the whole place is lighter, brighter, and hipper.

Dominguez, in full dress army uniform bedecked with medals and ribbons, was dining with his lady, the presumably pregnant Rose Marie. At their table was a paunchy middle-aged man who wore a madras sport coat and a slippery jet-black toupee.

"Hey, Sarge!" I called out.

Dominguez looked up and, without blinking, greeted me. "Lieutenant Lassiter."

I took the fourth seat at the table without being invited. A gigantic steak covered a plate in front of Dominguez. It had to be the dry-aged prime tomahawk, intended for two. Rose Marie had her own entree, a fish dish—I'd guess grouper—covered with bacon in a creamy broth. A black truffle mac and cheese potpie and a plate of asparagus made up the sides. Mr. Madras Jacket didn't seem to be eating.

"Mr. Torkelson, say hello to Lieutenant Lassiter, my CO in Desert Storm," Dominguez said. "Lieutenant, Mr. Torkelson is a stockbroker from Toledo."

"Proud to meet you, sir," Torkelson the Toupee said.

"Scram," I said.

"I beg your pardon."

Dominguez forced a smile. "Lieutenant's got PTSD," he whispered.

"Sarge, is that a gold trident on your lapel?" I asked. "You a Navy SEAL now, too?"

Dominguez opened his mouth, but nothing came out.

"Hello, Rose Marie," I said. "You look radiant."

"Thank you, Jake. Would you join us for dinner?"

"Depends who's paying." I turned to Torkelson. "Are you still here?"

He eased his chair backward and said, "Perhaps I should join my wife at the bar. Pleased to meet you, Sergeant. Thanks for your service. You, too, Lieutenant."

"Yippee-ki-yay, motherfucker," I said in my best Bruce Willis.

He retreated hastily, his toupee sliding a bit to starboard.

"Jeez, Jake. What are you doing?" Dominguez fidgeted in his chair, and his medals jiggled. "He hadn't picked up the check yet."

"Manuel, tell me everything you know about Benny the Jeweler."

"Benny? Ah, jeez. I can't do that."

I pulled out my cell phone, scrolled to the camera function, and took a picture of him.

"Hey, what's that for?" he said.

"I'm gonna e-mail it to a very dear friend of mine. Deborah Scolino. Assistant US Attorney."

"Yeah?"

"Those ribbons and medals. You're violating the Stolen Valor Act."

"Bull! I Googled it, Jake. Supreme Court struck down the law. Violates free speech. I know my rights."

"Well guess what, smart guy? Congress reenacted it, and President Obama signed it. Narrower law. Only applies when the defendant claims the honors to get a fraudulent benefit." I pointed at his plate. "That steak is about forty ounces of benefit, Manuel."

"You wouldn't rat me out. We're pals."

I started punching a phone number into my cell. It wasn't Deborah Scolino's. It was a take-out pizza place in Wynwood, but Dominguez didn't know that.

"Hold on, Jake." He sighed and said, "What do you want to know?"

"His full name, for one thing. His address. And every word he's ever said to you."

While Dominguez talked, I sawed off little pieces of his tomahawk steak. I didn't order anything because I would doubtless be picking up the tab. Within fifteen minutes I had everything I needed, including about eight ounces of medium-rare beef.

Benny the Jeweler was Benjamin Cohen. He had a retail operation in the Seybold Arcade downtown, an old building with several dozen jewelry shops. He ran a wholesale diamond business in the warehouse district near the airport. And he had a splendid waterfront home on Leucadendra in Gables Estates. Lately, the house had been filled with people. Private investigators a few stripes higher than Dominguez. Out-of-town lawyers. Security guards. Warehouse workers. Benny was scared. His employees were being summoned to a federal grand jury. FBI agents were trying to talk to the B-girls, bouncers, and bartenders at Club Anastasia. Some of them—Russians and Estonians—were quitting and flying home because of threats of immigration prosecutions. As best Dominguez could tell, Benny Cohen was the real owner of the club.

Dominguez flipped open his cell phone and gave me Cohen's private numbers.

"Is he still looking for Nadia Delova?" I asked.

"Like 24-7, Jake."

"To hurt her or help her?"

"That's above my pay grade, Lieutenant." Dominguez took a forkful of his mac and cheese and between bites said, "What are you gonna do, Jake?"

"Visit Benny, of course."

"He's a nice old guy. But he's surrounded himself with muscle, and he's nervous, so don't piss him off."

"I'll try to keep my PTSD under control."

"I'm serious, Jake. Don't cross him."

"You think he's capable of ordering a hit?"

Dominguez patted his lips with a napkin. "You're talking about that B-girl on the beach the other night?"

I nodded.

"Benny had nothing to do with it."

"And you know this how?"

"'Cause he had me following her off and on."

"Why?"

"Benny was thinking maybe she'd lead me to the other one, Natasha."

"Nadia."

"Yeah. The friend was his path to Nadia, so no way he would have her killed."

"If you were really following Elena, Manuel, you'd know where she was last Wednesday night. Late. After work."

"I wasn't following her that night. But I know where she was."

"How?"

"I was following you. That's the night you and the lady lawyer met with her in the Russian church."

That rocked me. Manuel was telling the truth, almost a first for the con man. "The gray Range Rover?"

"That's me. When I wasn't following her, I was tailing you."

"Damn, I should have known. You tell Benny about the meeting at the church?"

"Nah."

"Why not? You're working for him."

"'Cause me and you are pals. You never did wrong by me. Till tonight, anyway. I didn't tell Benny because I didn't want you to get messed up."

"Thanks, Manuel."

I peeled three hundred-dollar bills out of my wallet and put them on the table. Dominguez frowned. "Will barely cover the wine, Jake."

I emptied my wallet and headed home, happy I'd parked at a meter, because I couldn't afford the valet.

-37-

Let's Make a Deal

I was sitting in my office the next morning, speed-reading the state's discovery documents. Skimming the autopsy report on Nicolai Gorev, I could nearly hear the bored, matter-of-fact voice of the medical examiner dictating his notes: "The missile proceeded through the frontal pole of the brain, perforated the cerebral peduncle, then impacted with the occipital bone."

All the while, I was planning my visit to Benny the Jeweler.

Benjamin Cohen.

The true owner of Club Anastasia. Boss of the Gorev brothers. Target of the federal investigation. Someone I would not be able to intimidate with my in-your-face tactics. Which is why I would take Victoria along. She had a talent for getting people to talk, winning them over with sincerity and trust.

Victoria.

My gut was still tied in knots when I thought how close she had come to being killed. I could not have lived with that. In the aftermath of Elena's death, my feelings were all jumbled. I'd pushed Victoria to the back of my mind, telling myself for the umpteenth time that she was my client's lady.

We'd formed a bond through a shared, horrific experience. The bond was steeped in emotion and dipped in blood. A danger there. The emotional connection transitioning to the sensual. No way! Friends, yes. Possibly close friends. Even that, I sensed, would not be a happy prospect for Solomon.

The phone rang. My secretary, Cindy—she had not yet graduated to "assistant"—told me it was the State Attorney.

"You mean an assistant state attorney?" I said.

"Nope. The one and only Raymond Pincher."

I picked up the phone and cried out, "Sugar Ray! Sugar Ray! Who'd you frame today?"

It was my imitation of his very own singsong, preacher's voice.

"Wrong Way! Wrong Way! Who'd you score for today?"

Damn, he was good.

"The Jakester, my man!" he continued. "The mouthpiece who took the *shy* out of *shyster* and put the *fog* into *pettifogger*."

I should never have let him get started.

That Ray Pincher became chief prosecutor of Miami-Dade County was something of an upset. He had fought his way out of the Liberty City projects. Literally. He boxed middleweight in the Police Athletic League and won a bunch of Golden Gloves fights. Then, a U-turn to a Baptist seminary for a year, but that didn't seem to be his destiny.

Quick with the quip as well as his fists, he set his eyes on lawyering. Scholarships to Florida State and Stetson Law School followed. He was a decent young prosecutor with spellbinding closing arguments. He ran for state attorney while still in his thirties. His slogan, of course, was "Elect a Real Crime Fighter." Billboards featured Pincher, in shaved head, bare chest, and boxing gloves. He won easily and these days never even faced opposition for re-election.

We were friendly but hardly friends. I used to see him in the gym. Once he invited me to spar, wearing puffy gloves and head-gear. I outweighed him by seventy-five pounds, and I've never lost a bout against the heavy bag, but he had this pop-pop jab that black-ened both my eyes. Quick sneaky hands.

He also caught me with a left hook to the groin that bent me double.

"Too tall, too tall, gets whacked in balls."

His explanation.

"You calling to apologize for indicting my client?" I said now.

"I incite. Grand jury indicts. I also invite. How's about lunch?"

Now that was a first.

"You paying, Sugar Ray?"

"No sass, fat ass. This is your lucky day."

"Yeah, why?"

"A friend of mine over on Northeast Fourth Street wants me to charge you with something, but we can't seem to find a crime."

"Your friend being Deborah Scolino."

"Jakester, just what did you say that got her federal panties in such a bunch?"

"Only that the theme of my case would be to blame her for Gorev's murder."

"Well, she's a little high-strung, so that would do it. Anyway, the lady and I met yesterday evening. You'd probably call it a 'con-spiracy of sovereigns taking place in the shadows,' except we had dinner on the patio of the Biltmore." He chuckled to himself. "I do appreciate a man who can turn a phrase, and you, Jake, are second only to me."

"Get to the point, Ray. I've got mobsters to visit."

"Soho Beach House. One hour."

He hung up, and I put on a tie.

The Soho Beach House is a fancy oceanfront hotel, private club, public restaurant, and spa. A few months ago, it's where LeBron James, Dwyane Wade, and Chris Bosh ate salads and guacamole as they decided their future . . . and that of the Miami Heat. Maybe LeBron didn't like the salad dressing.

I got there on time and found Pincher in the courtyard of the Italian restaurant on the hotel grounds. His table was under a silver buttonwood tree laced with pin lights. Glass lanterns hung from wooden trellises overhead. Three of the four seats at the table were taken. Pincher, of course. Plus Assistant US Attorney Deborah Scolino and Miami Beach Detective George Barrios.

"In one corner," I said, taking the empty chair, "the city, the state, and the federal governments. In the other corner, little old me. Doesn't seem like a fair fight."

Only Pincher cracked a smile. "Jake, you're gonna like what we've got to say."

I ordered a Peroni, fried anchovies, and meatballs, and listened.

"What's the biggest weakness in the state's case against Solomon?" Pincher asked.

"Motive," I said. "Barrios has some bullshit theory that Solomon was having an affair with Nadia Delova and got talked into doing the crime."

"Or tricked into it," Barrios said. "Either way, he's guilty."

"Except it's not true. The Russian woman was a client, nothing more."

"Well, sir," Pincher said, "today we've got a dead-solid perfect motive."

I sipped my beer and said, "Wake me up when you get to the part I'm supposed to like."

Pincher nodded toward Barrios. "Detective, you do the honors."

"Jake, remember when I told you we traced the Glock to a guy in New Jersey."

I chewed a spicy meatball and said, "Owns a courier service. No record. Name is Littlejohn."

"Does business as Littlejohn Couriers, Inc. We looked into it. Little family corporation, but it doesn't really own anything but the name. The trucks are registered to a Florida corporation whose stock is owned by a Bermuda trust. The trustees are officers of a bank in the Cook Islands. Are you following me?"

"Not really. I don't even know where the Cook Islands are."

"A bit east of New Zealand, and that's where the feds come in."

Deborah Scolino put down her fork. She had been nibbling eggplant caponata and now patted her lips with her napkin while still managing to scowl at me. Multitasking. "The Cook Islands don't give comity to American judgments and really don't cooperate with our law enforcement agencies. But we have ways of getting information."

"Sneaky NSA ways or old-fashioned bribery?" I asked.

"I'll ignore your slanderous innuendo," she said. "Mr. Pincher tells me it's just your way, and I shouldn't take it personally."

"Excellent idea," I said. "I didn't take it personally when we were sparring and he hit me in the balls."

Another scowl. Then she said, "Once you cut through the shell corporations and trusts, Littlejohn's trucks are owned by Benjamin Cohen. It's one of his businesses. Littlejohn is pretty much just a bookkeeper."

"And because of his clean record, Littlejohn is Benny's gun buyer."

"Exactly. When our agents confronted Littlejohn, he folded in about thirty seconds. Admits he buys weapons for Cohen, including the Glock that came from Houston and was used to kill Nicolai Gorev."

"So what's that got to do with Solomon?"

"Hang with us," Pincher said. He was eating a kale salad with apple and grilled chicken. Maybe planning on getting back down to middleweight range.

"We have warrants to tap Benjamin Cohen's phones." Scolino lowered her voice to a whisper, maybe afraid the Guatemalan busboy also worked for Benny. "Three days before Gorev is killed, Benny gets a call from one of our CI's who's playing both sides of the street."

"I'm shocked, shocked that a scumbag informant would do that," I said.

"The guy tells Benny that he's our real target, not Gorev."

"And Benny knows Gorev will flip on him," I ventured.

"In a Moscow minute," Scolino said.

"Giving Benny the motive to kill Gorev," I said happily. "So Benny gives Nadia the Glock and she kills Gorev, just like my client told Barrios at the crime scene."

Pincher cleared his throat. "Not exactly."

I thought I saw where this was going. "You don't have Nadia to testify. In fact, Ms. Scolino doesn't want you to have Nadia testify because my cross-examination will get the esteemed prosecutor a transfer to North Dakota. So, as of this minute, you can link the gun's ownership to Benny, but not its use as a murder weapon."

"But Solomon can."

"How? Benny gave Nadia the gun. She's the link."

"Think about it a second, Jake."

I followed instructions while Pincher gave me his campaign poster smile. After two seconds, I would have liked to knock out his pearly teeth. I've seen the state pull some shit in my time, but this was pretty much an all-time low.

"Sugar Ray, are you saying that, in a town filled with thugs and creeps and killers, a career criminal like Benny the Jeweler hires this half-assed lawyer to kill a Russian mobster?"

"If Solomon says so, we'll buy it."

"If Nadia said she was the shooter, you'd buy that, too."

"First one in the door gets the prize," Pincher said.

"We're still not ruling out that Nadia used her feminine wiles to get Solomon into the murder for hire," Barrios said.

I looked at Deborah Scolino. "Did he really say 'feminine wiles'? Doesn't that violate some federal statute?"

"The fact that Solomon looks pretty harmless is helpful," Pincher said. "Adds credibility to Benny's plan."

"How?"

"The whole Nadia passport deal was just a ruse to catch Gorev off guard."

"Still not following you, Ray. Maybe because you're making no sense."

"Noodle it. Nadia had been in Nicolai Gorev's office lots of times. Benny figured she wouldn't arouse his suspicion. And better to bring along this harmless-looking lawyer, rather than some professional hit man or a guy Gorev knows works for Benny."

"So your theory is that Benny hired *both* Solomon and Nadia to knock off Gorev? That's a helluva high-wire act. To say nothing of it being total bullshit."

"Gorev ends up dead with the murder weapon in Solomon's hand," Pincher said, "and Nadia flees with the contents of the safe. It passes the blush test—don't you think, Jake?"

"Funny, I thought our standard of justice was guilt beyond a reasonable doubt. Now I learn it's when the state's theory doesn't turn you beet red or make you laugh so hard you fart like cannon fire in the *1812 Overture*."

That left the three of them glowering at me, especially Deborah Scolino. I pictured her boss, the local US Attorney, reading her the riot act after Gorev got killed, because *his* boss, the Attorney General, had just reamed him out. That would have led to Scolino stomping her sensible shoes in a conference room filled with FBI agents and yelling that something had to be done to resuscitate the dead-in-the-water Benny Cohen investigation.

I am not one of those defense lawyers who thinks that our federal cops and lawyers are either incompetent boobs or vengeful agents of retribution. Most are hardworking and ethical and under-paid. Okay, there are examples of outright boobery that go back to ABSCAM and beyond. There was the anthrax investigation where a former army scientist was wrongfully named as a suspect—and later paid $6 million—and the FBI's false accusation against a hapless Atlanta security guard as the Olympic Park bomber.

Pincher let me sit there, stewing a moment, then said, "Jake, my man. We've known each other too long for you to be climbing on that high horse of yours. Get your ass down here on the mules like the rest of us."

"Fine, I'll wallow in the mud with you. What's in it for Solomon? Just give me the numbers."

Pincher beamed. "Yes, indeedy-do! Let's make a deal! In a nutshell, Solomon faces conviction for felony murder. Manda-tory life without parole. He gets that, right? He'll never see the light of day."

"Unless . . . ?"

"He lays out enough details to indict Benny Cohen for con-spiracy to commit the murder."

"Such as?"

"Benny gave Solomon the Glock. Nadia Delova was an acces-sory. Solomon was promised so much money, yada, yada, yada."

"And . . . ?" I said. "What's the quid pro quo? What do I get besides a thank-you note I can hang over the crapper next to my diploma?"

"Solomon has a clean record, if you don't count his contempt citations, which are basically parking tickets. The guy he aced was a piece of shit Russian mobster. Be thankful for that or we couldn't do this. We'll have to think a bit on what Solomon will plead to, but let's work backwards from the sentence. Say we recommend ten years. Out in eight and a half with gain time. How does that sound?"

Like a monkey with an accordion, I thought.

"Jesus, you must really want Benny Cohen," I said.

"You have no idea," Deborah Scolino said. "Among other things, Cohen has violated the Foreign Corrupt Practices Act with bribes to public officials overseas."

I shrugged. "So has Walmart, but I don't see you framing them for murder."

"You don't understand the scope of this. Benjamin Cohen has been the John Doe of our investigation from the beginning. The largest diamond smuggler on the East Coast. He's corrupted customs officers here and mining company executives in Russia."

Again, Scolino lowered her voice as if Kremlin spies might be listening. "Cohen has partnered with one of Vladimir Putin's closest associates. That's how they managed to reopen portions of a closed diamond mine in Siberia."

"The pit six hundred meters deep that Gorev talked about?"

"The Mirny mine. Officially closed. But a small part is working off the books. Benny gets the diamonds, and Putin reaps millions of dollars a year in kickbacks. It's official US policy to shut off the gravy train to the Russian president. From day one, the Cohen case has been all about Russian bribes and kickbacks to Putin. Not some credit card scam of B-girl joints. The Attorney General himself gets weekly reports."

"The Attorney General himself," I repeated, without overdoing the sarcasm.

Scolino's voice was now a whisper. "The president is also well aware of the investigation."

"Unless it goes to hell," I said. "Then the assistant secretary of the interior will take the fall."

"You have a patriotic duty here," Pincher said, as earnest as a TV preacher.

"To help your country," Scolino added, in case I didn't get it.

I looked at Barrios. I thought he might start whistling a John Philip Sousa march, but he kept quiet.

"Benny Cohen ever kill someone or have them killed?" I asked.

"Other than Gorev, you mean?" Pincher said.

"Yeah, if that's the picture you want to paint."

"We have no intelligence on that," Scolino said.

"So you're basically framing a nonviolent criminal with murder."

"I'll ignore that," Scolino said.

"So what'll it be, Jake?" Pincher said. "Solomon's fate is in your hands. Life without parole. Or dancing in the streets in eight and a half years."

"That's still enough time for you to steal his girlfriend," Barrios said, taking his shot at me.

"I'll convey your offer to my client, as required by the rules," I said.

"But will you recommend it?" Pincher pressed me.

"Chill, Ray. I'll drive straight to the jail and call you later."

"Tell you what we can throw in. Solomon can choose the facility. I hear Sumter up in Bushnell has decent food. Plus classes in auto mechanics and masonry."

I hadn't finished my meatballs and anchovies, but my hunger was gone. I remembered my first conversation with Victoria, expressing my frustration about the system. Well, after all these years, I just realized there's not a damn thing wrong with the system. It's just the flawed human beings who run it. People like Pincher. Scolino. Barrios. And me.

"Like I said, Ray, I'll pass it along."

"That's my Jake, playing it close to the vest. Like a peekaboo boxer."

I slid back my chair and stood. "Ray, if we do this deal, you'll get some headlines for convicting an international criminal of murder. Scolino here dodges a bullet, and Barrios has solved yet another major crime."

"Not just us, Jake," Pincher said. "Word gets around that you and I have a close working relationship—it'll be great for your business. Clients will ask, 'How'd you get that great deal?' And you'll just smile that crooked smile of yours. They'll be crawling all over each other to pay your fees."

"Something for everybody," I said, leaving without saying good-bye.

Jailhouse Lawyers

I drove west across Biscayne Bay on the Julia Tuttle, headed for the jail. While waiting for the valet to deliver my car, I had called Victoria to meet me for our sit-down with Solomon. I left out all the details of my lunch date, wanting to tell the story only once.

Feeling cruddy. It's my own damn fault they offered a dirty deal. Hell, I'd practically invited it when I taunted Scolino that day in my office.

"Feel free to give Pincher a preview of my closing argument. Maybe the two of you will come up with something that won't cost you your job."

I planned to keep the jailhouse meeting brief. I figured Solomon would turn down the deal, probably angrily, but I wasn't going to push him one way or the other. If he didn't take it, Victoria and I would pay a visit to Benny Cohen. International criminal and pal of Putin.

On the phone, Victoria had said she would take the Metrorail to the jail, so we could travel in one car to Benny's place. Which would not have been a problem, except it started to rain.

Not *rain*, as in an afternoon shower.

Rain, as in summer in Miami. Monsoon rain. Amazon rain. Noah, finish-the-damn-ark rain. Great gray sheets pouring from a black sky, pounding my windshield, disabling my wipers, and tattooing my roof like Max Weinberg on the drums. A lightning bolt zigzagged out of the death clouds and struck one of the little islands south of the causeway; the thunderclap rattled my windows. My old canvas top wasn't exactly leaking, but little droplets appeared along one seam.

Victoria had planned to walk from the Civic Center Metrorail station to the jail. It's only a couple of blocks, but today a person could drown. I tried calling her cell. Under the low-hanging ceiling of otherworldly clouds, no service.

My big, fat Caddy tires were hydroplaning, so I slowed down. Either that, or risk flying over the guardrail and turning the old Eldo into a boat. Years ago, I'd had a CD player installed, so now I slipped my favorite Leonard Cohen into the device. In his distinctive gravelly voice, Leonard was half singing, half talking:

"Everybody knows that the dice are loaded,
Everybody rolls with their fingers crossed."

Well, I knew that, but thanks for reminding me.

Once on the mainland, I took I-95 south, then west on 836, exiting on Northwest Twelfth Avenue. Instead of going to the jail, I headed toward the Metrorail station, next to Jackson Memorial Hospital. I found Victoria huddled under an overhang, waiting for me. Somehow she knew I'd come get her, knew I wouldn't let her walk through the storm. So far today, that was the only thing that I felt good about.

* * *

Solomon had lost more weight, appeared even paler, and seemed depressed. Well, he wasn't staying at the Four Seasons. Victoria looked away, maybe thinking she might cry if she kept her eyes on the man she loved.

"Can you make another run at getting bail?" Solomon asked. "This damn place is getting to me."

"It won't work," I said. "Judge has ruled."

Solomon didn't curse at me or tell me what a lousy lawyer I was. I would have preferred that. Instead, he seemed to just shrink into himself. He'd lost the spark that defined him.

We have some mutual friends from the courthouse. One is Marvin the Maven, a retired guy in his eighties who drifts from courtroom to courtroom, looking for the best action and dispensing advice on picking juries. A few months ago, I ran into Marvin in the corridor. He'd just left a courtroom where Solomon was defending a pair of six-foot-two-inch South Beach models, identical twins named Lexy and Rexy, who were fighting several thousand dollars in fines for parking in handicapped spaces.

"You know how the son of a gun won?" Marvin asked me.

"Bribed the jury," I guessed.

"Claimed the girls had anorexia, so they get to park in the handicapped spots. Now, that's chutzpah. Solomon's like Barnum and Bailey. Whenever he tries a case, there's always a dozen clowns crawling out of a little car."

But Solomon didn't look like a ringmaster now. More like one of the circus cats, gone mangy and lazy from being kept too long in a cage.

I shot a look at Victoria, who nodded, her signal for me to start talking. Then I told them about my meeting with our dedicated public servants who wanted Solomon to lie to make their case against Benny Cohen. A case that was part criminal and part political.

"That's despicable," Victoria said.

"Did Pincher tell you how long the offer was open?" Solomon said.

"No, but I promised to call him today. If you want, I can ask for more time."

"What!" Victoria's eyes flashed from me to Solomon and back again. "You two aren't seriously considering this."

"Not my call," I said. "I wouldn't take it, and I wouldn't advise a client to take it. But your partner is sophisticated. If he determines it's in his best interest to plead, you won't hear me yelling about truth, justice, and the American way."

Her head whipped toward her lover. "Steve! What are you thinking?"

"Life without parole. Losing you forever. There'd be nothing to live for." He looked at me. "Is there any play in the numbers?"

"Pincher would never open with his best deal, so I'm thinking there's some. They want Benny Cohen so badly, they might give you the key to the city and a ticker-tape parade to rat him out."

"Realistically, Lassiter. What can you get me?"

"Pincher offered ten. I can counter with eight. With gain time, that's six years and . . ."

I was still doing the math when Solomon said, "Nine months. Six years and nine months. I can do that."

"Steve!" Victoria gestured with both hands, palms turned upward. "What the hell?"

He didn't respond.

"Jake!"

I didn't respond. Communication with her two men wasn't going well today.

Solomon was clear-eyed and focused as he said, "Lassiter, the only way I can make this decision is for you to give me an accurate assessment of my chances at trial."

Unlike most clients, he was taking an analytical approach. I admired that.

"I don't know yet. Everything's fluid and changing daily. I want to meet with Benny Cohen."

"He'll talk to you?"

"He's had me followed. I think he'll want to have a few words."

"About what?" Solomon said.

"He's wondering if we know where Nadia is. I'm wondering if he knows anything that can help our defense. We'll play some cat and mouse with him. I'd sit down with the devil himself to keep you from getting convicted of murder."

"Or copping to a phony plea," Victoria said.

"That, too," I agreed. "And right now, Benny Cohen is the only avenue we've got."

-39-

All You Need Is Love

I made two phone calls from the jail parking lot. First I danced with Ray Pincher to buy more time.

A counteroffer of eight years in the can was "within the realm of possibility," he allowed. And sure, Solomon could take a couple of days to think it over. Big decision, after all.

Then my cold call to the cell number Manuel Dominguez gave me. Benny Cohen answered with a languid, "Mr. Lassiter, I've been expecting to hear from you."

* * *

With Victoria riding shotgun, we took I-95 to the end where it dumped us onto South Dixie Highway. Also called US 1. Or Useless 1, if you prefer. Turned left at LeJeune, rounded the circle where Granny did her fishing in the Gables Waterway, and continued south along Old Cutler Road under its canopy of Japanese banyans.

The rain had stopped, and by the time we hung a left on Arvida Parkway, the sun was blazing, steam rising from the pavement. It's an everyday occurrence in Miami and possibly in hell, if that's not redundant.

The rent-a-cop in the guardhouse waved us through. We took a left onto Leucadendra and found Benny Cohen's place on 450 feet of waterfront. You could have docked a cruise ship behind the house.

The place was your typical two-story Miami mansion. Orange barrel-tile roof. Towering royal palms framing a circular tile drive-way that could handle parking for a hundred of your closest friends. Pillars out front to either hold up the second floor or just make the place look more stately than it was.

Also out front were two large men in dark suits on this scorching-hot day. They stood in the shade of a portico, waiting for us to get out of the Eldo.

"Let's do this," I said to Victoria.

"What's our game plan?"

"Not sure I have one. Just play it by ear."

"I knew it!" She leveled me with that Victoria Lord glare. "I just knew it."

"Sorry I don't have all my questions typed on color-coded cards."

"Men!" she said, opening the car door and stepping out.

Apparently, Solomon and I had similar failings, I figured.

Once we were on the portico, the two men frisked us for weap-ons, then used a magic wand to check for wires. One of them ush-ered us into a two-story foyer. Spiral staircases peeled off from either side to the second floor.

"Mr. C is on the patio." The Dark Suit led us through a room the size of a football field toward a set of French doors. The floor tiles were beige. The walls were a muted neutral color in the same family. The crystal chandeliers were large but without all the doo-dads you often see in these houses. Despite its size, the house tended toward the understated. You might even call it boring.

The French doors had a splendid view of the infinity pool, a tanning ledge, and the wide expanse of waterway that led to the Bay. The Dark Suit politely held the door, and we exited the house onto a covered patio with ceiling fans and a long granite table.

"I'm Benjamin Cohen." The little man got up from the table, bowed toward Victoria, and extended a soft, pudgy hand for me to shake. "People call me Benny the Jeweler."

"Jake Lassiter," I said. "And this is Victoria Lord."

He smiled as if we were old friends overdue for a visit. He wore a cream-colored silk guayabera with buttons that looked like gray pearls. His dressy slacks had a houndstooth pattern, black with that same cream color as his shirt. His shoes were loafers in a soft black leather with those silver buckles that resemble a horse's bit. I'd guess Ferragamo or Gucci. If he stood on his tippy-toes, he might be about five feet five.

He looked to be somewhere between fifty and eighty. It was impossible to tell. Smooth, tight skin. Not a wrinkle on the forehead and the eyes with just a bit more slant than you might expect. He'd had some work done. Lots of work.

"May I offer you anything?" A lot of New York in his voice. "Lemonade. Something stronger? A little bite to *nosh* on?"

We both declined.

"So. How do you like my house?"

"To tell you the truth, the colors are a little bland," I said.

"Jake! That's impolite," Victoria admonished me.

"Better resale value," Benny explained.

"Me, I like to live in the present," I said.

"Understandable. Who knows when tragedy will befall any of us?"

Maybe it was a threat. Maybe just chitchat.

"Do you know how I got into my business, Mr. Lassiter?"

I shook my head.

"Started as a diamond polisher in New York. For old man Slutsk. An orthodox Jew, of course. Do you know why the Jews got into the diamond business?"

I said I did not.

"Let's say you were a Jew in Lisbon in the fifteenth century. You could be in the cattle business or the diamond business. But if there came a time when Portugal decided to expel the Jews, as they did in 1497, it's a helluva lot easier to travel with diamonds than with cows."

"Makes sense," I agreed.

"Those were the same Jews that Spain expelled in 1492," Victoria added. "Just when they thought they had sanctuary, boom, it happened again in Portugal."

"Smart *maidel* you got there, Mr. Lassiter."

"Princeton and Yale," I told him.

"Anyway, from old man Slutsk I learned everything about diamonds and how to treat people."

"So he was a good boss," I said.

"Diamonds, he knew. But good boss, my *tuches*! He was the worst *momzer* in midtown. He read Talmud all morning and screamed at his workers the rest of the day. I learned to do everything the opposite. I treat my workers like family. Pay them well. Send doctors when their kids get sick, presents when they get married. I could never tolerate a person who mistreated his underlings."

"That's a good trait," Victoria said.

"Take Nicolai Gorev, for example. Greedy and stupid. I told him not to charge so much, he'd get in trouble with the credit card companies. Plus he cheated the girls, withheld their wages, forced them to have sex. I shed no tears for him." He turned toward me. "So, Mr. Lassiter, what is it you want?"

"Top of my list. Evidence my client is innocent."

"No, no, no. That's what Solomon wants. But you, *boychik*! In life, I mean."

"You want to chat about life?"

"These days, I don't get a lot of visitors. And the ones who come are either Russian goons or beautiful young women who cannot carry on a conversation." He gave a sly little smile. "With the exception of one *shayna maidel* named Nadia, but we'll talk about her in a moment."

I'd dated a couple of Jewish women, along with virtually every other ethnic group, including Seminole Indian, so I knew he'd just said "pretty girl" in Yiddish.

"Okay," I said. "I just want to be happy. Like everyone else."

"And what will make you happy? Money?"

I shook my head. "Money's never been the goal."

"Prestige then? Chamber of Commerce Man of the Year. Honors in the community."

"I don't give a crap about that stuff."

"Now we're getting somewhere. Since we've ruled out those things, what brings you happiness?"

"Mr. Cohen . . ."

"Benny."

"Benny, I don't really think much about it. I just go about my life day to day. Stuff happens. Some good. Some bad. I don't know what's at the end of the rainbow, or even if there is a rainbow."

He smiled, but a bit sadly. "An honest self-appraisal from a decent man. Now, may I tell you what would bring you happiness?"

"I'm not sure you can. You can speak for yourself, but you don't know me."

"*Feh!* We're just alike."

"You and me? Doubt it."

"You! Me! Ms. Lord! Mr. Solomon! Even Nadia Delova. All of us, good people. We want the same thing. Love!"

He sang it then, with a nasal twang, not sounding a bit like the Beatles. "All you need is love, love. Love is all you need."

"Benny, I know you're trying to tell me something, but subtlety sometimes eludes me. Why not just hit the nail on the head?"

Victoria stepped in. "What he's saying, Jake, is that he's in love with Nadia."

"She's got an ass like a ripe fig," Cohen said.

"How sweet." Victoria turned to me. "Mr. Cohen is also saying he would never hurt Nadia."

"Bingo!" Benny said. "A *yiddishe kop* you've got, Ms. Lord. A Jewish brain."

"I'm Episcopalian," she said. "So you would like Nadia to come back to you?"

"Such a smart question. What you are really asking in a gentle way is whether I know Nadia has found a young man. Of course I know. And despite my feelings for her, I understand. Why would she want an *alter kocker* like me, anyway? I wish her the best. You see, Ms. Lord, that is true love. The same feeling that Mr. Lassiter has for you."

"We're not lovers," Victoria fired back, a bit quicker than necessary.

Benny waved his hand. "Not yet! But I watched on the security monitor as you two sat in the car. I saw your body language, how close your heads were when you spoke to each other. Then I saw a little spat, as lovers do. I know about your nighttime travels. The Russian church. The beach. The meals you've shared. Your common purpose."

"Our common purpose is to keep Steve Solomon out of prison," she said. "Steve is my lover."

"For now, yes. When he is in prison, what then?"

"It's my job to keep him out of prison," I broke in.

"Then you would have to be both a magician and a mensch. A magician to accomplish the task, a mensch for wanting to."

"Benny, I was hoping you could help us."

"I doubt it, but tell me what you know, and we'll take it from there."

"The feds want you for smuggling stolen diamonds, but they need someone to draw them a road map. An eyewitness who can place the diamonds in your hands. They thought Nicolai Gorev was their guy. They'd charge him, and he'd flip on you. But now that he's dead, maybe Nadia can do it, if she knows enough."

"That sweet child will never tell the government a thing."

His statement gobsmacked me. I had expected him to say that Nadia doesn't know anything. But instead he said she wouldn't talk, inadvertently conceding that she *could* nail him. But so far, she hadn't. I remembered Deborah Scolino telling me that she didn't trust Nadia's denials when it came to Benny's business:

"Nadia said a lot of things about Nicolai Gorev that were surely true. But when it came to Benny the Jeweler, she was evasive."

Now I wondered just how deep was Benny's professed love for the Russian Bar girl? Was he really comfortable with her on the loose? I needed to poke around a bit to find out.

"I would be remiss if I didn't ask you a question, Benny," I said. "How do the diamonds get to Miami?"

He coughed up a laugh, delighted that anyone could ask such a foolish question. "What is the expression I'm looking for?"

"Maybe it's 'Ask me no questions, I'll tell you no lies,'" I ventured.

"No, another one. From the movies. 'I could tell you, but then I'd have to kill you.' Yes, that's it!" Another chuckle. "What else do you have for me?"

"I know you gave Nadia the gun that killed Nicolai Gorev, and that could be a problem for you."

Benny thought a moment before replying. "If you know that, it means the federal stooges told you. Which also means they want something from you. Oh, Mr. Lassiter, I hope you don't let your client do anything stupid. Or perjurious."

Benny the Jeweler was no fool. He'd figured out the government's play.

"I'm trying, Benny. But I need a reasonable chance to win his trial."

"The damned Glock." He made a tsk-tsk-tsk-ing sound. "My mistake, entirely. Personally, I hate guns. I gave it to Nadia because she felt she needed it for protection."

"So you didn't hire Nadia to kill Gorev?"

"Of course not. He was a useful idiot. But I was foolish to give her the gun, which I suppose she gave to Solomon, who used it to kill Gorev. Or maybe she killed him. Who knows? I wasn't there."

"Why would she do that? And why would Solomon?"

"Nadia was in an impossible position. The federal government forced her to wear a wire to get immunity."

"She told you this?"

"Until the shooting, she told me everything. Every time she walked into the US Attorney's office, she would call me afterward. Loyalty. Add that to love, Mr. Lassiter. That's what we all need. Love and loyalty."

"So she told you she was going to have a meeting with Gorev."

"I wish she had. If she'd told me about her passport, I'd have ordered Gorev to give it to her. Same for the back pay."

"She had to know you would do that for her," I said. "Meaning she didn't go for the passport at all. Or to get Gorev on tape for the feds. She went there to kill him."

"It's possible," he agreed. "She could have thought that with Gorev gone, I would no longer be at risk, and she wouldn't have to testify. Run away, yes. But testify, no."

"So your theory is she did it for you," I said.

"I was kind to Nadia. Generous. She was not used to men treating her well. So, yes, *boychik*, I think she might have killed Gorev so he couldn't incriminate me."

"You've been looking for Nadia," Victoria said. "Why?"

"Obviously not to harm her."

"It's not obvious to me," I said. "She could still come back and rat you out to save her own hide."

"I want to pay her, not kill her."

"Hush money?"

"Going away money. For her and her young man." He lowered his voice to a conspiratorial whisper. "Do you know where she is?"

I said yes just as Victoria said no.

Benny laughed, the sound of a small dog yipping. "Now you sound more like a married couple than ever."

"So who's telling the truth, Benny?" I asked. "Victoria or me?"

"Ms. Lord, of course. If you knew where Nadia was, you'd be there, not on my pool deck. Mr. Lassiter, you *meshugenah* shyster. You lied to extract more information; then you would have thrown me a bum steer. 'She's in San Diego.' Or whatever popped into your head."

The old bastard was still sharp, I thought. *Best to remember that.*

"If you find her, tell her I will give her half a million dollars," Benny said. "No strings attached. She can go to Rio with her man or wherever they want. I don't care. Just not back here where the feds could grab her. And for you two, a hundred thousand for your honeymoon."

Victoria started to say something. Undoubtedly, a strong denial of any nuptials. I stifled her with a wave of my hand. "Thank you, Benny. We'll let you know."

"Tell her one more thing," Benny said. "That I think of her every night as I fall asleep. With fondness in my heart."

-40-

Whore's Rules

Victoria was troubled. There was something about Benny Cohen that raised the hair on the back of her neck. His faux gentlemanly pose. His philosophy of love and loyalty. His personal story with Nadia.

"Are you buying all that lovey-dovey talk?" she asked Lassiter on the ride to his office.

"Obviously you are not."

"I don't take at face value the sweet words of old lechers who give diamonds to B-girls in return for sex, then claim to have fallen in love."

"So you're prejudiced against old lechers?"

"Plus the guy is a diamond smuggler."

"That seems more relevant to me on credibility, but call that a guy reaction."

Victoria stared out the windshield. The sky had turned gunmetal gray once more, but no new thunderstorms. Yet.

Without warning or preamble, Lassiter said, "Why does everybody think we're a couple?"

Victoria kept her eyes straight ahead. "They don't. They think *you* think we're a couple."

"Not the way I'm hearing it."

"That was part of Benny's act. To distract us. He's a clever old fox."

"I don't know, Victoria. Maybe he sensed something between us."

Not this again, she thought. "Do I have to call another Code Yellow?"

"I'm not putting the moves on you. I'm just asking. It may help in my future relationships."

"That's different." Victoria thought he sounded sincere and deserved a serious reply. "If you want relationship advice, I can help you. First, you might try dating an appropriate unattached woman."

"You mean no more fleeing felons?"

"I'm being serious, Jake."

"As for dating, I thought guys and girls just hung out these days playing video games and getting tattoos."

"Not guys your age."

"Ouch! Message received."

"I'm glad. Some men, you swing a hammer at them, they think you're into home improvement."

"But as for that Code Yellow, last time we talked, you'd hoisted the flag for Code Green."

"Damn it, Jake!" She couldn't believe he'd gone there. They had both avoided any mention of that embarrassing night. "I gave you major points for being a true gentleman—"

"A real mensch, you mean."

"But now when you bring it up—"

"By 'it,' you mean your shameless come-on?"

"You lose all your points along with your mensch-i-ness."

That shut him up for a while. They picked up I-95 and headed for the I-395 flyover to the MacArthur. If traffic was light on the Causeway, they'd be in Lassiter's law office in fifteen minutes.

"Back to your question about Benny's bona fides . . ." Lassiter said.

Victoria was thankful to talk about the case.

"Suppose Benny really was in love with Nadia," he continued. "Is it credible that he's offering all that money and wishing her happy times with her true love?"

"You're a man. What do you think?"

"'All you need is love.' Maybe that's right for you and Solomon. Maybe even for me. But Benny's not like us. He was full of crap about that. Lifetime criminals like Benny and the Gorev brothers are sociopaths. By definition, they don't feel the give-and-take of human emotions."

When Victoria didn't respond, Jake shot a look at her. She was looking in the passenger wing mirror.

"What is it?" he said.

"There's a gray Range Rover that's been behind us all the way since Old Cutler."

"Manuel Dominguez. Benny Cohen isn't done with us yet."

* * *

Victoria realized she was hungry on the stairs leading to Lassiter's second-floor office. Maybe that's because she was inhaling the aroma of a piquant picadillo with garlic, sugar, and raisins coming from the Cuban restaurant on the first floor.

They settled into chairs on opposite sides of an old oak table in the mini–conference room. Lassiter said, "Let's sum it up. What we know and what we don't."

"There's a confrontation in Gorev's office. Nadia demands her passport and back pay, but she uses some language about federal crimes that makes Gorev suspicious. He threatens her, making reference to a pit six hundred meters deep that we now know is the Mirny diamond mine in Siberia. He also mentions the jeweler, who we now know is Benny Cohen and is Gorev's boss. Gorev accuses Nadia of telling the government about Aeroflot 100, which presumably is the flight she took to New York."

She noticed Lassiter nodding his approval at her summary. They were working well together.

Lassiter took over from there. "Solomon tells the cops at the scene that Gorev pulled a gun and ordered them to strip to see if either one was wearing a wire. While Gorev is watching Solomon, Nadia slips Benny's Glock out of her purse and fires the shot that kills Gorev. Then she robs the safe, inexplicably takes Gorev's gun, and leaves by a back door, locking Solomon inside. Oh, she also tosses the murder weapon to Solomon, who panics and fires two more shots into the door when Gorev's thugs try to break in. He's got the murder weapon when the cops arrive." Lassiter raised his eyebrows. "It is, if I may say so, one of the shittiest stories a client has ever told me."

"Then, Steve told us to stop looking for Nadia," Victoria said. "I couldn't figure out why, but you did."

"Because I don't look at Solomon through the gauzy, soft focus of love."

"You sensed Steve was admitting he lied to the cops. Nadia didn't shoot Gorev. Steve did. At that time, we were still hoping Steve fired in self-defense because we were relying on his story about Gorev having a gun. Since then, Nadia told me on the phone that Gorev was unarmed. No Stand Your Ground. No self-defense."

"Leaving us where, Vic?"

"Well, you think we're stuck with the crazy story Steve told the cops."

"Any change now, he'd be torn to shreds on cross based on his prior statements."

From somewhere outside, a police siren wailed. From downstairs, the aroma of marinated meats and spicy sauces grew stronger. "I still think Steve should tell us the whole truth now," Victoria said. "Even if it contradicts his first story, and even if it's painful to me."

"Then tell which story at trial? Like I said back in the jail, I don't have many rules. But I won't introduce testimony I know to be false. If Solomon tells us he's the shooter, I can't let him take the stand to say Nadia pulled the trigger."

"I swear, Jake, the way you run roughshod over everything, I can't believe you're such a wuss on this."

"Even a whore's got rules. I do a lot of things, but I won't lick ass."

"God, you're disgusting."

"It's a slippery slope, Victoria. Once you start using perjurious testimony, what's next? Fabricating phony documents? Destroying evidence?"

"I can't believe I'm being lectured on ethics by you."

"And I can't believe you're fighting me on this, Vic. All I can think is that you're too close to the case. Your personal stake overwhelms your usual good sense."

"You had no problem when I lied to the cops about Elena's cell phone."

"Gray area. But this isn't."

"These lines you draw. So damn arbitrary."

"But they're *my* lines."

Victoria was now, by equal measures, hungry and frustrated. So much for working well together. But then again, she and Steve always squabbled over strategy and ethics. Maybe this give-and-take would lead to the same kind of synergy she had with Steve in court.

Lassiter said, "There's also the practical problem that the state has Solomon's story at the scene on tape, which makes it ten times more powerful. He changes it now—even if the new story is true, which it isn't—we're dead when Pincher plays the tape and impeaches him with his own words."

"So in Lassiter's world, it's ethical to win with perjured testimony as long as your client hasn't told you it's perjurious."

"Of such microscopic distinctions our law is made. Now, keep going. What else do we know?"

"The federal government will give away the store to convict Benny Cohen of something. If Steve lies to make a murder conspiracy case, he's looking at less than seven years in prison. And Mr. Ethics—that's you—doesn't seem to have a problem with it."

"Technically, Solomon hasn't told me the murder-for-hire story is false."

She sighed in exasperation. "We know Benny Cohen gave Nadia the murder weapon, but because we can't believe a word he says, we don't know if he told her to kill Gorev. We also don't know if he wants to throw her a wedding shower or kill her."

"What else?" Lassiter said.

"In my one phone conversation with Nadia, she said, and I'm quoting here, 'I know what your man told the police. It did not happen that way.' But she never told me precisely what did happen. She admitted she brought the gun but implied that Steve fired it, which is pretty damn confusing. How did the gun get from her purse to Steve's hands?"

"So it all comes back to Nadia," Lassiter said. "The missing brick in our wall."

They were both quiet a moment. Then Victoria said, "I know what you're thinking."

"Let's hear it, kiddo."

Before she could answer, there was a knock at the door. A waitress from Havana Banana downstairs.

"Lourdes!" Lassiter greeted her. "Please thank Jorge for his kindness."

She smiled and served them a steaming platter of lechoncita, shredded roast pork with onions and a mojo sauce. And another platter of chicken tarimango, grilled chicken breasts with mango and a tamarind sauce. The sides were black beans and rice. A flan and a tres leches cake for dessert. Oh, and for starters, four—not two—icy mojitos with white rum and fresh mint leaves.

Lassiter tipped Lourdes, who retreated down the stairs, and they sipped at the mojitos.

"You were saying . . ." Lassiter said.

"You've changed your mind. Now you want Nadia."

"Just to talk to her. Don't ask her to come to Miami. First, because it's too dangerous for her. And second, if Pincher drags her to court and she says what he wants, it's the nail in the coffin for our case."

"When we spoke, she told me not to call her again and hung up on me."

"I'm not talking about a phone call. We need a face-to-face with Nadia, and by 'we,' I mean you."

"You mean just knock on her door and say hello?"

They started eating. Sharing plates. Just as she did with Steve, Victoria thought. Lassiter's pork was spicy, her chicken sweet. It was a nice combination. The first mojito had gone down quickly.

"Can you find her, Vic?"

"I don't know. Do you have the discovery I wanted from Anastasia?"

"Just came in yesterday." Lassiter pointed to a pile of cardboard boxes in the corner of the little conference room. "Every credit card receipt, charge-back, letters from angry customers, notices from the Better Business Bureau, the zoning department, Noise Abatement Office, and electricity and water bills for the last year."

"Have you gone through it?" she asked.

"Hell, no. You're second chair. That's your job."

Victoria wondered if that was the reason, or was it because she was a woman and the task was so damn clerical in nature. "Nadia told me she's staying with her boyfriend. She wouldn't say where but indicated it was far from Miami. She said he came to a food products convention on the Beach about three months ago. He spent fifty-three hundred dollars in one night. Nadia got access to the credit card terminal at the club and reversed the charge. If all the records are there, I can find the charge and the credit, and we'll have the boyfriend's name, if nothing else."

"That's a start."

"And if we find Nadia, just how do I get her to talk to me?"

"What does she want?"

Victoria thought about it a moment. It was a complex question but perhaps with a simple answer. "To live in peace and harmony with the man she loves."

"What do you want?"

Victoria smiled just a bit. "The same. With Steve."

"What's keeping Nadia from her goal?"

"Fear. The feds want to subpoena her. Alex Gorev wants to kill her. Benny . . . well, we don't know what Benny wants."

"What's keeping you and Solomon apart?"

"The so-called justice system, as you like to put it."

"So you and Nadia have a lot in common. And while you're talking, figure out if there's anything she can say that's helpful to us or can lead us to something helpful. Because if not, Solomon is gonna take that plea. He'll set up Benny Cohen on a phony murder charge and take his own felony conviction. He'll be disbarred, and even though he'll serve less than seven years, he'll come out a different man. It'll be like he's been in a coma all those years and never fully recovered. Neither his life nor yours will ever be the same."

Lassiter had drained his first mojito and took a long pull on the second one. "And goddamn it, Victoria, I will do everything in my power to keep that from happening. If there's any way to win this case, we're gonna do it. Together. And you two can have that peaceful life."

Victoria's eyes welled with tears. Despite their bickering, she felt a growing bond with Lassiter. A swirl of emotions she would not express because he would misinterpret them. She was deeply in love with Steve. At the same time, she felt a stirring warmth for Lassiter, a good man, sturdy as an oak. If not for her love for Steve, this was a man she could . . .

No, I will not go there.

She reached across the desk and took Lassiter's hand, giving it a long, fond squeeze.

He took a fork to the tres leches cake, smiled, and said, "Code Yellow, kiddo."

-41-

Pretzel Man

I was impressed with how quickly Victoria worked.

One hour and twenty minutes to find the charge and reversal slips that revealed the man's name.

Gerald Hostetler.

One day in April, he charged $5,328 on his MasterCard at Club Anastasia. Forty-two hours later, someone with the initials "N. D." reversed the charge from the club's credit card terminal. It had to be him. And her.

Victoria clicked onto Google for the rest. A lightning-fast search revealed that during the same week in April, a snack foods convention took place at the Eden Roc. One of the speakers, Gerald Hostetler, addressed the crowd on "Branding Unique Snacks in the Twenty-First Century." The convention website listed Hostetler as president of Hostetler Pretzels and Chips. There was a headshot of a man about thirty-five years old in a white apron, holding a tray of beer pretzels. He had blond hair that was just starting to retreat, giving him a high forehead, and a smile that said he loved his work.

The Hostetler Pretzels and Chips website listed the address of a plant in Lancaster, Pennsylvania. Victoria found Gerald Hostetler's home address on a pay site, along with the information that he'd never been charged with a crime, had never been married, and had graduated from East Stroudsburg University, where he'd lettered in track all four years. At the time, he held the school record in the ten thousand meters.

That interested me. Distance runners are their own breed. Skinny. Self-sufficient. Patient. Able to endure and conquer pain. Often loners, which may explain Hostetler's apparent lack of a wife or girlfriend when he met Nadia. I had no such excuse.

Victoria found the website for the local newspaper, the *Lancaster New Era*. In the archives was a feature story on Hostetler and his business. Seems he employed three-dozen women to hand-roll each pretzel. Time-consuming and expensive, but that's the way his great-great-grandfather, a German immigrant, made the pretzels in the late 1800s. Gerald Hostetler was a man of tradition and old values. I figured I might like the guy.

Google Maps had a fine photo of Hostetler's home, not far from the Susquehanna River. The house was built of stone and might have been a hundred years old or more. Maybe it was his great-great-grandfather's. Family ties. I liked that, too. The house had a trimmed lawn and rose beds in the front yard. Lush pine trees towered like sentinels at the property line, and a single fir tree thirty feet tall stood near the brick path that led to the front door. I would bet a hundred bucks that Hostetler decorated the fir tree each Christmas. And another hundred bucks that he was as solid as that house.

With the Internet, this was just so damn easy. About eleven minutes for everything, once we had his name. Just amazing. When I started practicing law—not long after the days of rotary phones and IBM Selectrics—it would take a PI a week with boots on the ground to get the information we had gathered.

Victoria was scouring the American Airlines website. "There's a nine fifty p.m. flight to Philadelphia," she said. "I'll stay in a hotel near the airport and drive to Lancaster in the morning."

"Assuming you find Nadia there, your meeting will require some delicacy," I said.

"Oh, my God. Instructions from the bull in the china shop about delicacy."

"All I'm saying. Nadia may not have told Pretzel Man anything. Benny the Jeweler. The Gorev shooting. The federal investigation. Peel her away from him before you get into anything substantive. And then approach everything very gingerly."

"Jake, do you remember why you sent me to talk to Elena, instead of your trying to do it?"

"I think I said something about you being good at feminine things."

"That 'empathy shit,' you called it."

"Not as articulate as I would like, but you got the point."

"Just trust me, okay?"

* * *

I drove Victoria to the Solomon-Lord house on Kumquat and waited twenty minutes while she packed a carry-on. Then we headed north on LeJeune toward the airport. In front of me was a Jeep with a sailboard on top and the red-and-white "diver down" decal pasted on the body, just above the license plate. In case we didn't already get the point, there were two bumper stickers: "Divers Do it Deeper" and "Have You Gone Down Lately?"

Actually, no.

Still, that was a lot less offensive than the old bumper sticker from the Cocaine Cowboys days: "Honk if You've Never Seen an Uzi Fired through a Car Window."

No thanks.

I looked in the rearview mirror and that's when I saw the gray Range Rover two cars behind me. *Damn.*

"I'm not letting you out in front of American," I said.

"Why not?"

"I'm thinking Bahamas Air."

"That's Concourse H. I'd have to walk all the way back to D."

"I want to throw off Manuel Dominguez. He's following us."

She sneaked a peek in her wing mirror. "The Range Rover?"

"Yeah. If he gets out and tries to follow you, I'll intercept him and you'll have plenty of time to lose him."

"Be careful, Jake. And be quick. Or they'll tow away this old piece of junk."

I pulled the Eldo behind a limo at Concourse H. The Range Rover stopped three cars behind. For a reason I cannot explain, I leaned over and gave Victoria a peck on the cheek. A husband sending his wife off on a business trip, maybe.

She touched my cheek with one hand and gave me a gentle pat. Then she leapt out of the car, grabbed her carry-on from the backseat, and hurried inside. In the rearview, I spotted Dominguez in army fatigue pants and camo Windbreaker scoot out the passenger door of the Range Rover.

I turned off the engine and swung out of the car. Dominguez was already through the sliding glass doors when the parking cop yelled at me, "Hey, fellow. No unattended vehicles. You'll be towed."

"My wife forgot her driver's license," I shouted. "Back in a jiffy."

Yeah, I said "jiffy." It seemed the word an old married guy would use.

The cop didn't say go and he didn't say no. In a second, I was inside the terminal.

I caught up with Dominguez at Concourse E. He was fifteen paces behind high-stepping Victoria when I grabbed him from behind by the hood of his camo Windbreaker.

"Hey!" he yelled. "Whoa! The hell?"

I yanked hard, spun him around, and pushed him into a store that sells coconut-covered chocolate patties and dried mango slices dipped in sugar. Except for four years at Penn State—or was it five?—I have lived in South Florida all my life and have never, ever seen a Miamian eat chocolate coconut patties. The airport stores also used to sell miniature orange trees that people would take home to die on their Manhattan balconies, but I haven't seen those mutant plants in a while.

"Jake! It's you!" Dominguez gasped when he turned around to face me.

"Whadaya doing, Manuel?"

"Flying to Nassau. Hitting the casinos."

"You passed the Bahamas Air concourse. I'll walk you back to the TSA line."

"Not necessary, pal." He shot a look in the direction Victoria had walked, but from inside the store, neither of us could see her.

"C'mon. I'd love to see what the metal detector finds."

"I'm not carrying. Jeez, Jake. I'm a convicted felon. I can't get the permit."

I slammed my right forearm under his chin and pinned his neck against the wall. A gurgling sound came from his throat, and his face turned red. Over at the cash register, the cashier reached for her telephone. Not much time. I ran my left hand up and under his Windbreaker. Leather holster. Metal gun.

"You want to talk to me, Manuel? Or should I call a cop? You're carrying a concealed weapon. In an airport, no less. Not to mention you're violating the probation I got you."

"Jeez, Jake."

"Think quick. The cashier is calling security."

"Let's get out of here," he pleaded. "I'll tell you whatever you want to know."

I hustled him out the door, and we headed back toward Concourse H.

"I was supposed to follow you and the lady," Dominguez said. "Benny figured, sooner or later, you'd lead him to Nadia. But I had a different plan."

"Yeah?"

"I was gonna warn you. Don't bring the Russian girl back."

"You have my cell number. Why not call?"

"I just decided on the way over here. I'm afraid what Benny will do to her."

"You're full of shit, Manuel. You're afraid I'll rip your throat out."

"Trust me, Jake. Benny has these guys around the house. Not like me. Tough guys. I listen to them talk. If they find Nadia . . ." He let his words drift off.

"At least you got her name right. What else do you know?"

"Benny's a diamond smuggler, and Gorev worked for him."

"No shit."

"Jeez, Jake, I'm trying to help. If you tell me what line of crap Benny fed you, I can give you the facts."

We exited the sliding doors into the exhaust fumes of the outer terminal. Miraculously, my beloved Eldo was still there.

"Benny told us he loves Nadia," I said. "She killed Gorev or had Solomon do it to protect him. If Benny finds her, he'll give her half a mil as a wedding present."

"That's a crock, Jake. Nadia robbed Gorev's safe of Benny's diamonds and ran off with another guy."

Benny's diamonds!

So that's what was in the freezer bag Solomon saw Nadia take from the safe. Benny's love-is-all-you-need shtick had clearly been a charade. First because Nadia stole his property. Second, because it's possible the diamonds could be linked to Benny in front of a federal grand jury.

"Benny's offered a hundred K to whoever brings the B-girl back," Dominguez continued. "Two hundred K if they get the diamonds, too. They can do whatever they want with her for a couple days. Then Benny will personally kill her."

"So much for the Beatles," I said.

"Huh?"

The gray Range Rover pulled up to the curb, Rose Marie at the wheel. She waved at me, and I waved back. "I won't be a party to a murder, Jake," Dominguez said. "You gotta know that's true."

"I appreciate that, Manuel."

He reached over and gave me a man hug, his handgun digging into my ribs. I am not a hugging kind of guy, especially not as the huggee. But etiquette kept me from stomping on his instep.

"What are you gonna tell Benny?" I asked.

"That I followed you two to the airport and the lady lawyer got on a flight for the Bahamas. Maybe he ought to send a couple tough guys to Nassau."

I studied him a second. He was, after all, a con man at heart. When he lied, there were no tells. No blinking eyes or turning away. No coughs or squeals in the voice. But I had known Dominguez a very long time, and my sixth sense had me believing him.

He opened the passenger door to the Range Rover and was about to hoist himself inside. "One more thing, Jake. No matter what Benny told you about the shooting, I heard him say there's no way Nadia killed Gorev."

"Do you remember his exact words, Manuel?"

"Of course. In my business, you gotta have a photogenic memory."

I didn't correct him. I just asked, "So, what'd he say?"

"I can't do the accent so good, but Benny said, 'That *maidel* never pulled a trigger in her life. You ask me, her schlemiel of a lawyer did it. But the diamonds. The diamonds, she took.'"

-42-

The Chrysler

Several cars behind the Range Rover sat a late-model dark-gray Chrysler 300 sedan. Four doors. Black walls. Nondescript.

The license plate did not say, "US GOVERNMENT—FOR OFFICIAL USE ONLY." The Chrysler wore the standard Florida plate with the orange, the blossoms, and the old nickname, "Sunshine State."

An FBI agent named Louis Palbone sat at the wheel. He wore gray slacks, a white shirt, and a blue blazer, and his grease-stained tie was at half-mast. Palbone was in his late fifties and nearing retirement. He had already placed a down payment on a fishing lodge in Everglades City. He'd planned on being a fishing guide for at least twenty years. On stakeouts, he often daydreamed of chasing bonefish and permit, snook and redfish.

The passenger seat was empty. Lauren Dunlap, his young partner, was inside the terminal, following the woman lawyer. Lauren had two Ivy League degrees, engineering and law, and somehow decided to become an FBI agent. She was so gung ho, she worked nights and weekends without filling out time sheets.

Palbone went back to daydreaming. Islamorada. Not for deep-sea fishing. He'd never cared for that. But the backcountry channels in the middle Keys were humming with mangrove snapper and mullet. And tarpon! He was pondering the use of crab as bait when the pleasantly rocking boat in his mind was interrupted by an unpleasant voice from the backseat.

"What's taking her so long?"

Deborah Scolino. The pain-in-the-ass assistant US Attorney. Ever since her confidential informant had screwed up and fled, Scolino had been a total bitch.

"Dunno," Palbone said. "It's a big airport."

Deborah Scolino gave a little snort, and Palbone tried to get back into daydreaming mode, but his mood had soured. He despised Scolino, but then he hated most government lawyers, especially the deadly earnest ones. Funny thing, he didn't mind the criminal defense lawyers so much, even though they cross-examined the bejesus out of him. At least most of them had a sense of humor, and he enjoyed the sparring. As far as he could tell, Scolino had no life outside work. He wondered if she even knew how to ride a bicycle. As for fishing, the only hooks she'd ever baited were deals with lowlife informants.

"You should have followed Lassiter," she said.

"He's not going anywhere. Jeez, his car is sitting right there."

"So where's Agent Dunlap? I'm gonna call her cell."

"Not a good idea. She could be standing right next to Lord."

Impatient, Palbone thought. If there's anything you need on surveillance, it's patience. Plus a convenient place to piss.

Scolino put her phone down.

"There's Lassiter!" she shouted in Palbone's ear. "With the man he followed into the terminal."

Palbone watched the big lawyer and the guy in the army fatigues and Windbreaker. He remembered Lassiter as a second-string linebacker with the Dolphins. No speed but a hitter. He looked as if he could still take care of himself.

"Look, they're hugging!" Scolino said.

"I see. I see. Maybe a couple of queers."

"Palbone, you're a Neanderthal."

"Hey, I watch the sports. Some football players been coming out of the closet lately."

"Jesus. I thought the FBI was doing sensitivity training."

"That's what some of us call 'nap time.'"

"Palbone, you are so burned out, your ashes are cold."

"No shit." He squinted through the windshield. "Hey, I recognize the guy in the fatigues."

"Why didn't you say so? Who is it?"

"When I was staking out Benny Cohen's house, that guy would come and go. I think he works for Benny."

"I didn't expect this," Scolino said. "Lassiter in bed with Benny Cohen. And, no, Palbone, I don't mean they're gay."

Scolino's cell rang. Caller ID said "Unavailable."

"Yes?" she answered in a conspiratorial whisper Palbone found amusing.

Scolino hit the speaker button. On the other end of the line, Special Agent Lauren Dunlap said, "American Flight 944. Arrives Philadelphia twelve thirty a.m."

"Did you get a seat?"

"Boarding now. Subject is three rows ahead."

The line clicked dead.

"Palbone, didn't you used to work in the Philadelphia office?"

"Yeah. Back when William Penn was laying out the streets."

"Who do you still know there?"

"At this time of night, no one."

"Call the duty agent. Tell her to line up two cars."

"Her?"

"Him or her. Get with it, Palbone. Two cars. Four agents. Have them at the airport at half past midnight. I don't know if Lord is being picked up, if she's taking a cab, or renting a car. But we can't lose her."

Great, Palbone thought. Some Philadelphia agents lived across the river in New Jersey. Some were far west of the city near King of Prussia off the turnpike. Wherever they lived, four very pissed-off agents would be pulling all-nighters. Because of one very paranoid assistant US Attorney in Miami.

Palbone saw Scolino typing on her cell phone browser. *Now what?*

"There's a seven a.m. flight to Philadelphia," she said. "I'll be on it and catch up with the team. You, Palbone?"

"You sure you don't want the Eighty-Second Airborne, too?"

"I take that as a no."

"Take it as a hell no."

Deborah Scolino didn't seem to care. She was working something over in her mind. "Jake Lassiter and Benny Cohen," she said. "I never would have guessed."

-43-

The Dew Drop Inn

The thought came to Nadia Delova in the early morning while curled up with Gerald in the fluffy sheets at the inn, and it brought a smile to her face.

I am in love with a pretzel baker from Pennsylvania.

Not just any pretzels. Hand-rolled, sourdough Pennsylvania Dutch beer pretzels. How proud Gerald was. The best flour, the best yeast, the best malt. Everything with a personal touch. After the pretzels popped up from the boiling soda ash, little old ladies salted them and placed them in ovens Gerald's grandfather had used.

On the cans was the slogan: "Hostetler Pretzels: Hand-rolled, hand-salted and hand-baked."

No mention, however, that this sweetly traditional way of baking furnished only a hand-to-mouth living. Nadia would like to help with that.

She knew better than to say, "You would probably make more money with new machinery." Because Hostetler Pretzels and Chips Company was steeped in family and history and love. As for the chips, they had stopped making those forty years ago. No way to compete with the major companies. Thankfully, the factory had been in the family for four generations, so the building and land were owned outright. So was his old stone house. Gerald could take home a middle-class income, but that was all.

Now Gerald breathed deeply as he slept in bed next to her. They had made love. Three times. As a lover, Gerald was caring and giving . . . and grateful. As if he couldn't believe his good fortune that such a goddess of a woman would bestow her gifts on him. As opposed to Benny. A small man, and what he lacked in size he did *not* make up for in technique.

Pump-pump-pump. Ahhhh.

The *ahhhh* being Benny's. Not hers. Then he would topple off her like a sparrow shot from a tree limb.

Benny treated her as he might a prized possession, like his Bentley. There was the diamond pendant, of course. And the other presents. Prada purses. Valentino shoes. Which, ironically, helped create her persona as the wealthy and wild European tourist looking for a hot time. Instead of a lying, swindling, watch-stealing Bar girl, which, let's face it, was what she was.

But now there was Gerald, and she felt true love for him. The dear man had taken her to the Dew Drop Inn, a bed-and-breakfast in a three-story Victorian home, located just off the Old Philadelphia Pike. The day before, they had visited an amusement park called Dutch Wonderland. They had ridden the merry-go-round and the twister and had banged into each other in bumper cars. An old-fashioned place filled with families. Nadia had watched the laughing children, faces plastered with cotton candy. It had been years since she'd even thought about having children of her own, but now she did. Now, with Gerald, she felt ready.

She had met Gerald sitting at the bar in the Clevelander. Elena had given him the thumbs-down. No expensive watch. A brown suit that yelled department store rack. But Nadia wanted to go for him, so she did it solo. There was something about his mild, handsome face. The blondish hair, receding just a bit. He had been talking to the bartender, telling him, very politely, that the pretzels in the little bowl were overcooked and oversalted. The bartender had said he ordered the extra salt. A thirsty customer is money in a bartender's pocket.

Nadia had slipped onto the next bar stool and said hello. She asked if he liked French champagne and American jazz. He said he'd never encountered much of either one, but why the heck not?

It only took two vodkas to knock him sideways at Anastasia. Then came the bottles of champagne, and he whipped out his credit card without her urging. Within an hour, he was trying to buy the black velvet painting of the Kremlin that hung behind the bar.

Sometime during the evening, as Gerald was telling Nadia about the seventh-century French monks who invented pretzels to represent arms crossed in prayer, she started looking at him differently. He was drunk. Helpless. Adorable.

She put him in a cab and took him back to his hotel. Instead of fleecing his pockets for cash, she tucked him into bed and sat in a chair, watching him sleep, until she dozed off herself. The next morning, he awakened with a hangover and apologized in the event he had taken advantage of her the night before.

They spent the day together. Breakfast, lunch, dinner. No booze. Much talk. She told him about growing up outside Saint Petersburg. Always tall and gangly, at sixteen, she had suddenly become beautiful to others. She modeled, dropped out of school. Tended bar.

Then, with a deep breath she said the Lord's Prayer to herself in Russian, or at least the part about forgiving our trespasses:

"Prahsty nahm dahlgee nashee."

And she told Gerald Hostetler, square American guy from Pennsylvania, the truth:

"I am B-girl."

He looked at her with puzzlement. Did he not understand?

"Bar girl. I work for Club Anastasia. To take your money."

Still, he did not speak.

"I was arrested in Estonia and Latvia." Tears welled in her eyes. *"I have not been the person I wanted to be."*

She feared he would leave then, but he did not. He told her about himself. The factory passed down to him from prior generations. It barely made money, but he had thirty-seven employees. All those families depended on him.

"Back home in Lancaster, I belong to the Lutheran Church. I am very good with my hands. Maybe from rolling so many pretzels. So I volunteer for the bike ministry. We fix bikes for poor children. Some are teenagers who have gotten into trouble. No one looks after them. We take them on overnight bike trips. Camp out. Cook out. It's very fulfilling."

"Is wonderful thing to do," she said.

"I believe in redemption."

They spent the next night together in his hotel room and made love for the first time. And the second and third. She decided in the morning that this was a man she could love. Truly love, not pretend.

Gerald had a speech to give at his snacks convention, so she went to the club to process the reversal of charges on his credit card. When she returned to the hotel, he asked if she would like to see southeastern Pennsylvania. Of course she did. She would have gone anywhere with him.

There were things she did not tell Gerald. The criminal charge—the stolen watch—from an unhappy customer. The federal immigration violations. The threats that she would be charged with federal crimes, imprisoned, and then deported if she did not cooperate. Her decision to wear a wire and try to get Nicolai Gorev to say what the damn government woman wanted. If that was the only way she could be free to join Gerald, then she would take the risk.

Gerald went home to Pennsylvania. Afraid of facing Gorev alone, she hired Solomon, the lawyer she saw on television shooting the guns. Of course, no one was supposed to get hurt. All she really wanted was her passport and the money—more than $20,000—that Gorev owed her. Then she would join Gerald with more than a suitcase filled with thongs and cocktail dresses.

How had everything spun so dangerously out of control? Her happiness at being with Gerald was tempered by the death of Elena. She blamed herself for that. Then there was Solomon charged with murder. That was partly her fault, too. Gorev's death. Okay, he was swine. Stealing the diamonds. That was spur of the moment.

She knew how to open Gorev's safe by watching him pay the girls. Foolish man used the postal code from his first strip club in Latvia as the combination to the safe. She would need a story to tell Gerald about the diamonds. Would he believe she inherited them from an old Russian aunt? Maybe. There was such a sweet air about him, like the aroma of freshly baked bread.

But now the dangers seemed to come at her from every direction. The murderous Alex Gorev after her. And the federal government. And Solomon's lawyers. And Benny. She had thought she could trust him. How foolish. A few days earlier, she had called Marina, one of the other B-girls. Marina said that Benny's men had slapped her around and demanded, "Where's Nadia, bitch?"

Why did this surprise me?

For God's sake, she had stolen Benny's diamonds. But even worse, Benny would know she could destroy him if the federal government found her. She had lied before, telling the government woman she knew nothing about smuggled diamonds. But she knew enough. She had seen enough. If she testified truthfully, she could send Benny away to prison for the rest of his miserable life.

The last few days, she had pushed these thoughts out of her mind, but now they came swirling back. Maybe she was living in a fairy-tale world like Dutch Wonderland. She did not know what to do. Should she tell Gerald everything? He was smart and honest.

But maybe too honest. He would probably want her to cooperate with the government. Return the diamonds. Testify. Not realizing the risks. She knew about the American witness protection program. Move away. New names, new identities. But Gerald could not move his factory. His life was here.

Most likely, the government would just deport her to Russia, where friends of the Gorev brothers would find and kill her.

I can see no way out.

Next to her in the bed, Gerald stirred. Blinked his eyes open. Smiled at her.

"Are you hungry, hon?" he said.

"If you are."

"The scrapple and venison sausage are first rate here."

Gerald gave her a peck on the lips and headed into the bathroom to shower. Nadia was just getting out of bed when her cell phone rang. A 305 number. Marina's.

"Allo," Nadia said.

"Ay, *bubeleh*!" Benny Cohen said. "Why you stay away so long?"

Nadia felt her throat tighten. She shot a look at the bathroom door. Closed, the shower running.

"Hello, Benny. Where's Marina?"

"She lent me her phone. Sweet girl."

"Did you hurt her?"

"Never! She handed the phone to Tony of her own free will . . . after he broke her wrist. I know where you are, *bubeleh*."

I never told Marina where I am, so how did he find out?

She went to the window, parted the curtains, and looked outside. She imagined Benny outside with his thugs in a rental car. But no. Nothing suspicious.

Benny coughed up a laugh and sang a little tune off-key: "It's better in the Ba-ha-mas."

Just like the television commercial. But what was he talking about?

"My plane's at the Nassau airport right now. Two of my men are there. You'll recognize them."

He thinks I'm in the Bahamas.

How could Benny get it so wrong? Welcome news. At least for now.

"Come to the airport," Benny said, "and save them the time of looking for you. They won't hurt you. They'll bring you home."

"They'll drop me into the ocean."

"*Oy!* You confuse me with Alex Gorev, that barbarian. This is Benny, the man who loves and forgives you. The man who can protect you from Alex. You know what he did to Elena?"

"I heard."

"Then come home to Daddy. And bring my property with you. I have a reward for you."

"Okay, Benny. I'll come to the Nassau airport. Two hours, okay?"

"Don't disappoint me, *bubeleh*."

The phone clicked off.

She tried to relax but could not. She had bought time but how much? What would the next call be? Who would be at her door? Room service or assassins? She had tried running away from her problems but now knew she would have to face them.

I cannot live like this.

-44-

At Long Last . . . Pravda

Victoria drove past the Hostetler Pretzel and Chips plant near downtown Lancaster. The building had to be a hundred years old. Three stories of red brick. Some of the mortar had turned mossy green, but the place gave an impression of solidity and strength. She remembered something Jake had said about constructing a legal defense.

"One brick at a time. Place the brick exactly in line with the one next to it. Smooth the mortar to the same depth each time. It takes a while to build a wall."

Gerald Hostetler's forebears had doubtless laid the bricks straight enough for the building—and the business—to last a century.

She had spent the night in a hotel near the Philadelphia airport, then hit the road at 8:00 a.m., piloting her rental Ford Fusion to Lancaster County. A straight shot west on the Pennsylvania Turnpike, then a short drive on US 222, and she was in the small city that dated from before the Revolutionary War. She stopped at a farmer's market downtown for a glazed donut and coffee.

Now she eased the Ford into the pretzel factory employee parking lot. Windows down, she smelled the dough baking. Spotted a marked spot for "G. Hostetler."

Empty.

She'd been hoping the spot was filled, that Gerald was at work, and Nadia at his house alone, arranging flowers or whatever.

She drove off, using the rental car's GPS to find Hostetler's home. It only took ten minutes to get there. A clean, quiet neighborhood. The house was two stories of stone with bright-green shutters and two chimneys. Probably old fireplaces. No car in the brick driveway. But there were three days' worth of newspapers.

Damn.

They were out of town, and no way to tell when they would return.

Victoria wondered, *What would Jake do?*

Empty house. Quiet neighborhood. Probably walk around the back and jimmy open a window.

Then she wondered, *What would Steve do?*

Something involving deception, she figured.

She went with Steve and picked up her cell phone.

"Hostetler Pretzels and Chips," said the chirpy voice on the phone. "This is Edna."

"This is Margaret Lee at the Sheetz store over in Mechanicsburg," Victoria said. "Is Mr. H there?" Thinking "Mr. H" would be just the right touch of familiar but not overly so.

"Not yet," Edna said. "We're expecting him around noon."

Great.

"Anything I can do to help?" Edna asked.

"I'll just call back. Love your extra dark pretzels, by the way."

"Thank you kindly. We bake 'em a tad longer. Hard as heck not to burn 'em."

Victoria looked at her watch: 11:10 a.m. She drove half a block and pulled up to the curb in the shade of a pine tree. Rolled down the windows, killed the engine, and took in the scent of the pine needles warmed by the summer sun. She kept her eyes on the Hostetler house in the sun-visor mirror.

Twenty minutes later, a gray Buick Lacrosse pulled into the driveway.

Yes, Gerald would be a Buick man. A V-8, if they still made them.

Feeling like a shady PI, Victoria watched as Hostetler, in khakis and a blue polo, exited the driver's door and hustled around to open the passenger door.

Chivalry is not dead in Lancaster, Pennsylvania.

As he held the door open, two long legs stepped out. The rest of Nadia Delova followed. She wore a bright floral sundress, tight in the bodice with a swingy skirt and strappy summer sandals. Hostetler popped the trunk and removed two overnight bags. Ever the gentleman, he rolled the luggage to the front door, where Nadia was already waiting. He unlocked the door and placed both bags inside. They stood there a moment, talking.

Then he took Nadia in both arms and kissed her. A long, slow, loving kiss, his left hand cradling the back of her head, her long dark hair cascading over her bare shoulders.

The kiss lasted long enough for Victoria to contemplate the length of time it had been since Steve had kissed her like that. Well, before he was jailed, of course. But truth be told, some time before that. Three months? Six months? She couldn't remember.

Why don't I know? Was it something I've pushed out of my mind?

So much to work on with Steve . . . if we can keep him out of prison.

The long, soulful kiss turned into an even longer hug, the two of them gripping each other, as if they couldn't bear to part from say . . . lunchtime to dinner.

Victoria found herself filled with a longing for Steve—the old Steve—and filled with jealousy, too. What a jumble of emotions.

I'm jealous of a fugitive who's in love with a pretzel baker.

Finally, the couple untangled. Hostetler gave Nadia a last quick kiss, headed back to his waiting Buick, and drove away. Yes, he'd be at the plant by noon. Victoria figured Gerald Hostetler was not a man to be late.

Victoria waited five minutes, then walked to the house and rang the bell.

Nadia opened the door a moment later, a puzzled expression crossing her face.

"Da?" she said.

"Nadia, I'm Victoria Lord. We spoke on the phone."

Nadia's hand flew up to her mouth. "I told you not to call me again!"

But she made no move to close the door.

"We should talk, for your own good," Victoria said.

"How did you find me?"

"It wasn't that hard. And if I could do it . . ."

"I know. The government. Alex Gorev. Benny."

Nadia shot worried looks up and down the street, then grabbed Victoria's arm and pulled her inside, quickly closing and locking the door. She led Victoria into a large living room with traditional furnishings. An overstuffed sofa, chairs with carved wooden legs, and an oak coffee table with old-fashioned drawers. Nadia pulled the drapes closed and motioned toward one of the chairs.

"You sit. I will make tea."

In five minutes she returned with an ornamental teapot, two cups and saucers, and a plate of lemon cookies. The Bar girl had quickly become domesticated, Victoria thought.

Pouring the tea, Nadia said, "In a way, I am glad you are here. You are a needed reminder of the real world I have been avoiding. Since coming here, I have been living in a dream."

"Love will do that," Victoria said, "but the world always finds a way in."

"What should I do?"

Victoria sipped the tea. "Have you told Gerald the truth?"

"Only that I have an immigration problem. Which is like saying it gets a little cool in Siberia. The sweet man thinks everything will be solved by his marrying me. That I'll get green card. He doesn't know I face prison, then deportation."

"I relate to how you feel. Your fear of losing the man you love."

"Of course you relate. You are in love with Solomon."

"We are both afraid of losing the light of our lives." Victoria felt silly saying it. A soap opera cliché. But she meant it, and she thought Nadia would respond to the emotional overload.

"Exactly!"

Victoria nibbled at a cookie and decided to plunge ahead. "Perhaps I can help you with your problems in Miami. But you must tell Gerald everything."

Nadia sighed. "What a test that will be for him. Of his love for me, I mean."

"I watched him kiss you. I think he will pass that test."

"I can hope."

"You will need a lawyer in Miami," Victoria said.

"Can you represent me?"

"I have a conflict of interest because of Steve's case, but I can find someone to help."

"I will trust you, then. Do you know about the diamonds in Alex Gorev's safe?"

"Benny's. You stole them."

"Will they prosecute me for that?"

"It depends what information you have to trade. To make a deal, you'll have to be honest with the government. Do you have information that ties Benny Cohen to diamond smuggling?"

"*Da.* I know plenty."

"Does it have anything to do with Aeroflot 100?"

"Everything." Nadia gave Victoria a knowing smile. "But before we talk about that, you didn't come here just to help me. You want to know what I will say if the government makes me testify in Solomon's case."

"Yes."

"But do you really want the truth? *Pravda?*"

"Yes. At long last, *pravda.* The truth, Nadia."

"Is simple story. I paid Solomon to help me get my passport and back pay. I told Nicolai I was quitting to get married, and he laughed at me. Then I made a mistake. I told him I would not be part of his wire fraud and money laundering and racketeering. He knew those were not my words. That they had come from the government."

"Then what?"

* * *

"Take off your dress!" Gorev orders.

"I have taken off my clothes for you for the last time."

"I am not going to screw you. I am looking for wire."

"Nicolai, I would never—"

"Are you working for the government or for the jeweler?"

"I work for you only."

"Nadia, my little Nadia. Why?"

She pulls a Glock nine millimeter from her purse and aims it at Gorev with both hands.

"Whoa, whoa, whoa!" Solomon says.

Her hands shaking and the gun wobbling, Nadia says, "I just want my passport and money you owe. Forget everything else."

Gorev barks a laugh. "First your lawyer wants to sue me. Now you want to shoot me. At the sound of gunshot, Alex and Sergei will break through that door and cut your heart out. So stop this foolishness, gerla."

"Nadia, let's put down the gun, okay?" Solomon says.

"Lawyer is not as stupid as looks," Gorev says.

Solomon reaches over slowly with one hand. Nadia removes her left hand from the gun but is still holding it in her trembling right hand, pointing the barrel at Gorev. For the moment, the gun is partially in Nadia's right hand and partially in Steve's left hand.

"Do me favor, lawyer," Gorev says. "Hit magazine latch and remove bullets."

"Where's the safety?" Solomon says.

"Idiot! Glock has no safety. Why do you think I want magazine out?"

It all happens in seconds.

Nadia takes her index finger off the trigger and lets Solomon take the gun.

Solomon's right index finger slips into the trigger guard as Nadia lets go. With his left thumb, Solomon hits the magazine latch.

Filled with fourteen rounds, the magazine slides from the Glock's grip and hits the floor with a startling noise. Solomon's index finger jerks back—a movement as light as a baby's touch—and the round in the chamber fires.

The gunshot hits Gorev squarely between the eyes.

* * *

"It was an accident!" Victoria felt her heart racing. "Steve never meant to shoot Gorev, did he?"

"With the magazine gone, he didn't even know there was a bullet in the chamber."

"But it's not the story Steve told the police." Victoria shook her head sadly. Instead of telling the truth—or better yet, clamming up until she arrived at the scene—Steve had invented the story of Gorev threatening them with his gun and Nadia shooting him. As lies so often do, that one required another. Steve then told the far-fetched tale of Nadia pulling a switch, taking Gorev's gun with her—thus explaining its absence at the scene—while leaving Steve with the murder weapon.

Oh, what a tangled web we weave . . .

"Why did your man not tell the truth?" Nadia asked.

Victoria shrugged. "Because he panicked. Or maybe he thought the police wouldn't believe him. Or he feared he'd still be charged with manslaughter, even if they did believe him."

"What can I do to help him, Victoria?"

Before she could answer, a noise far louder than a gunshot rocked the room as a battering ram blasted through the front door. As splinters flew and light from outside streamed through the opening, three men with guns burst inside.

"On the floor!" one man screamed. "Now!"

-45-

Enter the Cavalry

Two men wore blue nylon Windbreakers with "FBI" emblazoned on the back.

The third man's Windbreaker said "US Marshal."

Walking in behind them, stepping gingerly over the splintered wood, was a woman in a gray business suit and black pumps. Assistant US Attorney Deborah Scolino. She brandished no gun. Instead, she waved two blue-backed documents as she spoke.

"Ms. Delova, we have a warrant to search these premises and a warrant for your arrest on federal immigration charges. Upon your return to Miami, you face indictment for conspiracy, wire fraud, money laundering, and racketeering. Additionally, there is a state bench warrant for your arrest on grand theft charges involving a watch. Finally, you could very well face indictment as a conspirator in the murder of Nicolai Gorev, though that will be up to the State Attorney."

"Don't say a word," Victoria said. She'd had enough of blabbermouth defendants.

"Ms. Lord, I assume you are not Ms. Delova's attorney, given your blatant conflict of interest."

Victoria ignored her and repeated, "Don't say a word, Nadia."

"You may leave, Ms. Lord. In fact, you are ordered to leave."

"Nadia, she's trying to frighten you."

"Is working," Nadia said.

"Ms. Lord! Would you like to be arrested for obstruction?"

"You have no obligation to speak to anyone from the government," Victoria said.

"I was just getting to that, Ms. Lord," Deborah Scolino said, scowling. She recited the Miranda warnings.

When she was finished, Victoria said, "Nadia, exercise your right to remain silent."

"This is your last warning, Ms. Lord. You can leave carrying your purse or wearing handcuffs, your choice."

"I do what Victoria says," Nadia said. "I exercise my right."

"I'm leaving now, Nadia," Victoria said. "Be strong."

"What about Gerald?"

"I'll talk to him. I'll give him the names of several very good lawyers in Miami. Have faith."

"Tell Gerald I love him."

"He knows. But I will."

Victoria headed for the shattered door.

"Your boyfriend should have taken the deal," Scolino called after her.

"The deal was dirty," Victoria called back.

"Nightmare scenario for you. We don't need Solomon's testimony against Benny Cohen now that we have our witness. And even worse for Solomon, Pincher has her, too. Ms. Delova may be silent today, but she'll be singing to the grand jury for me and in state court for Pincher. Basically, Ms. Lord, Solomon just became dispensable, and that makes him dead meat."

46

Nadia and the Feds . . . and Benny

Three days after Nadia's arrest in Pennsylvania . . .

United States District Court for the Southern District of Florida

In Re: Investigation of Benjamin Cohen

File No. 2014-73-B

Statement of Nadia Delova

October 2, 2014

(CONFIDENTIAL)

Q: My name is Deborah Scolino, assistant United States attorney. Please state your name.

A: Nadia Delova.

Q: Let the record reflect that also in attendance today in the Office of the United States Attorney is Marcia Silvers, esquire, attorney for Ms. Delova. Additionally, with my permission, Mr. Gerald Hostetler is here. You have asked for their presence, is that correct, Ms. Delova?

A: *Da.* I need them both or I will say nothing and sign nothing.

Q: Subsequent to your return from Pennsylvania, is it true that we have had extensive discussions with your lawyer and your . . .

A: Fiancé. Gerald is my fiancé.

Q: Ms. Silvers and Mr. Hostetler have been present during these discussions.

A: *Da.* We have talked and talked.

Q: Very well. Have you had a chance to review the document the government has prepared?

A: [Examines document] These are the things I have said.

Q: And you are willing to repeat these statements under oath to the federal grand jury investigating Mr. Benjamin Cohen?

A: I will say these things because they are true. I took Aeroflot 100 from Moscow to New York carrying uncut diamonds hidden in lining of my luggage. All the girls took that flight and carried diamonds from Mirny mine. Was our job.

Q: Why that particular flight, Ms. Delova?

A: Like I told you hundred times. The Gorevs had their man working Aeroflot 100 at Sheremetyevo Airport in Moscow. There was no risk. That is why we never took the Transaero nonstop flight to Miami. Too much risk. So we fly Aeroflot to JFK where US Customs looks for drugs and weapons only. Diamonds were sewn into compartments and were never found.

Q: When you landed at JFK, did you meet Mr. Benjamin Cohen?

A: He was waiting at hotel near airport. He opened my suitcase, tore out the lining, and removed the diamonds.

Q: You saw him do this?

A: With my own eyes. He told me it was the only time he went to New York for the diamonds. He always waited for them to be delivered by one of his men, someone he could trust would never testify against him. "No hand-to-hand transaction, *bubeleh*, except with you." That is what he told me. And that is why the US government love me so much. I am your big eyewitness. Also reason Benny want to kill me.

Q: [By Ms. Silvers] Nadia, please just answer the question and refrain from editorializing.

A: [By Ms. Delova] Sorry. Usually, driver delivers girls and diamonds to Nicolai Gorev in Miami. Gorev was middleman, again to protect Benny. This time, was different for reason I already say.

Q: [By Ms. Scolino] So why this one time did Mr. Cohen take the risk and come to New York?

A: He had buyer in city who could not wait. Benny took diamonds to Manhattan that night.

Q: Thank you, Ms. Delova. Do you fully understand the nature of the documents you are about to sign?

A: I testify against Benny. You drop all charges against me. Gerald marry me, and I get green card.

Q: And by Gerald, you mean Mr. Hostetler.

A: Who else would I mean? He is the only Gerald I marry.

Q: I am led to believe you will be giving a statement to State Attorney Pincher in the Gorev shooting, is that correct?

A: *Da.* I will tell him shooting was accident.

Q: Well, we'll see what he says about that, won't we?

A: [Witness does not respond]

47

Use a Gun and You're Done

There are no accidents, Jake." Ray Pincher exhaled a blue puff of cigar smoke in my face. "Freud said that."

"I'll be sure to keep him off the jury. C'mon, Ray. You heard Nadia's story."

"Sure. In her *opinion*, Solomon was supposedly unloading the Glock when it accidentally discharged."

"Exactly. The magazine hit the floor with a bang. Solomon was startled and pulled the trigger."

"So she opines."

We were in the state attorney's office, atop the Richard E. Gerstein Justice Building. Pincher was perched on the edge of his desk, a hundred certificates, plaques, and photos arranged gaudily on his mahogany walls. His merit badges from the Elks, Rotarians, and probably the International Order of Odd Fellows. A crystal glass humidor sat on his credenza. It was filled with Cohibas. Real ones. From Cuba. Illegal. That probably made them taste better to the chief prosecutor.

I had come to plead Solomon's case. Accident. Not first-degree murder, the charge he faced under the felony murder rule. And not even manslaughter.

"Ladies and gentlemen of the jury. This wasn't a crime. It was just an unfortunate accident."

Here was my dilemma. Reducing the charge to manslaughter wouldn't keep Solomon out of prison. Manslaughter is a second-degree felony with a maximum penalty of fifteen years. When a firearm is used, Florida has a tricky little law called "10-20-Life." Or in the words of the televised public service announcements: "Use a gun, and you're done."

It's all very complicated, what with sentencing guidelines, firearm enhancements, and conflicting statutes, but you can take this to the bank. Manslaughter committed with a gun carries a possible thirty years in prison. Yeah, draconian. I know. Welcome to Florida, the Sunshine State.

And just what is manslaughter? That's tricky, too. The statute says it's the "killing of a human being by culpable negligence without lawful justification."

And what is culpable negligence? Well, it's worse than mere carelessness. It's an action that shows reckless disregard for human life. Let's say you shoot a gun into the air to celebrate New Year's, and the falling bullet kills someone. Or you leave a child in the car on a broiling summer day. Or you get in a fistfight in a bar and the other guy cracks his head on the floor and dies.

Manslaughter?

I'll give you a lawyer's answer. Guilty, if the jury says so. Not guilty, if it says that. Truly, manslaughter is one of the shadowy areas of criminal law.

"It was an accident, plain and simple," I told Pincher. "At worst, simple negligence. But not culpable negligence to support a manslaughter charge."

Pincher blew a smoke ring and tapped ashes into a wastebasket. With any luck, the building would burn to the ground.

"Were you listening, Jake? Accident is just the B-girl's opinion. But she's a fact witness, not an expert. I'll be filing a motion in limine to strictly limit her testimony to what she saw and heard. You won't be able to cross her as to what she *thinks* happened or what was supposedly in Solomon's mind."

"I don't care about your fancy motion," I said. But I was lying. I cared a lot. Even if Nadia tried to help us, Pincher could put her in a straitjacket if the judge granted his motion. Obviously, I couldn't let Sugar Ray sense my worry. First rule of a trial lawyer: *never let them see your fear.*

"So the battle lines are drawn," he concluded.

Not really. We hadn't discussed a plea. There's always a duel to see who cries uncle first. Would the State Attorney make an offer or would I ask for one? Having seen Sugar Ray box in Golden Gloves, I knew he liked to skip around the ring before settling down to business. I would try to wait him out.

"You know, Jake, I always teach our young prosecutors to simplify their cases. I tell them to state their theory in one sentence. One simple Anglo-Saxon sentence with a noun and a verb and damn few adjectives. You want to hear mine?"

"Hit me with your best shot," I said. "Or a combo, if you've got one."

"Solomon takes the gun from Nadia and shoots Gorev right between the eyes."

"Solomon's not that good a shot."

"That's your defense?"

"Our defense is that Solomon was a good Samaritan, trying to defuse a nasty situation. It was a brave, heroic act. He simultaneously disarms Nadia and ejects the magazine, and the gun accidentally discharges."

"A gun doesn't accidentally discharge. Someone—your guy—pulled the trigger."

Pincher took the cigar from his mouth and gave me that irritating *gotcha* smile. "I've got an expert witness who'll testify about the Glock's safe action split trigger. You can't fire with any sideways pressure. You gotta have your finger all the way in the guard and pull straight back."

"And my expert witness will testify about the Glock's light trigger, only five pounds of pressure. We've got exhibits showing all the accidental shootings that have plagued police forces for years. A lot of cops shoot themselves in the leg while reholstering."

"Fine and dandy," Pincher said. "Sounds like a jury question then. I'll do my job, you'll do yours, and the solid citizens of Miami-Dade will go into their little room, come out, and tell us who's right."

"Enough dancing." I caved, losing the cry-uncle battle. I just wanted to get out of the toxic mixture of cigar smoke and prosecutorial bullshit. "What are you looking for, Ray?"

"You first."

"*Nol-pros* the indictment before I embarrass you in front of the voters and ruin your otherwise stellar career."

Pincher pointed the Cohiba at me as if it were a dagger. "Nice try, but screw you, Jake. Make a real proposal so I can respond."

"If you reduce the murder charge to something along the lines of assault, I might be able to convince Solomon to plead. The court withholds adjudication so he can keep his Bar license. No prison time, six months' home confinement with an ankle bracelet, plus three years' probation. If he kills any more Russian gangsters while he's on probation, you can send him away."

Pincher was surprised to find his Cohiba had gone out. He struck a long match and slobbered a bit getting the tobacco flaming again. He enjoyed making me wait. One puff, and then he said, "I

247

love this about you, Jake. Always thinking big. Dreaming. Others may see it as a flaw, but I admire it."

"Save the lube job and let's get to the sex."

"I've got one offer. Don't even think about a counter. Solomon pleads to manslaughter, fifteen years."

"That's bullshit!"

"Go to trial and lose, I'll ask for the max. Life if it's felony murder. Thirty years if it's manslaughter with a firearm."

"When you were kissing federal butt and they needed Solomon to nail Benny Cohen, you offered eight years. That's when you supposedly believed Solomon was guilty of murder. Now you damn well know it's an accident and you want fifteen years on a plea."

"Oh, the bewildering perplexities of the law."

"That's crap."

"Our case just got stronger. You no longer have that empty chair to point to."

"I've got better."

"How?"

"Your immunized witness, Nadia Delova, is the only one who profited from this so-called crime. You're giving her a free pass on the shooting and the diamond robbery."

"She's given the diamonds to the government. It's part of her deal."

"You mean the feds found them in her boyfriend's house in Pretzelville, Pennsylvania."

"Same difference."

He blew another smoke ring and watched in admiration as it rose toward the ceiling. It was an old ceiling, probably filled with asbestos. Maybe Pincher would inhale a spore one day and die a painful death.

"Forget the accident defense!" I exploded.

"I already have. That's your theory, not mine."

"Not anymore! You're playing hardball; so are we."

"I always like it when you get pugnacious. Let's hear it, Jake."

"I'm changing our entire defense, right here and now."

"This I gotta hear."

"You've charged the wrong person. That's our case, Ray. And you know the beauty of it. It's consistent with what Solomon told the cops on the scene. Nadia planned the whole thing. She killed Gorev and robbed him, taking his gun, framing my client, and fleeing the state with the diamonds. Now she's got a sweetheart deal from the feds and the state. I'll chew her up and spit her out on cross."

He made a *tut-tut-tutting* sound with his tongue. "Shame on you, Jake. You know very well, not a word of that is true."

"It doesn't matter what I know, Sugar Ray. Let's just see what the solid citizens of Miami-Dade have to say when they come out of their little room."

-48-
Caring about Justice

"All this time, Lassiter, you've been saying you wouldn't let me lie on the witness stand," Solomon said. "One of your sissy rules."

"Hey, don't diss me for the one thing I do right."

True confession. My rule against presenting false testimony wasn't based solely on morals. It's partially self-preservation. I learned a long time ago that my client is not my friend. Basically, I'm a lifeguard trying to save a drowning man in rough seas. A man who'll push me under just to stay afloat himself. If they had the chance, ninety-nine out of one hundred clients would flip on me to save themselves. I can picture the scene:

"Honest, Mr. State Attorney. I didn't want to do it, but Mr. Lassiter told me to lie on the witness stand."

What prosecutor wouldn't rather destroy a pain-in-the-ass defense lawyer than your run-of-the-mill criminal defendant?

Notwithstanding what I had told Pincher, I hadn't yet made up my mind what to do. I was still looking for a way to win without violating my principles or losing my ticket to practice law.

"Until today, I never lied to a judge or let a client perjure himself at trial," I told Solomon.

We were in the lawyer's visitation room at the county jail. Just the two of us, facing each other over the steel table. I was glad Victoria wasn't here. I didn't want to hear her disapproval.

"And now you just told the State Attorney I'm gonna testify falsely," Solomon said.

"Not in so many words. I said you were sticking with your original story."

"My story was false. Is this your new strategy? Falsely pinning the shooting on Nadia?"

"I don't know. I'm considering it."

"Victoria thinks Nadia will try to help us."

"Operative word *try*. What happens if Pincher intimidates her? Or her command of English fails her? Or she simply decides you're not worth the risk of alienating the government? Or . . ."

"Yeah?"

"Or the jury believes every word she says and still thinks it was manslaughter."

He pulled at the front of his orange jail smock. The air-conditioning must have been on the blink, because we were both sweating, and the air tasted stale and salty.

"So make up your mind, counselor. What's our strategy?"

"Nadia tells her story on direct. As limited by Pincher, it's a simple story. You took the gun from her and shot Gorev. On cross, I force her to admit she had the motive; she stole the diamonds; and she fled the state. I hit hard on her B-girl job, which basically consists of lying, trickery, and thievery. If I destroy her credibility, there's a chance we create a reasonable doubt that you ever touched the gun."

"But if you can't shake her, I go to prison and you go on to your next case."

"Nope. When the trial's over—win, lose, or mistrial—I'm quitting."

"Quitting what, Lassiter?"

"The practice." I stood and paced in little circles. The room was too small for big circles. "I've been thinking about it for a while. When Pincher offered you that dirty plea, I thought some more. Then today, after inhaling his cigar fumes, I decided. I'm gonna coach football at this little prep school in Vermont."

"Holy shit." Solomon dropped his head into his hands. "I told Victoria hiring you was a mistake. My only hope is a 3.850 motion."

"Hey, I haven't lost yet. Too early to be talking about ineffective assistance of counsel."

"I want a continuance. File the motion tomorrow."

"Why?"

"So new counsel can get up to speed. You're fired."

"Not so fast. Let's think logically about our chances. Why should the jury believe this conniving Bar girl when she says you pulled the trigger?"

"Oh, I don't know. Maybe because it's true."

"Hell, boy! Truth doesn't matter. Evidence does. Credibility does. I can rip her to shreds."

"You've lost your mind, Lassiter."

"I want to win, Solomon. For you and for Victoria. But what I really want is to rub Pincher's face in the mud. And when it's over, I want the jurors to carry you out of the courtroom on their shoulders while whistling 'God Bless America.'"

"Now you're delusional."

I banged my right fist against the concrete wall. And then my left. Hard enough to hurt. My hands, not the wall. Solomon's eyes bugged. Was I going to clobber him next? He glanced at the door, maybe wanting to yell for a corrections officer.

"A good lawyer is part con man, part priest," I said.

"No idea what you're talking about."

"The con man promises riches if you hire him. The priest threatens hell if you don't."

"I get it. So what?"

"I've lost my religion. Why should I care about justice?"

"Are you asking me, or is this some philosophical debate you're having with yourself?"

I paced some more. "The state and feds came to us with a filthy deal. If you nailed Benny Cohen for conspiracy to kill Gorev, you'd get leniency."

"You've been practicing law for twenty years, Lassiter, and you just learned the government plays rough?"

"I'm not talking about their everyday overzealousness. Unreliable informants. Entrapment. Overcharging. Deals with scumbags. This was different. This was criminal."

Solomon was quiet a moment. "Let's say we do it your way and stick with my story to the cops. At the end of the day, what are the odds the jury will believe Nadia pulled the trigger?"

"They don't have to believe she killed Gorev. They only need a reasonable doubt that you did."

He processed that, and his look told me I wasn't really fired. Not yet. "But after you tear her to shreds, to use your term, you want me to testify she pulled the trigger."

"That's what I was getting to. We might create reasonable doubt without ever putting you on the stand."

"Bullshit! I'm testifying, even if I don't know yet what I'm gonna say."

"Just listen a second, Solomon."

"If I don't testify, I piss off the jury. And don't tell me about the judge's instruction that they're not to hold it against a defendant who keeps quiet. Jurors will think I'm hiding something."

"Solomon, how often do you let a defendant testify?"

"Seldom. But that's because they usually have criminal records that will come out on cross-exam. Or they're stupid. Or both. Doesn't apply to me."

"But there's another reason to keep you off the stand," I said. "Pincher has the recording of you being interrogated at the scene. On the tape, you say Nadia brought the gun, which she will have to admit when she testifies. You say she robbed the safe, which she will also admit. You say she shot Gorev, and here's the beauty of it. Pincher can't cross-examine a tape recording. What you said to the cops will be preserved for eternity in the jurors' minds and Pincher can't impeach it . . . *unless* you take the stand."

"And you keep your virginity intact by not letting me lie."

"That, too. But most important, I keep you from being cross-examined and screwing up."

Solomon rubbed at a three-day growth of whiskers with the knuckles of his right hand, thinking it over. Then he shook his head and said, "I don't like it. And Victoria will hate it. We should go with the truth. Accident. I'll take the stand and explain I lied to the cops because I panicked. Nadia's story will support accident, and your job will be to keep the jury from coming back with a manslaughter conviction."

I looked at him in silence, fully appreciating the irony. Shyster Solomon insisting on the truth and my semiethical self pushing for a shady defense.

"Are we on the same page, Lassiter?"

I headed for the door. "Not even in the same book, pal."

-49-

Bending the Law Like a Pretzel

Rain pelted the overhead canvas awning. The humidity was roughly a zillion percent. But Gerald Hostetler seemed to be enjoying his grouper sandwich and fried conch fritters, Victoria thought. He was not a difficult man to please.

"Freshest fish sandwich I've ever had," Hostetler said, smacking his lips.

Victoria smiled and sipped her iced tea.

They were outdoors at Garcia's, a fish joint on the Miami River in a seedy part of downtown Miami. Victoria couldn't get near Nadia, who was in protective custody in a two-bedroom suite at the Hyatt. Gerald and Nadia had one bedroom, two federal marshals had the other. Assistant US Attorney Deborah Scolino left strict orders: no visitors.

Nadia was spending her third day testifying before a federal grand jury. Next week, she'd be the star witness in state court in the case of *State v. Solomon*. Today, while Solomon and Lassiter were meeting in the jail, Victoria was trying to find out just what Nadia would say on the witness stand. It had been Lassiter's idea.

"Why don't you just take Nadia's deposition?" Victoria asked.

"I have my reasons," Lassiter said.

"But without it, you can't impeach her with prior statements."

"And neither can Pincher."

"She's Pincher's witness! Why would he want to impeach her?"

"Maybe he won't like what she says. Talk to the Pretzel King and see if you can find out whether she'll try to help us."

Victoria slipped a tortilla chip into the fish dip and said, "Gerald, I'm very happy it's working out for Nadia. And that she has you at her side."

He shrugged. "I'm in love. What else could I do?" Then he looked at the bowl of fish dip. "They should serve pretzels with that."

"I suppose you know why I asked to see you."

"Of course. And we're willing to help. Nadia blames herself for Steve being prosecuted."

Hostetler began sharing everything he'd observed the last seventy-two hours in a hotel conference room, including the fact that the morning started with pastries that weren't up to Pennsylvania Dutch standards. "Marcia Silvers, Nadia's lawyer, was there every day, of course. She was tenacious. It took most of the first day, but she wouldn't allow Nadia to speak to the grand jury until an immunity deal was hammered out. Nadia's been testifying now for the last day and a half."

"So it sounds like everything's fine on the federal charges." Victoria waited. She didn't know how forthcoming Gerald would be when they got to Steve's case. In the river, a freighter loaded with cargo containers steamed east toward open water, doubtless bound for a Caribbean island.

When Hostetler didn't volunteer, Victoria asked, "And State Attorney Pincher?"

"Oh, of course! I'm sorry. We met yesterday on Solomon's case. He allowed me in the room but ordered me not to reveal a word. Said it could be obstruction of justice."

"So you won't tell me what was said?"

Hostetler shot glances left and right. No one who remotely looked like a cop was nearby. Just a couple of ponytailed river rats, guys in their sixties in baggy shorts, T-shirts, and flip-flops, their skin sun-scorched the color of tea with the texture of old leather. The men were slurping down bowls of conch chowder.

"Pincher is a bully," Hostetler whispered.

"Indeed."

"He thinks I'm a pushover. Happens a lot. Being misjudged. Especially by city people. Maybe because I was always taught to have manners. 'Yes, sir.' 'No, ma'am.' A handshake is a contract; a man's word is gold. It's the way I was raised."

"And . . . ?"

"I never shook Pincher's hand. Never promised to keep quiet. He thought he'd bulldozed me. But he hadn't." There was a note of pride in his voice.

"Did he give Nadia immunity for the shooting and robbery of Gorev?"

Hostetler nodded. "As long as she testifies against Solomon. And she has to tell the truth or face perjury charges. That's the only thing immunity doesn't cover. Pincher was quite threatening about that. He repeated over and over that Nadia would go to prison if she lied."

"What else did he say?"

"He did a practice question-and-answer session with Nadia to see how she would respond in court. And he kept interrupting. 'Never use the word *accident*,' he told her. 'Never say he didn't mean to fire. Not a word about Solomon's intent. Only tell what you saw. Solomon took the gun and pulled the trigger. I'll handle the rest.'"

"Anything else?"

Hostetler dipped a piece of conch fritter into hot sauce and popped it into his mouth. "One thing I didn't understand. Pincher asked Nadia whether Steve knew she had a gun, and she said yes. She had shown it to him. Then he asked if Steve told her not to bring the gun into the meeting with Gorev, and Nadia said no. Pincher seemed happy with that. He said it was consistent with what Steve admitted to the police. Then Pincher looked at Scolino and said, 'Heads we win. Tails we win.'"

Victoria felt as if her heart were gripped in a vice. How would they ever defend the case?

"Do you know what he meant, Victoria?"

She took a breath and said, "Pincher isn't going after manslaughter, except as a backup. He's sticking with felony murder. The death of a robbery victim, even the accidental death, is first-degree murder with a mandatory sentence of life in prison without parole."

"Jesus H. Christ. Pardon my French."

"Pincher's theory is that Steve was in on Nadia's plan to take property from Gorev by force. An armed robbery. Then it doesn't matter if Steve shot Gorev accidentally or purposely. Or even if Nadia shot him. They're both guilty of murder. Only Nadia has immunity and Steve takes the fall. That's the 'heads we win.'"

"And the tails?"

"The judge will instruct the jury on lesser included offenses."

"Manslaughter?"

"Exactly. If some jurors think it's murder and some think it's a pure accident and the verdict should be not guilty, they're likely to compromise and convict Steve of manslaughter. Jurors don't know the penalties. The ones who threw in the towel on innocence would probably be shocked to learn Steve could face thirty years for manslaughter."

"I had no idea," Hostetler said.

They were quiet a moment. In the river, a lone paddleboarder rode the current toward the open bay.

"Nadia says you love Steve very much," Hostetler said. "That your relationship has withstood stress and outside pressures, just as ours has. She'll do everything she can for you."

"I appreciate that, Gerald."

"But she can't risk perjury."

"I understand."

Victoria's mind drifted to Steve in that hellhole. She thought of her life with him and his life—if it could be called that—without freedom. She also thought of Jake, who had risked his life at Club Anastasia and had strapped on a gun to protect her that fateful night with Elena.

With all of this whirling through Victoria's mind, she considered all those lofty notions engraved on marble pediments.

"Justice the Guardian of Liberty."

That's what it says high above one entrance to the Supreme Court building. And then on the opposite side of the building:

"Equal Justice under Law."

And let's not forget about those signs above the bench in Miami courtrooms.

"We Who Labor Here Seek Only the Truth."

Maybe it was time to dispose of the pretty phrases. Maybe it was time to dive headfirst into the murky waters where Steve and Jake swam. She remembered one of "Solomon's Laws."

"If the facts don't fit the law, bend the facts."

"Gerald, maybe there's something Nadia could do at trial to help us, but it's not without risk."

"Is it legal?"

"It's not black-and-white."

"Meaning what, Victoria?"

"What I'm asking Nadia to do is in the shadows. In the gray between light and darkness."

"I'm really not sure what that means."

"Sometimes, Gerald, people break the law so clearly you can hear it crack like a tree branch snapped in two. But other times, like a baker twisting a roll of dough into a pretzel, you only bend the law. You don't tear it. You don't break it. You end up with something better than the ingredients you started with. And the final result is beautiful to behold."

-50-

The Vulture and the Chicken

It was our last visit to the jail before trial, and my client and my cocounsel were both furious with me.

"Lassiter, you two-hundred-thirty-pound sack of shit!" Solomon yelled at me.

"Two forty-five," I corrected him.

"Whatever. You can't do this," Solomon said. "Vic and I have talked, and we think it's a huge mistake."

Victoria nodded in agreement. "If you make Nadia look like *La Femme Nikita*, the wicked assassin, she'll never help us."

"She *can't* help us."

"You don't know that! I gave Hostetler a plan that might work."

"Did he ever get back to you?" I asked.

Victoria shook her head, and her shoulders slumped. "He's not returning my calls."

"Then we have to assume Nadia can't—or won't—do what you asked. You took a helluva risk, Victoria, and I admire that. If Hostetler had ratted you out to Pincher—if he'd told him what you asked Nadia to do—you'd have been indicted for obstruction."

"I'm always amazed by the actions you admire," she said.

"Anyway, Nadia's help is just whiskey under the bridge. Pincher's going for felony murder, and if we claim accident, he'll probably get a compromise verdict of manslaughter. We all know it. We have to go all in."

"Which is? Say it aloud, Jake. Just the way you'll tell the jury."

"Solomon didn't shoot Gorev. Nadia did. Pincher, the dumb ass, gave immunity to the murderer."

"You might want to leave out the 'dumb ass' in your opening statement," Solomon suggested.

"Jake, have you considered this?" Victoria asked. "If you don't attack Nadia in opening, maybe she'll walk into the courtroom, take a look at Steve and me, and—"

"What? Feel sorry for you? I can't rely on that. Here's the way it's gonna be. I lay down a barrage of artillery on Nadia in opening. On cross, I force her to admit every crime she ever committed and a few she's only thought about. Then we use Solomon's taped statements to the cops to bolster our theory while keeping him off the stand."

"Seriously, Lassiter," Solomon said, "what are the odds that'll work?"

I shrugged. Clients always want you to give a prediction like a meteorologist forecasting the chance of rain. "If I had to guess, I'd say we have one chance in four of acquittal."

"One in frigging four! I told you from the beginning, Vic. This guy's a loser. A burnout. Jesus, he told me he's gonna take down his shingle and teach high school in New Hampshire."

"Coach prep school football in Vermont."

"You need a rest home, dude."

Actually, I didn't feel like a burnout. The adrenaline rush was starting. It always comes with a murder trial. Tomorrow morning, we would pick a jury. Today, I felt like a knight, slipping into my brigandine vest. Now, where the hell was my sword?

"Jake, have you thought this through?" Victoria asked calmly. "Your strategy is so risky. It's all or nothing."

"Exactly," I said. "It's just like life. Breathe it in."

"Breathe what in?"

"The pure air of a windswept beach or a mountain peak."

"You're starting to worry me a bit." Her tone was gentle, as if trying to coax a cat down from a tree.

"No worries. Jump off the bridge without a bungee cord," I said.

She considered that a moment. "Okay, I get it. Take risks. Is that what you're saying?"

"Face your greatest fears. Indiana Jones in a pit of rattlesnakes. Donald Trump on food stamps. Sugar Ray Pincher hitting you below the belt. It's all the same thing. Win or die."

"It's my life, not yours!" Solomon snapped. "You said one chance in four, and I'm supposed to be happy?"

"Forget the odds! One in four or nine in ten. What difference does it make? They're just numbers, Solomon. Meaningless predictions. Who can tell where lightning will strike?"

Victoria appeared baffled. To her, I must have looked like Tarzan, swinging on a vine, screaming like an ape.

Very softly, she said, "Do you feel okay, Jake?"

"Spectacular. Do you know those black vultures that fly circles around the courthouse?"

"Of course. They're supposed to be the souls of lawyers doing endless penance. Or maybe it's judges."

"I saw one today. As ugly as sin, as dark as Dracula's heart."

"Not possible, Jake. The vultures don't come until November, just like the tourists."

"This one wasn't flying. He was on the banks of the river by the Justice Building. Devouring a chicken."

Victoria's eyebrows arched. "A chicken on the river bank?"

"I figure it was a Santeria offering from a defendant's family."

"Okay, so you saw an out-of-season vulture . . ."

"It was a message, a sign."

"So which one are you?" Solomon asked. "The vulture or the chicken?"

I shook my head. "It's not that literal. The vulture represents a dragon, and that would be Pincher, who thinks you're dead meat."

Victoria and Solomon exchanged worried looks. After a moment, she said, "Jake, are you grounded enough to take on the pressure of a murder trial?"

"Relax, Victoria. When I walk through the swinging gate into the well of the courtroom, I'll be wielding a sword in one hand and an axe in the other. Just like the Vikings in old Norse tales, I'll either slay the dragon, or they'll carry me out on my shield."

51

The Collective Genius

I have a confession to make.

I hate voir dire.

I despise prying into other people's lives because I wouldn't want them prying into mine. But it's damned necessary. If your client is charged with murder, you *must* ask prospective jurors if they have had any family members murdered. In *every* case, you have to ask jurors if they've ever been a victim of a crime. Essentially, you must force these poor schnooks—already peeved at having been summoned to the courthouse—to relive the worst moments of their lives.

Some lawyers think that jury selection is the most important part of trial. More than opening statement, cross-examination, or even closing argument. I don't know if that's true because jury selection is such a crapshoot.

Deep-carpet law firms hire psychologists to interview jurors after cases are over, and the results are scary. Most jurors forget about 70 percent of the judge's instructions on the law. In deliberations, jurors spend about half their time discussing their personal experiences.

Jury consultants lay down all sorts of rules. If a blue-collar worker puts on a suit to come to court, it shows respect for the judicial system, which translates to a pro-prosecution juror. Aw, I don't know. Maybe he's just trying to con a lady juror into going out with him, a slick move that translates to a defense juror.

I often violate the unwritten rules about what kind of juror will favor one side over the other. Once, I left the wife of a cop on a jury—an absolute no-no—in a case I couldn't win unless I proved that the arresting officer lied. I cross-examined the officer relentlessly until he sweated so profusely that his hands stripped the varnish off the rails of the witness box. The cop's wife turned out to be the foreperson, and I won an acquittal. Why? I had sensed in voir dire that she was immensely proud of her husband, who had won a basketful of commendations, and I hoped she would be offended by a perjurious cop. It worked . . . that time, anyway. My point is, you just never know.

In Florida, we only have six jurors. The legislature wanted to save time and cut costs . . . and to hell with justice! The smaller panel makes my job tougher. It's much easier to hang a jury with one holdout if you're dealing with twelve citizens. Maybe you remember the stage play made into the hit movie about a jury that starts out eleven to one for conviction and ends up acquitting. Well, it wasn't called *Six Angry Men*.

In capital cases, we still get a dozen jurors, just like a carton of eggs. Because the state was seeking a maximum of life imprisonment in Solomon's case, we were seating the usual six-pack.

In theory, jurors are supposed to go through a four-step process. They assimilate the facts gleaned from the evidence, weigh those facts, learn the law from the judge, then apply the law to the facts. In reality, they determine if the defendant looks guilty and guess which witness is telling the truth. Okay, I'm overstating my cynicism. My point is that jurors can't help themselves. They're swayed by their life experiences as much as the evidence and the law. Still, with all my bellyaching, here's the strange thing.

Juries usually get it right!

Honestly, I don't know how. Maybe film director Billy Wilder said it best. He was talking about movie audiences, not juries, but the point holds true: "Individually, they're idiots. Collectively, they're a genius."

* * *

At the defense table, my client and cocounsel, despite hating my trial strategy, were nonetheless working peacefully with me on voir dire. Solomon scribbled notes on a legal pad while Victoria used her color-coded three-by-five note cards.

Having lost weight, Solomon's neck didn't fill out the collar of his white dress shirt, and he had that jailhouse pallor. As the venire filed into the box to be questioned, he locked a maniacal grin into place. Frankly, the Joker in *Batman* had a more natural smile.

"Relax," I told him. "You look like an axe murderer."

"The panel looks stupid," he said.

"Shhh," Victoria said.

"I mean, how smart can they be?" Solomon continued. "They couldn't even get out of jury service."

* * *

State Attorney Ray Pincher stood, smiled at the prospective jurors, and told them, "All I want, and all Mr. Lassiter wants, is a jury that's fair and impartial."

Speak for yourself, Sugar Ray.

I want a jury that will rule in my favor, even if a dozen eyewitnesses saw my client shoot a nun on Ocean Drive at high noon. Failing that, I'd take jurors who truly believed in the presumption of innocence and would hold the state to its burden of proving guilt beyond every reasonable doubt.

Whereas Pincher wanted jurors who believed the old canard "Where there's smoke, there's fire." Meaning, if Steve Solomon was sitting in the dock, by golly, he must have done something shitty . . . be it murder or manslaughter.

Voir dire is a two-lawyer job. One asks the questions; the other listens to the answers and observes. I did the talking and Victoria the observing. She watched, not just the person answering but the others in the box, too. Assessing body language is an essential tool of the practice.

In a day and a half, we had our six jurors and two alternates. Three men and three women on the active panel, all presumably citizens, good and true. It was a fairly typical Miami jury, which is to say, it had a lot of hyphens. Two Cuban-Americans, one Colombian-American, one Haitian-American, one African-American, and one plain old Caucasian.

Judge Melvia Duckworth gave her preliminary instructions. In addition to the age-old admonitions against discussing the case with family and friends, there were a few new ones. No texting, tweeting, blogging, or Facebooking about the case. No Instagrams, Pinterests, or Googling to look up information.

I'd tried cases before Judge Duckworth and I liked her. She was an African American woman of about fifty-five who had been a captain in the Army Judge Advocate General Corps. Most of our trial judges these days seem to come out of the state attorney's office, and many are prosecution oriented. In the military, JAG lawyers switch sides. One day a prosecutor, the next day a defense lawyer. Maybe they should make civilian prosecutors do the same thing. Many are plagued with a disease I call emotional scurvy. Instead of lacking vitamin C, they've been shortchanged of empathy.

In the past, on motion calendars when the judge was being particularly stern with me, I would call her "Captain Duckworth," instead of "Your Honor." She generally smiled and responded by calling me "Buck Private Lassiter." I always appreciated a judge with a sense of humor. Plus she always gave the defense bar a fair shake, and not all judges do.

Now, with the jurors having taken their oaths and ready to do justice, or a reasonable facsimile thereof, the judge said, "We'll stand down for fifteen minutes, folks. That's a recess. Then the state will present its opening statement."

52

A Simple Case of Murder

While the jurors were peeing, Sugar Ray Pincher sashayed over to the defense table, ostensibly to talk.

He would never do this with the jury in the courtroom. Fraternizing between opponents might give the jurors the idea that this was just a game played by friends.

I actually enjoy the camaraderie with the other side. I think of LeBron James and Kevin Durant, chatting it up before the game, then elbowing each other in the gizzard once the buzzer sounds.

Pincher slid his butt onto the table as I printed on a legal pad: *ACCIDENT! FIREARMS STUDY: GLOCK PROPENSITY FOR UNINTENTIONAL DISCHARGE.*

Pincher, of course, was using his sneaky ability to read upside down. He hadn't really come over to ask if my backyard mango tree was heavy with fruit. He wanted to see what folders I'd pulled out of my briefcase for opening statement.

"So how's Kip doing in school?" he asked, as if he really cared.

"Playing a little football." I kept writing. *DOUBLE TRIGGER INSUFFICIENT TO PREVENT HUMAN ERROR. ACCIDENTAL DISCHARGE NOT A CRIME.*

"Hope he's got more speed than his uncle." Pincher loved to needle me.

"I just hope he's smarter."

With that, Pincher gave me a playful punch on the shoulder and whispered, "I knew you were full of hot air the other day."

"Huh?"

"Claiming Nadia was the shooter. That's a dead end, no pun intended. Accident's your only defense, and you know it."

He showed me his pearly politician's smile and headed back to the prosecution table.

Yeah, I knew he'd be coming over to take a peek, so I gave him a little misdirection. Sort of like that trick play in football, the fumblerooski.

* * *

"Mr. Pincher, is the state ready to proceed?" Judge Duckworth asked.

"We are, Your Honor."

"Mr. Lassiter?"

"Locked and loaded, Your Honor."

The judge turned to the jury. "The attorneys will now present their opening statements. What they say is not evidence and is not to be considered by you as evidence. Rather, the attorneys will tell you what evidence they *believe* will be presented during the trial." Shooting a glance at the prosecution table, she said, "Mr. Pincher, please proceed."

Sugar Ray Pincher strutted toward the jury box. He was a toe walker, probably from his boxing days, so each step had a little bounce.

Not wanting to invade the jurors' personal space, he stopped about three feet away from the rail.

"Good afternoon, folks." He spent a couple minutes thanking the jurors for leaving their exciting lives to drive through frightful traffic all the way to the Justice Building in order to do their civic duty. Then he got down to business.

"This is a simple case of murder. A cruel and vicious crime, cutting down an unarmed man, and, under the law, a very special kind of murder."

A nice tease. Who's not dying to hear what makes it so damn special?

"It's not my place to explain the law, but rather to introduce the evidence, to present you with the facts. At the conclusion of the trial, Judge Duckworth will instruct you how to apply those facts to the law. She will define this very special charge of felony murder, which is a homicide committed during the commission of a felony.

"In this case, the evidence will show that the defendant, Mr. Solomon, participated in the robbery of the victim, Nicolai Gorev. And in the course of that robbery, Mr. Solomon shot and killed Mr. Gorev. It doesn't matter if the defendant intended to shoot the victim. It doesn't matter if he accidentally fired the gun. Once he was in on the robbery, he is guilty of felony murder, no matter the circumstances of the shooting."

Solomon was poking me in the ribs. Sure, I could have objected. After having promised the jury that he was going to discuss the evidence and not the law, Pincher was doing the opposite. Strictly speaking, it was an improper opening statement. But I only object when the opposition draws blood. Technical objections don't interest me, and they piss off the jurors.

They wonder: just what's the defense lawyer afraid of?

Besides, I wanted to know if Pincher dared go one step further.

"Here's another thing about felony murder," Pincher said. "While the evidence will clearly show that the defendant pulled the trigger, he would still be guilty of felony murder even if his cocon-spirator did the shooting."

There it was. An absolutely true statement of the law. But Pincher had to be wary of that outcome. If he had immunized the shooter in order to convict the less culpable defendant, he ran the risk of jury nullification: jurors so incensed at the prosecution that they wouldn't follow the law. As a former linebacker, I intended to blitz right through that opening in the offensive line.

"There are only two persons alive who can tell you what happened in Nicolai Gorev's office that July day. One is the defendant," Pincher said, pointing an accusing finger at Solomon, "and the other is a woman named Nadia Delova, the defendant's coconspirator. Now, the defense will make much ado about the fact that Ms. Delova received immunity from the state in return for her testimony. But that is the way the system works. Not every state's witness is Mother Teresa. All we care about is that our witnesses tell the truth. And you will be able to judge for yourself when Ms. Delova testifies whether the defendant was part of her planned robbery that turned into a homicide. You will judge Ms. Delova's credibility as she swears under oath that Mr. Solomon pulled the trigger and killed the victim. And you will judge the credibility of Mr. Solomon, for we will play an audiotape of a statement he vol-untarily gave at the crime scene, and I suggest you will find his account highly imaginative, farcically fanciful, and ludicrously lacking in all credibility."

"Objection!" I called out, getting to my feet.

"I was wondering how long you'd keep your powder dry, Mr. Lassiter," Judge Duckworth said. "Please state the grounds of your objection."

"Too many adjectives. Or maybe they're adverbs. I always get them mixed up."

"I assume you're saying that Mr. Pincher is engaged in closing argument, rather than opening statement," the judge helped out.

"Precisely," I said.

"Sustained. Now, Mr. Pincher, please confine your remarks to statements of what you believe the evidence will show. Save your editorializing for your press conferences."

Pincher bowed slightly toward the bench. "Thank you, Your Honor."

That's the way it goes. The party who loses the objection thanks the judge for the spanking.

Pincher stuck to the evidence for a while, hitting the highlights of his case:

That Solomon knew Nadia Delova was armed and did not ask her to leave the gun behind.

That during an argument with Nicolai Gorev, Solomon grabbed the weapon from Nadia and fired it, killing Gorev.

That Solomon's fingerprints were on the weapon and gunshot residue was on his right hand.

Pincher told the jurors the judge would instruct them on the lesser included offense of manslaughter. That would come into play if they did not find that Solomon conspired in the robbery, the crime giving rise to felony murder. By his tone, Pincher sent the message that Solomon's lack of participation in the robbery would be a highly unlikely finding.

"You will likely hear from the defense that all this was just one big mistake. An accident. An unintentional discharge of a firearm. That Mr. Solomon is not experienced with handguns and that the Glock he fired has a very light trigger pull. That the defendant never intended to even shoot the gun, much less kill Nicolai Gorev." Pincher cleared his throat, a guttural, dismissive harrumph.

"But you will hear expert testimony from the state's firearms specialist about the double trigger mechanism of the Glock, which replaces the traditional safety. You will hear from a second expert who tested the murder weapon and found it not to be defective. Yet a third expert will tell you that there is no such thing as an *accidental* discharge. The weapon will only fire if the trigger is pulled directly backward because of that double trigger safety. Now, here's where it gets a tad complicated. Yes, sometimes people might fire the weapon when they might not have intended to, but still, they pulled the trigger. I'll say it again. *They pulled the trigger!* And if you do that while pointing the gun at someone, even if you didn't intend to shoot him, that's manslaughter. You can't build an idiot-proof gun unless you build a better idiot."

"Objection!" I sang out. "I believe the state just called my client an idiot."

"Mere rhetorical hyperbole," Pincher said.

"Try not to fall in love with your own rhetoric," the judge said, tugging at the white filigreed rabat at her neck. "Tone it down, Mr. Pincher, and wind it up."

"It will be my pleasure," Pincher said, as if he had just been invited to tea.

I tuned out for the next several minutes, my mind drifting between what I intended to say when I stood up and wondering just when the leaves would be turning all those shades of gold and crimson in Vermont.

53

Tap-Dancing across a Tightrope

At the defense table, Victoria and I flanked Solomon, protecting our precious cargo from the slings and arrows of the prosecution. With the jury's eyes on me, I slid my chair back, buttoned my suit coat, and stood. I placed my big mitt on Solomon's shoulder and gave it a squeeze, as if he were my dearest friend. If the jury liked me, maybe some of that gold dust would rub off on my client.

Surely, this amiable big galoot of a lawyer would not represent a filthy murderer.

I walked several paces and planted myself like an oak in front of the jury box. I spread my legs to shoulder width, perfectly balanced. I did not hide behind a lectern. I carried no pad or notes. I would keep eye contact with the jurors throughout our little chat.

"I want to thank my colleague, the state attorney, for doing my work," I began.

They waited. Just what the heck was I talking about?

"But once Mr. Pincher chose to tell you all about our defense, I wish he'd gotten it right. We will *not* present evidence that Steve Solomon fired that Glock accidentally. We will present evidence from which you may reasonably conclude that Steve did not fire the gun at all!"

I was tap-dancing across the tightrope. I hadn't denied that Solomon fired the gun. I told the jury that they "might reasonably conclude" he didn't fire it. I hadn't lied. After all, I'm an "officer of the court," though in two decades of practice, I've never known what that meant. I also called my client "Steve" in an effort to humanize him. A first name is so much warmer than "defendant," which is a synonym for "scumbag."

"But since the state told you about our case, let me tell you about theirs. First, as the judge will instruct you, the burden of proof rests on the state's shoulders. That burden will be carried entirely by Nadia Delova, a Russian national who's in the United States illegally and who is an admitted criminal. That's right, the state's key witness is a diamond smuggler, an illegal immigrant, and a Bar girl."

Out of the corner of my eye, I saw Gerald Hostetler wince. He was sitting in the front row of the gallery. Nadia wasn't there, of course. As a witness, she was barred from the courtroom until her performance was needed.

"Let me tell you a few facts that Ms. Delova will admit from the witness stand. First, that she entered this country carrying stolen diamonds on behalf of an international gang of smugglers. Next, that she's been a Bar girl for several years in various countries. Her job, basically, is to lie to men and get them to pay thousands of dollars for cheap champagne. She does this by convincing them that she will go back to their hotel rooms and engage in sex."

I paused a moment and took inventory. An African-American woman on the jury, a churchgoing, hat-wearing lady of about sixty-five, was frowning. I hoped her disapproval was of Nadia Delova, not the big meanie painting her as a woman of the night.

"Let me make one thing clear," I said. "Ms. Delova is not a prostitute. A prostitute engages in a business transaction and delivers what is promised in exchange for money. Ms. Delova takes money and does not deliver. Nadia Delova is, basically, a liar and a thief."

Another pause to let those tough words sink in, then I started up again. "What will she say, this star witness of the state? She will admit that she feared and hated Nicolai Gorev, the manager of the bar where she worked, an establishment that existed solely for the purpose of thievery. She will testify that Gorev cheated her out of wages and forced her to have sex with him as a condition of employment. In short, the evidence will show that Nadia Delova, not Steve, had the motive to kill Mr. Gorev."

I moved half a step closer to the jurors. Just enough to establish intimacy without spraying them with saliva.

"Nadia Delova will admit that she is the one who brought the gun to the meeting, pulled it from her purse, and pointed it at Gorev. She is the one who robbed his safe, stole the diamonds, and fled to another state, leaving Steve Solomon behind to take the rap. A bum rap!"

I was into the flow and feeling good about my spiel. But not so good about myself. I felt like a creep. Everything I said was true, but forcing Gerald Hostetler to listen filled me with self-loathing. Still, what could I do? I had a client to defend. "Zealously," as the Florida Ethical Rules command.

"Now, let me tell you a little more about Mr. Gorev." Out of the corner of my eye, I saw Ray Pincher inch forward in his chair. His head was angled toward me and away from the jurors so they couldn't see his murderous glare. Yeah, if looks could kill, he'd be the one in the dock.

Stick around, Sugar Ray. I'm just warming up.

"The evidence will show that Mr. Gorev was a Russian gangster involved in fraud, racketeering, and diamond smuggling."

"Objection!" Pincher hopped to his feet and danced to the front of the bench. "The victim's character is not at issue here."

"Sustained. Mr. Lassiter, please try to avoid the thin ice. That's your one and only warning."

"Thank you, Your Honor," I said with as much humility as I could fake.

I turned back to the jury box. No one was asleep, always a good sign. At the prosecution table, Ray Pincher had changed his expression. Now he locked a tight little smile onto his face for the benefit of the jury. No way would he show I was scoring points. He had expected an opening statement laced with frills and finesse. *"Oh, please excuse Steve for accidentally shooting Gorev."* The full-bore attack with artillery and cannon fire had surprised him.

"There is even more that Ms. Delova will be forced to admit," I said, returning to my opening gambit. "She has received immunity from both the state and federal governments for all crimes she may have committed since entering the United States. What are those potential crimes? Immigration violations, theft of an expensive watch, diamond smuggling, and of course the robbery and murder of Nicolai Gorev. And what did she have to do to get that immunity? Testify in two cases. One is the federal diamond-smuggling case against the man who, not so coincidentally, gave her the gun that was used to kill Nicolai Gorev. The other is this case. That's right. Nadia Delova received immunity for her testimony against Steve Solomon.

"Now, why is that important? At the conclusion of the trial, Judge Duckworth will instruct you how to determine the credibility of witnesses. She will tell you that you are permitted to consider any—and I'm quoting now—'preferred treatment or other benefit' the witness received in order to get her to testify."

"Objection!" Pincher was up again. "Outside the scope of opening statement."

"Sustained," Judge Duckworth said. "You've both wandered onto my shooting range. Please stick to the evidence, Mr. Lassiter."

"Thank you again, Your Honor," I said, nearly snapping off a salute.

I smiled at the jurors and decided to wrap it up. "It's late in the day, and you good folks have sat here patiently while Mr. Pincher and I ran off at the mouth. So I'm going to sit down now." Then I held up a finger, as if I'd just remembered something. "But wait a second. I left something out. I never said who pulled that trigger, did I? Was it Steve Solomon, who stayed behind and gave a full statement to the police? Or was it Nadia Delova, who stole the diamonds and fled?"

I let the jurors hold their breaths. "At this point, I'm not going to answer the question or tell you how to decide the case. We'll have a chance to chat again in closing argument. For now, I want you to hear Ms. Delova's testimony and make up your own mind. In my heart, I trust each and every one of you to do justice. Thank you all very much for your attention."

I sat down, feeling a raging torrent of conflicting emotions. I was proud of myself for not telling any outright lies. But I still felt as if I'd been digging for worms, elbow deep in the mud. I needed to wash my hands and throw cold water on my face.

The judge began giving her end-of-the-day instructions, cautioning the jurors not to talk about the case with anyone and to be back at 8:30 a.m. sharp tomorrow. Next to me, Steve Solomon grasped my forearm with one hand and whispered in my ear, "Stupendous, Jake. They never took their eyes off you. Never blinked."

Victoria passed me a note. Just one word: *SWEET!*

The three of us stood, in respect, as the jurors filed out, followed by the judge, her robes billowing behind her. Then Solomon hugged me, like long-lost cousins at a family reunion.

"I take back every shitty thing I ever said to you," Solomon said. "You were awesome."

I didn't let the compliment blow me away. Clients routinely undergo a dozen mood swings in the course of a trial.

Ray Pincher waltzed over to my table, shoulders hunched forward, hands folded over his stomach, feigning pain. "Ooh, you sucker punched me, Jakie. Big-time."

"You'll get over it."

He straightened up. "Already have. You should have gone with accident. Maybe you could have sold that."

"You mean because that's what happened?"

"How the hell do I know what happened? I never know. You never know. We keep looking for justice, but it's nothing but stormy nights and dark alleys out there. Mysteries that can't be solved and secrets behind every door."

"What the hell are you talking about, Sugar Ray?"

"The one thing neither one of us ever has the balls to say to a jury. There's no recipe for justice. We grab whatever ingredients we can find and mix them in a big bowl. We turn up the heat and cook the mess until it boils over. Then, if we're lucky, what we've made doesn't smell like shit. As for your defense, Jake, I'm gonna prove it's just one big pile of turds."

54

Steve Solomon and O. J. Simpson

The state called Detective George Barrios as its first witness. No surprise there. Always start strong. And finish strong. The rules of primacy and recency. Jurors remember best what they hear first . . . and last.

Savvy and experienced, Barrios had testified in hundreds of homicides over twenty-five years. I was used to seeing him in a pale silk guayabera, where he took on a kindly Cuban *abuelo* look. In his dark suit, white shirt, and rep tie, he looked—and sounded—utterly professional. There was little chance he would make a mistake on direct or get tripped up on cross by a pettifogger, such as my own wily self.

Pincher took his time, starting with softball questions. He went through Barrios's background, established him as a veteran detective who'd solved some of the biggest murder cases in Florida and was currently chief of Miami Beach Homicide.

Next to me, Solomon squirmed a bit in his chair as Barrios summarized his career highlights. I could have objected. At one point,

Solomon scribbled on a legal pad, "WTF?" And later, "OBJECT!" But I kept quiet. Barrios's credentials wouldn't convict my client.

Finally, Pincher got down to it. Barrios arrived at Club Anastasia just moments after the uniformed cops. They were responding to a 9-1-1 call placed by the defendant. The jury got to hear the call, Steve Solomon hysterically shouting, "He's dead! I didn't do it! I didn't do it!" Then the sound of several gunshots, and Solomon, even louder, "They're shooting into the door! Get some cops here! I didn't do it!"

The 9-1-1 operator calmly asked where they might find the dead man and the caller who didn't do it.

Barrios picked up the story at the point he entered Club Anastasia. Two men, one of whom turned out to be the decedent's brother, were armed and screaming in Russian through the locked door to Nicolai Gorev's office. The men followed police orders to put down their handguns and lie on the floor, where they were cuffed as a precautionary measure.

Barrios called to Solomon through the door, asking if he was the person who called the police. Solomon said he was and opened the door.

"What did you observe when you entered the office?" Pincher asked.

"The defendant was standing with his hands up in front of a large wooden desk. A man we later identified as Nicolai Gorev was slumped at the desk with a single gunshot wound to the head. A nine-millimeter Glock handgun lay on the floor at Mr. Solomon's feet."

"Did Mr. Solomon say anything?"

"He was speaking quite rapidly. He said, 'I didn't do it. I didn't do it.' Several times."

"Then what happened?"

"A uniformed officer retrieved the Glock from the floor and as he was doing so, Mr. Solomon said, 'You'll find my prints on

that. And gunpowder residue on my hand, but I didn't shoot him.'
Another officer checked on Mr. Gorev and determined rather
quickly that he was dead. I frisked Mr. Solomon and found he had
no weapons on his person."

"What transpired next?"

"I told Mr. Solomon to be quiet until I could read him his
rights."

"Did he comply?"

"He did, and I read the Miranda warnings."

"How did Mr. Solomon respond?"

"He said he didn't need a lawyer because he was innocent."

I tried not to grimace, so I just ground my teeth. When you're
innocent, you *really* need a lawyer because of police and prosecution foul-ups. To say nothing of the average citizen's tendency to get
scared and confused when being questioned by cops.

"What happened next?" Pincher asked.

"Everyone started arriving at once. The paramedics, crime scene
techs, medical examiner personnel. I took a quick look at the office
door. It was quite heavy. Solid wood several inches thick, reinforced
with metal. There were two bullet holes on the inside and several on
the outside. Another officer and I took Solomon out of the office and
through the club where the decedent's brother and the other Russian
man had to be restrained, even though they were still cuffed. The men
were shouting at Solomon in Russian, so I can't tell you what they
were saying, but they were clearly making threats. It was apparent
they thought the defendant had shot Mr. Gorev."

"Objection, Your Honor!" I needed to stretch, so I stood and
feigned shock and horror. "For all his skills, Detective Barrios is
not a mind reader, and the thought processes of two criminals who
didn't witness the shooting are irrelevant."

"And I object to Mr. Lassiter's use of the word *criminals*,"
Pincher shot back. "There's no evidence that—"

"Sustained and sustained," Judge Duckworth ruled. "Move it along, Mr. Pincher."

"Thank you, Your Honor," Pincher and I sang out simultaneously, like a church choir.

"What did you do next, Detective?"

"We placed Mr. Solomon in the back of a marked vehicle, and I asked if he would answer some questions. He consented."

"Did you proceed to record a conversation with the defendant?"

"Yes."

Pincher spent a few minutes authenticating the tape recording. Yes, Barrios had a chance to listen to the tape. And, no, it wasn't edited or altered in any way. And, yes, it was a true and accurate recording of what was said.

The jurors leaned forward in their swivel chairs, Solomon sucked in a breath, and Victoria let out a sigh. Me? I just waited to hear the preposterous story I knew was to come.

The tape started playing. Barrios asked Solomon to state his name, occupation, and address, then repeated the Miranda warnings. Solomon had the right to remain silent. Anything he said could be used against him in court. He was entitled to a lawyer, and if he was dead broke, the very generous state of Florida would provide him with counsel.

* * *

"I got nothing to hide, Detective. Ask whatever you want."

"I'm just a dumb old cop. Why not tell me how you got locked in an office with a dead man and what appears to be the murder weapon, which you've already said has your fingerprints on it?"

"There were three of us. The dead guy. His name is Gorev. And my client, Nadia Delova. Should I spell that?"

"Sure."

"D-E-L-O-V-A. It's Russian. She's a B-girl, and Gorev owes her back wages, plus he was holding her passport. She hired me to get the money and the passport."

"How were you planning to do that?"

"My usual way would be to write a lawyer's demand letter first. But she said he'd never even read it, much less respond."

"So you arranged a meeting?"

"Not really. We just showed up."

"Tell me about the gun."

"Nadia brought it in her purse."

"So it's not your gun?"

"No, sir. I never touched it until after Gorev was shot."

"When did you first learn Nadia was carrying a firearm?"

"Not until we walked into the front door of the club."

"Did you object to her carrying the gun into the meeting?"

"Not in any substantial way."

"Well, did you suggest she put it in the car or otherwise not take it with her?"

"Not really, no."

"Did you actually see this gun?"

"She opened her purse, and yeah, I guess I peeked at it."

"What happened once you were inside Mr. Gorev's office?"

"I asked for Nadia's back wages and her passport. Gorev was belligerent. He accused Nadia of wearing a wire for the government. Actually, he accused us both. Anyway, he pulled a gun out of his desk drawer."

"Whoa now. There's a second gun?"

"Another nine millimeter. I think it was a Beretta."

"And where is the Beretta now?"

"I'm getting to that, Detective."

"Okay, Mr. Solomon. Just tell the story your own way."

"Gorev aims the gun at me. Orders me to strip to see if I'm wearing a wire. I start unbuttoning my shirt, and out of the corner of my eye, I see Nadia reaching into her purse for the Glock. Gorev sees it, too. He swings his gun toward Nadia."

"And then . . . ?"

"Detective, do you know how sometimes a moment gets frozen in time, like a snapshot?"

"No, tell me."

"I can see it now. Like a picture. Just a split second etched in my brain."

"Okay, Mr. Solomon. Describe that etching."

"Each one is pointing the gun at the other for a split second. Really just a nanosecond. Nadia fires. Hits Gorev in the forehead. But it's self-defense. Or Stand Your Ground. Or defense of another. Or all three. I'm a criminal defense lawyer. I know these things."

"That's way above my pay grade, Mr. Solomon. Just tell me what happened after Ms. Delova shot Mr. Gorev."

"The rest is sort of a blur."

"No more snapshots frozen in time?"

"I mean, everything happened really fast. Gorev's dead. Nadia pulls this picture away from the wall. There's a safe underneath, and she must have known the combo, because she only tries once and the door pops open. There's a bunch of foreign passports in there. She takes one plus a plastic bag."

"What kind of plastic bag?"

"One of those zippered freezer bags. Probably the gallon size."

"What was in it?"

"I couldn't tell."

"Did it appear heavy or bulky?"

"Hard to say. I wasn't really paying attention to the bag."

"Did it have currency in it? Her back wages?"

"No idea, and she didn't say anything about it. Then she goes through Gorev's desk drawer and comes out with a key. All very quickly.

Like she knew where everything was. She puts the plastic bag and the passport in her purse, along with Gorev's gun."

"Whoa! Hold on a sec. She took the victim's gun?"

"Yeah. That's why you won't find it. Then she points the Glock at me."

"Why'd she do that?"

"Maybe because I said we had to call the police."

"You left that part out."

"Sorry. Anyway, she's holding the gun on me with one hand and pulls back the drapes behind Gorev's desk with the other. And there's a door. She uses the key to unlock the door, tosses her gun—the Glock—to me, and leaves through the door, which locks again when she closes it, trapping me inside. That's when the guys in the club start yelling and shooting into the other door."

"And you shoot back."

"Twice. To protect myself. That's why my prints are on the gun. And probably residue on my right hand."

"Hold your horses, Mr. Solomon. All the stuff that happened in a blur."

"Yeah?"

"Well, you described it in pretty precise detail."

"I'm thinking it through now for the first time. It's not like I'm making it up."

"Not saying you are. I'm just puzzled as to a few things. First, that whole gun switcheroo. Why'd this Russian girl do that?"

"I don't know. Maybe she was trying to frame me."

"But you just said it was self-defense. That Nadia wasn't guilty of anything."

"I don't know. I'm a little shaken up."

"Next, the way you described Ms. Delova's actions. The shooting. Opening the safe so easily. Finding the key. It almost seems as if she'd had it all planned."

"Maybe. I guess."

"You wouldn't have been in on that, would you?"

"In on what?"

"Robbery. Murder."

"No!"

"But you knew she had the gun?"

"At the last minute."

"And then at the last second, she double-crosses you and leaves you there as she gets away with whatever was in the safe."

"She couldn't double-cross me. I wasn't in on anything."

"But you did go there with an armed woman to take back property and money allegedly belonging to her."

"Yes."

"So what went through your mind when Nadia told you she was taking a gun to the meeting?"

"How do you mean?"

"Did you wonder, 'Why bring a firearm?'"

"I don't know. I didn't give it a lot of thought."

"So why did she bring a weapon? Was she expecting a gunfight?"

"I couldn't say. What are you getting at, Detective?"

"Well, it looks all the world like she was planning to take the property at gunpoint if Gorev refused to give her what she wanted. And once you saw the gun, you must have known that."

"I wasn't thinking along those lines."

"Actually, this reminds me a bit of the O. J. Simpson case."

"What! How?"

"The second one. In Las Vegas. Where Simpson and some pals go into this guy's hotel room. O. J. said the guy had some sports memorabilia that had been stolen from him. So they take it back by gunpoint. Never shot the guy. Never even really hurt him. But O. J. got thirty-three years."

-55-

Using the Scalpel

I didn't want to cross-examine Detective Barrios. He hadn't lied or misled. The tape, as lawyers like to say, spoke for itself. Still, I was like a boxer who'd just been hit several dozen times without ever throwing a punch. I needed to score a few points . . . without getting knocked on my ass with a counterpunch.

So, my cross was not intended to bring Barrios to his knees, weeping and begging forgiveness for his deception. I couldn't do what the great trial lawyer Louis Nizer called "taking a scalpel to the hidden recesses of a man's mind and rooting out the fraudulent resolve." No, this was just an exercise in unearthing the hidden tidbits of helpful information that were buried beneath the topsoil of direct examination.

"Good morning, Detective," I began.

"Counselor," he replied with a nod and the faintest of smiles that said, "Take your best shot."

The trick on cross is to ask leading questions that can only be answered yes or no.

"Mr. Solomon told you he'd fired twice into the office door, correct?"

"Yes."

"And the techs found two slugs that matched the Glock, just as he'd said."

"That's true."

"And just as Mr. Solomon said, you also found slugs the Russians had fired into the outside of that door, correct?"

"Yes."

"The door to the safe was open, corroborating Mr. Solomon's story, isn't that right?"

"Well, someone opened it, yes."

"And Mr. Solomon was cooperative with you in all respects, was he not?"

"Yes."

"Did he ever refuse to answer a question?"

"No."

"He's the one who called the police to report the shooting, correct?"

"He called the police. I suppose we could quibble over whether it was to report the shooting or to rescue himself from the dead man's brother."

"Your Honor, would you advise the witness to just answer my question without embellishment?" I asked.

"I shall. Detective, you know the rules."

"Yes, Your Honor," Barrios said politely.

"No matter how you characterize it, Detective," I continued, "Mr. Solomon did, in fact, call the police and report the shooting, correct?"

"Yes."

"Whereas Ms. Delova fled the scene."

"That's true."

"And as you later learned, she fled to another state, where she was hiding out?"

"Yes."

"A fugitive from both state and federal charges?"

"Yes, she was."

"Until arrested and brought back to Florida by federal marshals."

"That's my understanding."

Those little morsels were about all I expected to get, but there was another seed I wanted to plant. I'd already been warned about attacking the character of the deceased, but I thought I could do it in a roundabout fashion.

"Anything else, Mr. Lassiter?" the judge asked.

"Just a couple more questions, Your Honor."

Judge Duckworth raised her eyebrows, her move-it-along-if-you-know-what's-good-for-you look. I couldn't tell if she was bored with cross or just wanted to recess for lunch.

"Mr. Solomon apparently told the truth about Ms. Delova taking Mr. Gorev's gun, didn't he, Detective?"

"I couldn't say. There's no way to know if there was even a gun in Mr. Gorev's desk to begin with."

"Well, your men inventoried the contents of the desk, did they not?"

"Of course."

"Did they find any firearms?"

"No."

"Now, this was an office with a heavy steel-lined security door, a hidden wall safe, and a secret back door, correct?"

"Yes."

"Apparently, Mr. Gorev's brother had a firearm, which he shot into the door?"

"Yes."

"And both Gorevs were gangsters with extensive criminal records in Russia, correct?"

"Objection!" Pincher shot from his chair. "Irrelevant. Mr. Gorev's character is not on trial here. Move to strike."

"Sustained. Motion granted. The jury shall disregard defense counsel's last question."

"Thank you, Your Honor," I said meekly. Telling a jury to disregard anything only emphasizes it, so I'd already accomplished my mission. "I'll rephrase. Detective, based on what you know of Mr. Nicolai Gorev's background, would you have expected him to keep a firearm in his heavily secured office?"

"Objection, Your Honor." Pincher was still on his feet. He knew where I was going and hadn't bothered sitting down. "Calls for speculation."

"Your Honor, I would agree, but for one thing," I said. "Mr. Pincher took half an hour detailing the detective's extensive experience until he sounded like a combination of Sherlock Holmes and Columbo. Twenty-five years solving the most difficult homicide cases in the history of Florida. For all practical purposes, the state established the witness as an expert qualified to give opinions on matters involving crime and criminals. I think the question falls within the penumbra of the detective's expertise."

I've always loved the word penumbra, *though I'm not entirely sure what it means.*

The judge peered at me over her reading glasses and allowed herself a little smile. The state can't appeal an acquittal, but the defense can appeal a conviction. So, in close cases, it's always safer for a judge to let a defense lawyer ask an iffy question on cross.

"Objection overruled. But, Mr. Lassiter, I'm keeping you on a tight leash on this issue." She turned to Barrios and said, "Detective, based on what you know of Mr. Nicolai Gorev's background, would you have expected him to keep a firearm in his heavily secured office?"

Barrios shot a glance toward Pincher. He wasn't looking for instructions. More like saying, "Hey, what can I do?"

"Based on my experience, yes, I would have expected Mr. Gorev to have a gun either on his person or within his reach . . ."

I knew there was a *but* coming.

"But I learned a long time ago that my expectations about people, based on prior experiences, often turn out to be wrong."

Half a loaf. But that was okay. I'd take it, because it would surely get worse as I sat down and Pincher announced, "The state calls Nadia Delova."

"Boom! Right in Head"

G ucci knockoff," Victoria whispered at the defense table.

She was referring to the outfit Nadia Delova was wearing as she walked down the central aisle, through the swinging gate, and toward the bench. A pin-striped charcoal-gray suit, white silk blouse with a bow, and black pumps with two-inch heels. Her face was scrubbed of makeup, her dark hair pulled back and up into a bun.

If they were casting Marian the Librarian for *The Music Man*, she'd have a shot at the role. Not that I could complain. Once I had my client, an alleged Ponzi schemer, order a doctor of divinity degree by mail. My conscience was then clear when I dressed him in a clerical collar for the trial. As I wouldn't let him near the witness stand, the state never had a chance to cross-examine him on his outfit, though the prosecutor winced every time I referred to the guy as "Reverend Slocum."

Back in the gallery, I saw Gerald Hostetler perched in the first row of the gallery. He was biting his lower lip as he watched the woman he loved take the oath to tell the truth, the whole truth, and nothing but the truth.

After his introductory questions, Pincher wisely defused my basic areas of attack before I had a chance to cross-examine. He had Nadia admit that she lied to enter the country, that she smuggled diamonds through customs, that she worked as a Bar girl, that she'd been convicted of petty crimes in Europe, that she stole diamonds from Gorev's safe, and that she fled to Pennsylvania after the shooting and robbery.

"What happened to those diamonds?" Pincher asked.

"I return them to USA government as part of my deal," she said in her fetching Russian accent.

In the broadest sense, that was true. But more precisely, US Marshals found the diamonds hidden in a drawer when they searched Hostetler's house. A small piece of ammo for cross.

"Tell the jury about your deal, as you call it."

"I testify before grand jury against smuggler named Benny Cohen, and government drop all charges."

"What instructions did the federal prosecutors give you?"

"Only one. To tell truth."

"And did you?"

"Every word."

"And a result of your truthful testimony, Mr. Cohen was indicted just days ago on multiple federal charges, was he not?"

"So I am told. Nicolai Gorev's brother, Alex, too."

"Now, in this case, what arrangement did you make with my office?"

"I testify. No charges against me."

"With what proviso?"

"Pro . . . ?"

"What instructions did I give you?"

"Same thing. Tell truth. All will be good."

Pincher turned his back to the jury, glanced at me, and gave me his irritating smile. Then he took Nadia through "the day in question," as he put it. He started with Nadia seeing Solomon's television commercial, where he wore cowboy garb and brandished a pair of six-shooters. To get the point across, Pincher played a video of the commercial for the jury.

And there was Solomon in living color, blasting away at some blowup dolls. A baritone voice-over intoned, "If you need a lawyer, why not hire a gunslinger?"

Solomon didn't so much look dangerous—as Pincher would have the jurors believe—as idiotic. But I still could have done without the video image of him firing pistols with both hands.

Once the video was finished, Pincher said, "Take us now to Nicolai Gorev's office . . ."

I said something like that to a witness once. *"Let me take you back to the crime scene . . ."* And the witness, not the brightest bulb in the chandelier, stood up and said, "Okay, let's go."

"And please tell the jury what happened in that office," Pincher continued.

Nadia recounted how Solomon asked Gorev for her passport and back wages and was rebuffed. How Solomon threatened a lawsuit and Gorev said he would wipe his ass with the papers.

"Then I make mistake," Nadia testified.

"I use words I heard from the federal lawyer. *Racketeering* and *money laundering* and *wire fraud*. I could see suspicion in Nicolai's eyes."

"What did he say?"

"He accused me of wearing wire. I said I was not. I work for him only, not government."

"Was that true?"

"No. I was wearing wire for USA."

"And the wire, the recording. What became of it?"

"I destroyed it. I am sorry."

"Pity. What happened next?"

"That's when Nicolai pulled the gun and told us to strip."

Pincher opened his mouth to ask the next question but froze in place, as if zapped by a paralyzer gun in a sci-fi movie.

After a moment, he said, "I'm sorry, Ms. Delova. For a moment, I thought you said Mr. Gorev pulled a gun."

"From drawer in desk. His Beretta. I'd seen it many times. But this was first time he pointed it at me."

"Now, Ms. Delova, you recall giving a statement in my office?"

"*Da.* Yes."

"Isn't it true you told me Mr. Gorev had no gun?"

"Objection! Counsel is both leading his own witness and attempting to impeach her."

Just where the hell was she going with this? I didn't know, and clearly, neither did Pincher. I just knew I loved the last answer and didn't want her to contradict it. Sure, she was lying. But she wasn't my witness, and I didn't give a damn. Why should I? She was trying to help us.

"Sustained," Judge Duckworth announced.

Pincher, an old pro, stayed calm. No gaping mouth or fluttering eyelashes. I'd bet his blood pressure hadn't gone up a point. "All right, Ms. Delova, just tell us what happened next and let's see where it goes."

"I tell Nicolai I will leave now and forget everything about passport and money, but he points gun at me and says, '*Nyet!* Sit.' Threatens me. Says if either of us is wearing wire, he will kill us both. Mr. Solomon says he does not work for government and starts to take off shirt to show he had no wire. While Nicolai watches him, I take gun from my purse. Nicolai must see me, because he quickly turns gun back toward me, and I shoot him. Boom! Right in head."

The courtroom went silent. But it was the silence of pealing bells. In my mind, at least, I heard the bells of Saint Mary's, accompanied by the bells of Notre Dame, and the cowbell Hilda Chester rang in the Ebbets Field bleachers. Or maybe it was just my tinnitus.

I turned on the instant replay in my mind. Rewatched the last minute of Nadia's testimony. She appeared and sounded credible. And why not? She was an accomplished actress. Telling all those men how handsome and sexy they were while picking their pockets.

Oh, bless you, Nadia Delova.

Now I had to run a double reverse with a flea-flicker pass at the end of the play. Instead of attacking Nadia, I had to protect her.

The only sound in the courtroom was the whir of the air-conditioning. And, oh yes, next to me, Solomon was hyperventilating. He had just listened to the state's star witness back his defense, and he appeared close to passing out.

After gathering his thoughts—which must have ranged from terror to fury—Pincher, as steady as a seventy-ton battleship, said, "Ms. Delova, do you remember taking an oath to tell the truth?"

"Yes. Just few minutes ago."

"And you remember your arrangement with the state of Florida?"

"Same thing. Tell truth."

"And even though you cannot be prosecuted for the shooting of Nicolai Gorev or the theft of his property, you can still be charged with perjury. You know that, right?"

Nadia nodded. "You tell me that many times. Five years in prison for one false statement. Ten years for two. And so on. Which is why I tell truth."

"Did anyone promise you anything for your testimony today?"

"Only you. Immunity."

"Well, did anyone threaten you?"

"Again, only you. Prison for lying. But I tell truth, so no problem."

Still unruffled, Pincher turned toward the bench. "Your Honor, permission to treat Ms. Delova as a hostile witness."

"Objection." I bounced from my chair so quickly, I nearly retore the ligaments in my left knee.

"In my chambers, now, all of you!" the judge ordered. "We stand in recess."

·57·

Hostile Witness

Judge Duckworth's chambers were dark and cool. An American flag stood on one side of her desk, a US Army flag on the other, complete with Revolutionary War cannon and the slogan "This We'll Defend." Otherwise, it was a typical trial judge's chambers, complete with the scent of old cracked leather and shelves of law books made obsolete by the Internet.

We gathered around the judge's desk. Pincher and one of his assistants. Victoria, Solomon, and me. Plus the court stenographer, ready to type away on her little machine.

"Well now," the judge began, "just what in the name of Ulysses S. Grant is going on?"

"I'm entitled to impeach my witness based on her prior statements," Pincher said.

"Just because Mr. Pincher doesn't like the testimony doesn't mean Ms. Delova is hostile to the state," I said. "It's not her fault he's placed the entire burden of proving his case on her. He can't just launch into leading questions of his own witness and attack her testimony."

"My questions will prove her hostility," he shot back.

"Let me see the transcript of Ms. Delova's deposition," Judge Duckworth said. "I'll make a preliminary finding on prior inconsistencies."

"I never took her deposition in discovery," I said.

"Really?"

"I'm actually quite a lazy lawyer."

"Either that, Mr. Lassiter," the judge said, a twinkle in her eye, "or you made a decision not to let the state know in advance just what you would ask the witness at trial."

"There's that, too," I admitted.

Judge Duckworth turned to Pincher. "Let me have a look at the sworn statement Ms. Delova gave to your office."

Pincher cleared his throat. It sounded a bit like the choking of a drowning man. "We never took a written statement."

"A recording then?"

"We didn't do that, either."

"Why in blazes not?" the judge inquired.

When Pincher hesitated, I answered for him. "Because the state would have been required to give me the statements in pretrial discovery."

That was true. Like a boxer head butting in a clinch, Sugar Ray always liked the element of surprise. Well, we both did.

"It was a strategic decision," Pincher said in his own defense.

"How's that working out for you?" the judge asked.

"I should still be permitted to impeach Ms. Delova based on what she told me in my office. It directly contradicts her testimony here today."

"And then what? You're a lawyer trying the case. You can't testify against your own witness. Or any witness for that matter. You just don't have the materials to impeach her, and I'm not going to allow you to treat her as a hostile witness just because her answers surprised you after you vouched for her credibility by calling her."

"Your Honor, I suspect skullduggery," Pincher said.

Yeah, he really said "skullduggery."

"Meaning what?" she asked.

"I should be permitted to ask Mr. Solomon and Ms. Lord about their contacts with my witness. Did they influence her in any way?"

"On my oath," I said, "I've never spoken to Ms. Delova in my life. In fact, I've never seen her before she walked into court today."

"Truly, Mr. Lassiter?" the judge said.

"I told you I was lazy."

"Your Honor," Victoria said. "I was with Ms. Delova the day she was arrested in Pennsylvania but have not spoken with her since."

"Thank you for that, Ms. Lord," the judge said. "Mr. Pincher, I'm denying your oral motion to treat your witness as hostile. You may ask her anything you wish on direct, but you may not lead or otherwise attempt to impeach her."

"For the record, note my exception."

"Unnecessary, but so noted."

"Now, do you have more questions for your witness?"

"Without the ability to impeach, no, I do not. Ms. Delova has become a defense witness, and I choose not to hear her tell the jury a second time that Mr. Solomon is innocent."

"Mr. Lassiter, do you have any cross?"

"Your Honor, Granny Lassiter didn't raise no idiot children."

"I take that as a no. Then we'll excuse Ms. Delova and Mr. Pincher can call his next witness."

Pincher massaged his forehead with both hands and said, "We request a seventy-two-hour recess in order to . . ."

"To what, Mr. Pincher?"

"To reformulate our case now that we lack an eyewitness."

"That's not a recess. That's a continuance. Motion denied. We're going to try this case to a verdict . . . unless you have anything you'd like to say to the court or to defense counsel."

"Yes, Your Honor." Pincher composed himself for a moment before turning to me. "Would a plea to aggravated assault interest you, Jake? Sentence of time served. Withhold adjudication."

"An hour ago, I would have taken it, Ray. But now, it's a non-starter."

Pincher sucked in a deep breath. So deep that if he'd been smoking a joint, he'd be halfway to the moon by now. He gave me a grudging little smile. "I don't know how you did it, Jake."

"Hell, neither do I."

He turned back to the judge. "Your Honor, the state cannot proceed and therefore will *nol-pros* all charges."

"As jeopardy has attached, that would be a dismissal with prejudice," the judge said.

"Of course. The case is over." Pincher shot a look at the court stenographer to make sure she was still typing. I knew what was coming next. The first draft of his official statement to the press. He spoke deliberately. "After due consideration, the state has determined that Nadia Delova killed Nicolai Gorev in self-defense. Gorev was a gangster and member of *Bratva*, the Russian Mafia. He was armed and threatened both Ms. Delova and Mr. Solomon, a distinguished Miami attorney. Under Stand Your Ground, Ms. Delova had every right to fire the shot that ended Gorev's life. In fact, she is to be commended for her bravery as well as her marksmanship."

Pincher turned to me as if for approval. I gave him a thumbs-up that wouldn't show up on the transcript.

"What about an apology?" Solomon said. "I want an apology on the record."

"Shut up, Solomon," I said. "You just got it. 'Distinguished Miami attorney.'"

"I need to go back in and thank the jury before sending them home," the judge said. "Anybody got anything else to say?"

Victoria wrapped her arms around Solomon's neck and kissed him. "I love you," she said. "And that's on the record."

-58-

Rapprochement

I can't thank you enough, Jake," Victoria said. "You were magnificent."

"Yeah, that goes for me, too," Solomon said. "And I apologize again for not trusting your judgment."

"Aw, jeez. My new BFFs. I think I'm gonna cry."

"Jake, be real," Victoria told me. "You pretend to have that hard bark, but you're cotton candy underneath."

"Okay, this is real. I didn't win the case. You did, Victoria. Whatever you told Hostetler worked. I just shut up and got out of the way."

It was just before noon the day after the trial ended, and we were in the bar at the Hyatt Regency downtown. Gerald Hostetler had called Victoria, saying Nadia wanted to see us. We were waiting for them while drinking mojitos and eating guacamole and chips.

"You're not really quitting the practice, are you, dude?" Solomon said, clopping me on the shoulder, all buddy-buddy. "Because I was thinking we could try a case together sometime."

"Funny," I said. "I was thinking we could try cases against each other."

"How?"

"There's a courthouse rumor that Ray Pincher isn't running for reelection."

"Oh no!" Victoria said. "You're not going to run for state attorney."

"Something to think about when I fall asleep in the hammock tonight, sipping a martini. Gin. Not vodka."

"I think it would be great if you're the chief prosecutor," Solomon said. "But I'd kick your ass in court. Being a defendant will make me a better trial lawyer, don't you think?"

"From personal experience, I know it will."

"Whatever the future holds," Victoria said, "we'll always be grateful to you, Jake."

"You're welcome," I told them. "So Victoria, what did you say to Hostetler that flipped Nadia?"

"Already told you. That you can bend the law like a baker twisting a pretzel. Just don't break the dough when you bend it."

"I always thought that was a little vague," I said.

"Me, too, Vic," Solomon said. "What's the rest?"

She poked her straw into the bottom of the mojito glass, crushing the mint leaves. "Nothing."

"Hey, babe, it's us you're talking to," Solomon said. "Steve and Jake. Your lover and my lawyer. We're a team . . . unless Lassiter gets elected state attorney. You can't hold out on us."

"I'm with Solomon on this one," I chimed in.

Victoria sipped at her mojito before answering. "Gerald was afraid if Nadia backed Steve's story, she'd be charged with perjury, so I broke down the case for him. There were three people in that office. One was dead. If the other two told the same story, no one could prove either one was lying. As a practical matter, she faced no chance of a perjury conviction if she backed Steve's story that she fired in self-defense."

"Nice work, Vic," Solomon said.

"Ditto," I said.

I spotted Hostetler and Nadia walking into the bar, pushing carry-on luggage. She was wearing a yellow polka-dot sundress that gave her a girl-next-door air of innocence. He wore a "Save the Ever-glades" T-shirt and jeans. They were headed back to Pennsylvania. The three of us stood as they approached our table.

A great deal of hugging commenced.

Victoria hugged Nadia, then Hostetler.

Solomon hugged Hostetler, then Nadia.

I just shook Hostetler's hand and said thanks to Nadia. Sorry, I'm just not that touchy-feely.

"I want to apologize to you in person, Steve," Nadia said. "So much trouble I caused you."

"It all turned out okay," he said.

"Could I speak to you privately?"

Solomon shot a look at Victoria, who shrugged a yes.

"I'll go check out, sweetheart," Hostetler said to Nadia, wheel-ing their luggage away.

Nadia and Solomon retreated to the far side of the bar, where they began whispering. Victoria watched a moment, then said to me, "What's going on?"

"No idea."

"You don't think . . . ?"

"What?"

"What I said before. That there was anything going on between them."

"No way, Victoria. Trust me. I can tell from their body lan-guage."

Which, of course, was precisely the moment Nadia kissed Solomon on the lips. Just a little kiss, not a long, lingering, can't-wait-to-hump-again kiss.

"What the hell!" Victoria said.

"Relax. It's just a Russian greeting."

"You're making that up. They already greeted."

We both watched as Nadia reached into her purse and handed something to Solomon. No way to tell from here what it was. Something small, though. It fit into the palm of his hand.

"Jake! What are they doing?"

I didn't know, so I didn't answer.

Solomon and Nadia hugged. Again. Just a quickie. Then she left to meet Pretzel Man at the front desk, and Solomon returned to our table.

When he sat down, nobody said a word for a long moment.

"Why are you blushing?" Victoria demanded.

"I'm not. I'm not." He was stammering. "I don't blush."

"Your neck is flushed. Do you have a fever?"

"I'm fine."

"What did Nadia give you?"

"I'm not sure this is the time or place," Solomon said.

"Why not?"

"Well, it's just that it's between the two of us."

"You and Nadia?"

"No! You and me, Vic."

"I'll leave," I offered.

"No, you won't," Victoria said. "I need a witness if I have sufficient grounds to slice Steve's throat. What did Nadia give you?"

Solomon reached into his pocket and pulled out a small brown cotton bag with a drawstring. He placed the bag onto the table. "Open it, Vic."

She looked at him dubiously, then picked up the bag, pulled the drawstring, and a rough glassy object a little smaller than a golf ball dropped into her hand.

"What is it?" she asked.

"Looks like quartz," I said.

"Uncut diamond," Solomon said. "Big one. Nadia estimates it'll be four to five carats when cut. She seems to know a lot about diamonds."

"I thought the feds recovered all the smuggled diamonds when they searched Hostetler's house," I said.

"They didn't get the ones Nadia buried in the backyard."

"So there are more?" Victoria said.

"Enough to build Hostetler a new factory," Solomon said. "Though they'll still hand-roll the pretzels. Anyway, Nadia wants you to have the diamond. I mean, I want you to have it."

"What are you saying, Steve?" she asked.

"Well . . ."

I fidgeted in my seat. "Solomon, am I sitting here listening to you ask Victoria to marry you?"

"Well. Yeah."

"Oh, my God," Victoria said.

"You're doing a shitty job of it, Solomon," I said. "Would it help if I left?"

"Damn right."

"I'm out of here, guys."

"Not so fast, Jake," Victoria said. "We're going to be seeing a lot of you."

"Why? Which one of you is gonna be indicted next?"

She ignored me and turned to Solomon. "Yes, Steve. Hell, yes! I want to marry you."

Solomon let out a long, low whistle like air escaping from a balloon. "Whoopee-ki-yay-yo!"

They leapt out of their chairs, embraced, and kissed. Slow and deep and long. So long I could have mixed a pitcher of martinis and polished off the first one. Just as I intended to do when I got home. But for now, I was still sitting while the two of them hovered above me, a-hugging and a-kissing. Making out is not a spectator sport, but there I was, the creaky third wheel. Sure, I was happy for them, but a part of me felt empty, too. Solomon was a lucky son of a bitch, and I was going home alone.

"Congratulations, you crazy kids," I said. "Now, may I leave?"

"Not yet, big guy," Solomon said, and they both sat down again. He gave me a straight-on, dead-serious look. "Jake, old pal, I want you to be my best man."

I was quiet a moment. Now I really wanted that pitcher of booze along with a bittersweet country song about dusty roads and broken hearts.

"C'mon, Jake. What about it?" he pressed me.

"Do I have to do a toast? I'm not good with cheerfulness and optimism."

"We'll call it closing argument and you'll be fine."

"You're not gonna write your own vows, are you? 'Love flew in my window on a seagull's wings.'"

"More like we met in a jail cell after being held in contempt," Victoria said.

"Are you sure about this?" I asked. "Not the marriage. My being best man."

"Relax, Jake," Victoria said. "You might have been joking when you called us your best friends forever. But the three of us? That's what we are."

I slumped in my chair. It's not that I'm antisocial. But coming from a fractured family, I'm not at ease at other people's festivities. Holiday dinners, communions, weddings? Not for me. Maybe joyous get-togethers remind me of what I've missed.

Solomon and Lord were reaching out to me, but I felt incapable of responding. Closeness with others, true friendship, had always been so elusive.

"Whadaya say, Jake?" Solomon said.

I let the question hang there a second, then said, "I really got a sense of Victoria when we were working on your case."

"Yeah?"

"You've got yourself a helluva smart fiancée."

"I know it, pal."

"And a terrific woman."

"I know that, too."

"You ever hurt her in any way, I'll beat the tar out of you."

"No worries, Lassiter. Now, are you in? You gonna be my best man?"

Still, I didn't answer. Then, apropos of nothing—at least nothing I was thinking about—Victoria said, "I've always wanted children."

"Me, too," Solomon agreed.

He fixed me with another serious gaze. If my cardiologist ever looked at me that way, I'd make sure my estate plan was in order. Now what?

"If we have a boy," he said, "do we have your permission?"

"To do what?"

"To name him Jake, of course."

Solomon was moving too fast for me. We'd spent the last several months arguing and insulting each other. Now he wanted me to carry his ring and to immortalize my name in his lineage. How do you say no to that?

"What about it, Jake?" Victoria said.

I sat up straight in my chair. Sometimes you just have to tighten your chin strap and charge full speed ahead.

"I really need to get home," I said. Disappointment crossed both their faces. "But before I go, let's have another round of drinks."

"Why?" they asked simultaneously.

"I gotta practice that wedding toast."

AUTHOR'S NOTE

Readers often ask, "Where do you get your ideas?"

Sometimes I rip them from the headlines. Not long ago, this story in the *Miami Herald* caught my eye: "Tears Flow Over Guilty Verdicts at End of 'Bar Girls' Federal Trial in Miami."

The subheadline read: "A Federal Judge Ordered the Three Convicted Bar Owners into Custody Immediately, Prompting Loud Wails by Relatives in the Courtroom."

Bar girls. Federal charges. Wailing relatives. It's all music to a crime novelist's ears. Reading the several-thousand-page transcript, I discovered a treasure trove of drama, humor, and chicanery. Take a look at the testimony of a Russian Bar girl named Julija:

Q: Did you encourage men who came to the clubs to drink?

A: I tried to make them as drunk as possible.

Q: And why is that?

A: Because sober men will never spend as much money as drunk men.

Q: Did the men pay several thousand dollars for a single bottle of cheap champagne?

A: Their minds were on B-girls, not on credit card slip.

Q: Did you ever offer the men sex?

A: No, because I was not acting as prostitute, but I gave them hope.

Q: By zipping down their pants?

A: Yes, touching them, kissing them, anything you can think.

Q: Giving them hope that they would have sex with you?

A: All my behavior was inclining to this.

Q: And once they signed the checks you disappeared, right?

A: Yes. Fast.

That's the moment *Bum Rap* was born and the chapter "Giving Men Hope" popped into my head, nearly fully formed. I knew Jake Lassiter would have to visit a B-girl bar, and I knew there would be a murder.

Bum Rap brings together Lassiter, the linebacker-turned-lawyer, and mismatched law partners Steve Solomon and Victoria Lord. Lassiter last appeared in *State vs. Lassiter*, nominated for a Shamus Award. Solomon and Lord were last seen bickering and bantering in *Habeas Porpoise*, the fourth novel of their Edgar-nominated series.

I hope you have at least half as much fun reading *Bum Rap* as I had writing it.

Paul Levine
Miami—November 2014
www.paul-levine.com

ALSO AVAILABLE

JAKE LASSITER SERIES

"Mystery writing at its very, very best." —Larry King, USA Today

TO SPEAK FOR THE DEAD: Linebacker-turned-lawyer Jake Lassiter begins to believe that his surgeon client is innocent of malpractice . . . but guilty of murder.

NIGHT VISION: After several women are killed by an Internet stalker, Jake is appointed a special prosecutor and heads to London and the very streets where Jack the Ripper once roamed.

FALSE DAWN: After his client confesses to a murder he didn't commit, Jake follows a bloody trail from Miami to Havana to discover the truth.

MORTAL SIN: Talk about conflicts of interest. Jake is sleeping with Gina Florio and defending her mob-connected husband in court.

RIPTIDE: Jake Lassiter chases a beautiful woman and stolen bonds from Miami to Maui.

FOOL ME TWICE: To clear his name in a murder investigation, Jake searches for buried treasure in the abandoned silver mines of Aspen, Colorado. (Also available in a new paperback edition.)

FLESH & BONES: Jake falls for his beautiful client even though he doubts her story. She claims to have recovered "repressed memories" of abuse . . . just before gunning down her father.

LASSITER: Jake retraces the steps of a model who went missing eighteen years earlier . . . after his one-night stand with her. (Also available in a new paperback edition.)

LAST CHANCE LASSITER: In this prequel novella, young Jake Lassiter has an impossible case: he represents Cadillac Johnson, an aging rhythm and blues musician who claims his greatest song was stolen by a top-of-the-charts hip-hop artist.

STATE vs. LASSITER: This time, Jake is on the wrong side of the bar. He's charged with murder! The victim? His girlfriend and banker, Pamela Baylins, who was about to report him to the authorities for allegedly stealing from clients. (Nominated for the 2014 Shamus Award.)

SOLOMON VS. LORD SERIES

(Nominated for the Edgar, Macavity, International Thriller, and James Thurber awards.)

"A cross between *Moonlighting* and *Night Court*. Courtroom drama has never been this much fun." —*Freshfiction.com*

SOLOMON vs. LORD: Trial lawyer Victoria Lord, who follows every rule, and Steve Solomon, who makes up his own, bicker and banter as they defend a beautiful young woman accused of killing her wealthy, older husband.

THE DEEP BLUE ALIBI: Solomon and Lord come together—and fly apart—defending Victoria's "Uncle Grif" on charges he killed a man with a speargun. It's a case set in the Florida Keys with side trips to coral reefs and a nudist colony where all is more—and less—than it seems.

KILL ALL THE LAWYERS: Just what did Steve Solomon do to infuriate ex-client and ex-con "Dr. Bill"? Did Solomon try to lose the case in which the TV shrink was charged in the death of a woman patient?

HABEAS PORPOISE: It starts with the kidnapping of a pair of trained dolphins and turns into a murder trial with Solomon and Lord on *opposite* sides after Victoria is appointed a special prosecutor, and fireworks follow!

STAND-ALONE THRILLERS

IMPACT: A jetliner crashes in the Everglades. Is it negligence or terrorism? When the legal case gets to the Supreme Court, the defense has a unique strategy: kill anyone, even a Supreme Court justice, to win the case.

BALLISTIC: A nuclear missile, a band of terrorists, and only two people who can prevent Armageddon. A "loose nukes" thriller for the twenty-first century. (Also available in a new paperback edition.)

ILLEGAL: Down-and-out lawyer Jimmy (Royal) Payne tries to reunite a Mexican boy with his missing mother and becomes enmeshed in the world of human trafficking and sex slavery.

PAYDIRT: Bobby Gallagher had it all and lost it. Now, assisted by his twelve-year-old brainiac son, he tries to rig the Super Bowl, win a huge bet . . . and avoid getting killed.

Visit the author's website at http://www.paul-levine.com for more information.

ABOUT THE AUTHOR

The author of nineteen novels, Paul Levine has won the John D. MacDonald fiction award and has been nominated for the Edgar, Macavity, International Thriller, Shamus, and James Thurber prizes. A former Miami trial lawyer, he also wrote more than twenty episodes of the CBS military drama *JAG* and cocreated the Supreme Court drama *First Monday* starring James Garner and Joe Mantegna. The critically acclaimed international bestseller *To Speak for the Dead* was his first novel. He is also the author of the Solomon vs. Lord series and the thrillers *Illegal*, *Ballistic*, *Impact*, and *Paydirt*. A graduate of Penn State University and the University of Miami Law School, he lives in Coconut Grove, Florida. Readers can sign up for the author's newsletter and be eligible for signed books and prizes at www.paul-levine.com. For more information about Paul Levine's novels, visit his Amazon Author Page at www.amazon.com/Paul-Levine/e/B000APPYKG.